W9-AVT-305

THE

LOST

GIRLS

OF

CAMP

FOREVERMORE

BOOKS BY KIM FU

For Today I Am a Boy

How Festive the Ambulance

The Lost Girls of Camp Forevermore

THE LOST GIRLS OF CAMP FOREVERMORE

KIM FU

HARPERCOLLINS PUBLISHERS LTD

The Lost Girls of Camp Forevermore
Copyright © 2018 by Kim Fu.
All rights reserved.

Published by HarperCollins Publishers Ltd

First Canadian edition

No part of this book may be used or reproduced in any manner whatsoever
without the prior written permission of the publisher, except in the case
of brief quotations embodied in reviews.

A portion of this novel appeared, in different form, in *Maisonneuve*.

HarperCollins books may be purchased for educational, business,
or sales promotional use through our Special Markets Department.

HarperCollins Publishers Ltd
2 Bloor Street East, 20th Floor
Toronto, Ontario, Canada
M4W 1A8

www.harpercollins.ca

Library and Archives Canada Cataloguing in Publication
information is available upon request.

Book design by Mark Robinson

ISBN 978-1-44345-359-2

Printed and bound in the United States
LSC/H 9 8 7 6 5 4 3 2 1

For JP

CAMP FOREVERMORE

THE GIRLS STOOD on the dock and sang the camp song, "Camp Forevermore." They sang in voices at worst bored or dutiful, but more often thrilled, chests swelling with unity and conviction, that feeling of being part of something larger than themselves, their brash, off-key voices combined into one grand instrument: "And I shall love my sisters/for-ev-er-more." In 1994, the song had echoed out over the Pacific Ocean for six decades.

They stood straight-backed and solemn-faced as soldiers in formation, even the ones who itched to squirm, to collapse into their natural, slumped posture, who were rolling their toes in their shoes and humming to themselves, squeezing their lips in their fingers to suppress a bubble of nervous laughter. Counselors dragged plastic bins of orange life jackets from one of the storehouses adjacent to the dock. The life jackets varied in size and some had broken buckles and split seams. The girls picked through to find intact jackets that fit, the process both hurried and cautious, drawing attention to their newly divergent bodies.

Ten-year-old Siobhan Dougherty snatched one and slid her arms through the holes. Would it reveal her to be too tall, too wide, too infantile, anything other than the universal girl-size implied by the unsorted bins? She fumbled to adjust the buckles and lengthen the straps, her fingers cold and stiff, until finally the jacket clicked shut. Satisfying clicks echoed up and down the dock. By some miracle, no one was left behind.

Two days earlier, Siobhan had stepped through the wooden gates of Camp Forevermore for the first time. The group of low log buildings in a man-made clearing, at the nexus of forest and sea, looked just the way it had in the brochure.

Upper-middle-class girls (and, as of 1976, a small group of need-based essay-contest winners) from up and down the northwest coast of North America, including both sides of the U.S.-Canada border, were sent to Forevermore, the name meant, like its religious and pseudo–Native American competitors, to project ancient knowledge. Nine-to-eleven-year-old girls would leave home fretful and finicky and return as capable, knowledgeable outdoorswomen, remade in the wholesomeness of woods and sisterhood. *The best of its kind,* crowed the brochure.

Siobhan wanted to be more like the heroines of the books she liked, about girl detectives and girl adventurers: tomboyish, scrappy, and resourceful, able to outsmart adults and survive without them, her body sun-brown and waiflike. She was, instead, a freckled, blue-eyed redhead, pale and dense as a block of shortening, who wasn't allowed to use the stove. The one time she'd been left alone at home after dark, she'd turned on all the lamps, the TV, and the stereo, needing a protective shell of voices and light.

Above all, she was looking forward to the kayaking trip, the central adventure of the first week. In small groups, the girls would kayak to a remote island and camp overnight. The brochure had stressed to parents that the overnight would *build character and an appreciation of the outdoors within safe boundaries*, but none of the pictures had adults in them. Just the campers, posing in their kayaks with their paddles triumphantly raised. Carrying firewood and military-style duffel bags in their twiggy arms, holding hands and jumping into the ocean. Bearing bold smiles of uneven teeth and no-nonsense braids and ponytails, these were girl pirates, girl spaceship captains, warrior princesses — the thrilling, independent societies of children that had existed only in Siobhan's books.

Even on that first, clear afternoon, the dark earth between the gravel paths and the deep green of towering pine, fir, and spruce trees contained the memory of recent snow and rain. The ocean at the far end of the camp was the color of slate.

Everything Siobhan was wearing was brand new: a black fleece she'd chosen for its silver heart-shaped zipper pull, her first pair of hiking boots, even her underwear. She felt a thrilling, terrifying dissolution of self. She was far from her parents, her classmates, anyone who had ever known her. She was curious to find out who she would be.

THE FIRST DAY passed in a blur. The girls were shuffled from place to place, given a lecture and a quick meal, hurried to an early bedtime and an awkward silence in the cabins with their counselor-chaperones. The morning of the second day, they faced a swimming test, shivering and exposed as they eyed one another on the dock, then timed as they swam for fifty meters parallel to the shore.

In sporty Speedo one-pieces, in childish frills and sea-creature patterns, the girls first noticed Dina Chang, a nine-year-old from Vancouver Island. There was nothing precisely remarkable about her appearance, her wholly prepubescent chest and legs and golden-brown skin in a black-and-white two-piece, but they could not keep their eyes off of her. Her every movement was magnetic. Girls brought her tied-together daisies, plastic bracelets, and toys they'd brought from home. Someone offered her the carton of chocolate milk from her morning snack. Dina shrugged and twirled a strand of her glossy black hair, like the attention was nothing new, no big deal.

During one of the swim tests, the girls' conversations trailed off as one by one they stopped talking to watch. The girl in the water was struggling. She kept stopping to tread and change strokes, from a frantic, ineffectual crawl—kicking up geysers of water without gaining any forward momentum—to a pathetic-looking doggie paddle, fighting to keep her head up, a tangle of dirty-blond hair plastered across her face. Andee Allen was ten years old and from Seattle, Washington. "One of the scholarship girls," someone stage-whispered. One of the girls they should feel sorry for and be extra kind to.

As the minutes ticked by and Andee continued to flounder in the water, the girls turned their attention to the counselors administering the test, particularly the one holding a stopwatch. They hadn't failed anyone, no matter how slow or poor her technique, as long as the camper could cross the distance somehow. But surely this was too much, and any minute now, they would jump in and tow or carry Andee to shore, and she wouldn't be allowed on the kayak trip.

The adults looked transfixed by Andee. When Andee finally swam a little closer, Siobhan could see why: the determined set of her mouth, the ferocity in her eyes. How much she wanted to finish. She would finish, no matter what. It would be cruel to stop her. And more to the point, if they ever *were* stranded in the ocean, Andee—who had been in the water for what felt like an eternity—would be the last to go down.

When Andee's hand slapped the far pillar of the dock, the counselors cheered. Two of them reached in and pulled her out by her forearms and the back of her swimsuit. Andee lay gasping on the planks like a fish in the open air.

THEY HAD KAYAK LESSONS for the rest of the day, their first tangle with the life jackets. At the outset, their neon-green kayaks crowded the shallows of the beach, knocking against one another like rubber ducks let loose in a bathtub. By late afternoon, each girl could escape a rollover, do a forward paddle stroke, and self-propel in a straight line.

At dinner, Siobhan was among the girls assigned to set the tables. Nita Prithi—eleven years old, from a midsize town in central California, in her third and final year at Forevermore —bossily led the group around, making the expansive gestures of a magician's assistant. "Here's where the forks and spoons are. Here are the cups. Here are the pitchers for water," she said. Nita was intimidating-looking, broad-shouldered with a heavy, clomping step, an oversize sweatshirt pulled down over early breasts, a wide mouth, and dark, expressive eyebrows.

Another group of girls carried the steamer trays of food from the kitchen. The mac and cheese was topped by pink flakes that might have been some kind of meat or fish, and green specks that might have been vegetables or mold.

The rest of the girls lined up with plates. Nita cut in front of Siobhan as though she hadn't seen her. Siobhan gave a little snort of protest. Nita turned and her gaze seemed to pass straight through Siobhan. Siobhan had known other know-it-alls, but Nita's commanding physical presence was something she'd never encountered in another girl.

"No cuts," Siobhan said.

Nita ignored her. She waved Andee into line in front of Siobhan, frontsies-backsies. By comparison, Andee looked scrawny and underfed, her hair deflated, little dog to Nita's big. They were cabinmates and, as of that morning—presumably since Nita had watched with the others as Andee fought her way out and back on the swim test—one of the many impenetrable friend-couples that had already formed. These partnerships made Siobhan feel lonely and slighted. She wondered why no one had picked her yet. The girl in the bunk above hers had started snoring the moment the lights went out, leaving Siobhan to listen to the girls in the adjacent bunks whisper and giggle.

"Hey," Siobhan said, tapping Nita on the shoulder. "I said no cuts!"

"Jeez," Nita said in a loud voice. She stepped out of line. "Go ahead. Get the mac and cheese that you want *so* badly." The rest of the girls tittered and Siobhan flushed.

At their tables, they were first taught the camp song, singing and banging their fists on the plastic tablecloths, louder and more confident with each repetition.

After dinner, arranged in a circle by the fire pit and waiting for the sun to go down, the girls were told to hold hands with two girls who weren't standing immediately beside them. Andee made eye contact with Siobhan and reached toward her. As Siobhan moved to meet her, Andee yanked her hand back and pretended to slick her hair with it, a schoolyard gesture Siobhan knew: too slow, so sad, too bad.

Then a miracle happened. Dina absentmindedly stretched her arm through the center of the circle, past a thicket of grasping, hopeful hands, and her hand locked on to one of Siobhan's. All of this happened in the space of a minute—Andee's rejection, Dina's soft fingers against Siobhan's right palm, another girl's hand grasping Siobhan's left. Forty independent girls morphed into a contiguous human knot. The game was to unravel themselves without letting go.

Siobhan looked down. Dina's hand had the same inexplicable glow as the rest of her, as if the falling, honeyed light struck her at a different angle than it did anyone else. The touch of her skin sent a silky, dizzying sensation of pleasure up Siobhan's arm and down into her abdomen.

ON THE THIRD DAY, the girls waited on the dock in their life jackets as they were divided into groups for the overnight kayaking trip. The counselors took turns reading out lists of names. Most of the counselors were athletic-looking young women, college students, former Forevermore sisters. The girls had judged them by their attractiveness, their apparent coolness or niceness, forming favorites and crushes. The blond one with a big, sunny smile and gentle voice. The one whose shorts were shorter than her camp T-shirt and looked like she was walking around without pants, reportedly seen smoking behind the shower building. The one who'd told the best ghost story at the previous night's fire circle, who'd raised her arms, held her hands as claws, and lowered her voice to a deep growl.

One of the group leaders for the trip wasn't technically a counselor, not anymore. She'd told the girls to address her by her first name—Jan—as they did the counselors, but a few hadn't been able to stop calling her "Ms. Butler." She had been one of the first campers at Forevermore, then a counselor, then an administrative staff member, on and off, for her entire adult life.

When Jan called Siobhan's name, Siobhan was secretly relieved. Jan was the least cool option, discussed with dread in the bunks of Siobhan's cabin, their excitement for the overnight trip tempered by physical exhaustion from the day of kayak lessons. But even though Jan was old—really old, older than the mental category Siobhan had for mothers, teachers, and aunts, old enough that one girl had accidentally called her "Nana"—Jan's solid form and no-nonsense mien were reassuring. As she did every day, Jan carried a small machete on

her belt, and Siobhan could easily imagine her felling a sap-
ling or skinning a rabbit. She had a thick pompadour of white
hair, and a healthy flush in her wrinkled, sun-spotted face. Her
clothes were made of rough fabric and had lots of pockets. She
looked replete with a different kind of knowledge, one that interested Siobhan more than whatever a college girl could teach
her about boys.

When Jan called Dina's name, Siobhan could feel the disappointment and envy of the girls in other groups. Siobhan
would make Dina her best friend by the end of the trip. She
was sure of it.

Jan continued calling names and Siobhan's initial relief
began to sink. ". . . Nita, Andee, and Isabel."

Nita and Andee had appeared at breakfast wearing matching friendship bracelets. Nita had brought a plastic case filled
with different colors of yarn to camp, which everyone knew
about, like Nita was a prison kingpin. Even girls who weren't in
Nita's cabin came knocking, asking for yarn, and to be taught
how to weave in her signature ten-strand chevron pattern.

Nita had bumped into Siobhan at breakfast, knocking
Siobhan's tray to the ground. It looked to everyone else like an
accident; even Siobhan wasn't sure. Nita had bent down to help
her. The tray had fallen straight down and slid forward, most
of the food remaining on the plate. "Right-side up," Nita said,
in a cheery, helpful-sounding voice. "That's lucky. You can still
eat it." She went to get a cloth from the kitchen to wipe up the
spilled water from Siobhan's glass.

The humiliation had been vague, unreportable, possibly
imagined. Siobhan had eaten her floor breakfast.

The five summoned girls gathered around Jan, holding
themselves in the bulky life jackets as though they were wearing wooden barrels on suspenders.

Nobody had heard Isabel Wen speak yet. She was eleven,

as old as Nita, but several growth spurts behind, more the size and proportions of a kindergartener. Her green tortoiseshell glasses warped her eyes, making them seem both magnified and faraway. Like Dina, she was from British Columbia, from a Vancouver suburb, and they were both — to Siobhan's eyes — Chinese, but they couldn't have been more different. They stood apart and gazed in opposite directions. Andee and Nita held hands and squeezed a signal to each other. While Jan double-checked her clipboard, in a quick flash of pink, Andee stuck out her tongue at Siobhan.

"Okay, sisters," Jan said, her voice low and crisp. "I'll help each of you launch, one at a time." She pointed to a tree leaning out over the water in the near distance. "Paddle over to the tree and wait for the rest of the group. Then we'll set off together."

Jan's group was the quickest to start onto the water by a wide margin. The other groups moved off the dock, onto the beach and the path, to listen to their leaders deliver longer speeches.

"To the tree, and then wait," Jan repeated to each of the five girls, sending them off. Siobhan went last, the meager lump of her sleeping bag and dry bag of clothes packed in under the rubber skirt. Jan's kayak, crisscrossed with bungee cords and three times the length of the girls' kayaks, carried everything truly important: food, water, first aid, and two three-person tents. Her kayak was red and a narrower, sleeker shape.

Siobhan passed Isabel as she headed for the tree. Her stomach fluttered: an exam, an adventure, the desire to be liked. Jan stopped paddling almost as soon as she launched. She floated on momentum past the girls, her kayak slicing through the water with loonlike grace.

After a comical length of time and some shouted instructions, the group was more or less clustered and stationary. Isabel's face had gone white. Siobhan feared Isabel was already seasick, though she must've gotten through the kayak lessons somehow.

"Okay," Jan began. "We've been assigned Lumpen Island. I'll lead. We're going to paddle for about an hour, then look for a good place to have a break and a snack. Another hour, and then lunch. One more hour and we should be at Lumpen Island, with lots of time to make camp. If you need a break before that, holler. If another girl is yelling, and it seems like I don't hear her, start yelling too."

"I watched your tests yesterday," Jan continued, "and it seems Nita is our strongest paddler. Nita, try to stay to the back of the group, and make sure we're all together, okay?"

Nita looked at Siobhan as she said, "Okay, Jan." Not just to rub in that she'd done the best on her test, but also, maybe, to express something more sinister. Maybe she wouldn't notice if Siobhan drifted away from the group. Maybe Siobhan would yell and yell and nobody would hear.

Later, as an adult, Siobhan will have dreams where, instead of the brightly colored plastic of their individual kayaks, she and the other four girls row a single wooden skiff, with Jan standing at the bow. In these dreams, Jan wears a double-breasted jacket with gold buttons and epaulets, and the girls are in rags. Jan has one boot up on the lip of the boat, and points forward with the tip of her machete.

NITA

1

AT THE END of her last, truncated summer at Camp Forever-more, Nita sat in a hard plastic chair in the police station. Her parents were in similar chairs on either side of her, and her feet were up in her father's lap as she dozed, limp after days of burned adrenaline, her eyelids weighted with relief. An unfamiliar woman's voice went back and forth with her mother's. And then another voice, a man who wasn't her father, added, "Don't worry. She'll be okay. You would be surprised what children can forget."

Nita stirred. In defiance, she wanted to hold on to this memory. The plastic chairs, the strangers' voices. But she felt it slipping away from her even as it happened, becoming clouded with sleep and doubt.

Nita had an impeccable memory for facts and figures. She had, almost accidentally, memorized a textbook page containing two hundred digits of pi as the single image of that page, rather than as a string of numbers, and could recite it for the amusement of her father and his colleagues. Yet, as her mother often pointed out, Nita seemed to have trouble with the events of her own short life. When asked, she couldn't remember if something had happened this year or the last, yesterday or the day before. Nita didn't mind. It felt intentional, like a super-power: she could clear out space for what mattered, replacing the dull homogeny of most days or the specifics of a bad day with more names, numbers, and information, until she was left with only a wordless remnant of how she'd felt. What had happened out in those woods? Fear, frustration. But also: power, control, knowing what to do and getting it done.

Her father's hands rested on a large blister on the back of her left heel, the skin translucent over a fat bubble of pus, and they both itched for him to pop it.

Afterward, as the Prithis drove from the ferry terminal to the airport hotel where they would spend the night, her father said suddenly, into the silence, "You had quite the adventure."

Nita could see her mother's profile only in snatches as they entered and exited the radius of each streetlight. Between two lights, her mother's disdain became — or disguised itself as — amused affection. For the first time, Nita saw her parents as separate people, a man and woman who had lived for years be-fore intersecting, before Nita. And she had a blueprint for the kind of man she could one day love. Someone like her father, affable and oblivious.

THAT SEPTEMBER, the pet store she passed on her walk home from school acquired a litter of golden retriever pup-pies. They bounced inside the window display like popcorn in an air popper. With their short snouts and black button noses, their pupils dilated to perpetual ecstasy, they looked like living teddy bears.

The puppies were gone the next afternoon, either sold or moved deeper into the store. Their image floated up in Nita's mind at night as she tried to sleep, and in that last hour of the school day, when even the teacher seemed twitchy and bored. She'd always wanted a dog, in an abstract way—a new toy, a special friend. The puppies made her feel something new, a goopy, aching sense of need. She had to have one.

She started her campaign the moment her parents arrived home from work. Her mother was an administrator at the hospital where her father was an anesthesiologist. "Mummy, Daddy, I want a dog," she announced, in a voice that failed to express the adult gravity, the serious and long-considered desire of her request. It had been three whole days since she'd seen the puppies. "I'll walk it, feed it, clean up after it. You won't have to do a thing."

"Ah," her father said, "let's not talk about this right now. I need my dinner."

Nita followed them into the kitchen, aware—but unable to stop it—that she was losing her composure, devolving into a little-girl whine. "I promise to take care of it all by myself. I want a dog! Oh, please. Oh, please please please." It was infuriating, this gap between her thoughts and feelings and what came out of her mouth. Her voice, low for a just-turned-twelve-year-old-girl, was nevertheless still in the high child-register the world was accustomed to ignoring. Whole universes stirred inside her, she felt, but she couldn't form them into words.

"Go upstairs, little elephant," her mother said. "I'll call you for dinner."

Nita stomped up the stairs, proving the nickname she resented. She lay down on her stomach in her bedroom, her ear against the heating vent, where she could hear her parents' voices in the kitchen if she strained. She thought the battle was lost for the day, and was surprised to hear her parents discussing the possibility of a dog in earnest. "I'm glad she wants a dog," her mother said. "Sometimes I'm afraid that . . ."

Nita's father prompted, "Yes? Afraid of what?"

After a long pause, her mother changed the subject. "Do you remember why we sent her to that camp?"

"Because she wanted to go. She begged to go."

"No, the first year. It was my idea. I thought she was too bookish, spent too much time inside. I was shocked that she loved it so much, that she wanted to go back every year. And it was so expensive and hoity-toity-seeming, and I was proud that we could manage it."

"It's not your fault," Nita's father said. "It was that crazy woman. Putting them in that situation. Pretending like she wasn't sick."

"No, I know—it's not that. It's just . . . Nita's just a little girl. She talks like a little girl, she wants little-girl things. She laughs when I'm silly. That's all I can see. I can't quite believe she did the things they say she did."

"She's a hero!" Her father raised his voice. "I'm proud of her. She saved herself. She saved the others. She deserves . . ." He faltered on what Nita deserved. "A dog," he said finally. "If she wants a dog, let's get her a dog."

That Saturday, Nita's parents left the house without telling her where they were going. She used their outing as she often did, a chance to graze through the cabinets, looking for any hidden treats. Finding nothing, she ate a handful of the raisins her mother used for cooking and a spoonful of jam.

She heard the front door open and her father's voice. "Go on, go on," he said. As Nita wiped the jam from her face, an enormous German shepherd crept into the kitchen, her parents walking behind. His tail was tucked between his legs and his head hung limply downward. Nita's parents beamed. Probably seeing an appealing show of submissiveness, a dog who knew his place. "Poor thing. He's been tied to a post in Cousin Harjeet's yard for two years," her father said.

The dog went immediately to Nita, who had stayed, terrified, in a chair at the kitchen table, her stomach sinking to her knees, the feeling that accompanies getting what you thought you wanted. *What have I done?* she thought. The dog quietly put a paw on each of her thighs and stretched to stand tall. Not excited and slobbering like the pet store puppies, those limp-tongued, golden bundles of pure joy in the shop window. Just poised there, sniffing her face, his breath as hot as a blast of air from a furnace and reeking of rotten meat. Up close, his brown eyes were disconcertingly humanlike, intelligent and probing.

"Hey, get down," Nita's mother said. The dog didn't react. To Nita, she added, "You'll have to teach him not to do that."

Nita touched the dog's ears gingerly. The dog dropped abruptly and turned to face Nita's parents, pinning Nita in the chair with his body, standing pointedly between her and them, claiming her.

IN A DELIVERY ROOM, more than twenty years later, Nita's thoughts were a slurry of effluvia and voided pain. Her sweat-drenched hair was plastered to one side of her face, the bones of her husband Sadiq's hand clutched in hers. The room was oddly dim beyond the reach of a standing work light pointed directly between her legs, as though she were giving birth to the sun. Like this was for them, the observers in sterile blue paper, and not her, her head kept purposely in shadows. Infinity eked out in seconds, each moment discrete, each one asserting its presence, demanding to be counted.

Her son, Evan, took his first breath. He transmuted from amphibian blue to shrieking red, screamed with the pain of the new world. The nurse beamed just like Nita's parents had while coaxing the dog forward, and Nita's stomach dropped in just the same way. The same thought: *What have I done?* And then, again: love, love like madness, love like murder.

• • •

NITA'S PARENTS HAD bought some rudimentary dog supplies, finding that Harjeet had none to give them. Still feeling festive, novel, Nita's father placed a dog bed on the floor of Nita's bedroom and gestured at it for the benefit of the dog, miming sleep with his hands tented under his head. The dog sniffed it once, and then climbed onto Nita's bed and lay down, placing his head on his paws. He stared at the family as if to see what they'd do. Nita's child-size bed frame, made of hollow, white-painted metal tubing, groaned in protest.

"You'll have to teach him not to do that," her mother said.

Nita changed for bed in the bathroom, too unnerved by the way the dog tracked her movements with his eyes to disrobe in front of him. When she returned, he hadn't moved. She nudged his butt gently with the heel of her hand, feeling his back hip bones shift as though loose and malleable under the skin. "Off," she said. "Off, you big wolf."

Sighing, she climbed into the bed with him. He gave off an extraordinary amount of heat. She was surprised the air didn't steam off his flank.

She rolled onto her side, turning her back to his collection of bad smells and the imprint of drool upon the sheet. She felt his nose prodding against her shoulder blade. And then a soft mouthing, a corner of her nightshirt clasped, teeth grinding on teeth. She stiffened. It seemed loving and threatening at once: *I could eat you, but I won't.*

THE FOLLOWING MORNING, the dog woke Nita just after 5 a.m. He didn't bark. He put all the force of his eighty pounds into his paws and bore down on her stomach. She screamed as her eyes popped open, his muzzle inches from her face.

He knew "sit," acquiescing as she attached the lead to his collar. Leash in hand, she opened the front door. While she was still processing her first thought, recoiling at the cold, vaguely frightened by the shadowy hedges in the streetlights, the dog bolted outside.

She was yanked behind, trying to bear down on her heels, gripping the taut leash as it shredded her hands. He wasn't running—the leash reduced him to an ambling speed, his feet scraping the concrete mechanically as he strained forward by the neck—but she was.

"Stop! Heel! Wolf! Wolf, stop!"

So she had named him.

Forty minutes later, she succeeded in dragging Wolf back into the front hallway of their house. As soon as the door closed, he was once again alert and obedient, like nothing had happened. She unclasped the leash and saw his fur was forced against the grain around his collar. She massaged his neck, and he bore it stoically.

She threw Wolf and a bowl of dog food into the enclosed backyard. "Here," she said. "You can run and romp and play by yourself, with nobody choking you. Okay?" She had to walk backward and nudge his prodding nose with the sliding door to get it shut, with her on the inside.

She passed through the living room again as she left for school. Wolf was still sitting by the back door, his breath fogging one spot on the glass, staring at her, the food untouched. Patient, ominous. He'll get bored and explore eventually, she reasoned. As she walked by the tall wooden fence of their front yard, she saw his nose poking at the small gap at the bottom of the fence, tracking Nita as she passed.

THAT AFTERNOON, as Nita was leaving school, the guidance counselor, Miss Taylor, took a flying leap out of her office —formerly a section of lockers in the hallway and a closet in the principal's office, hastily joined—and into Nita's path. "Nita, I'm glad I caught you. I've been trying to get a hold of your parents to schedule a meeting, but no one ever answers the phone."

Miss Taylor was the tallest woman Nita had seen in real life. Her pulled-back hair was a whisper from the low ceiling, and her long, drooping necklace of wooden beads seemed to elongate her further. Her limbs were slender, her head ovular and in line with her narrow torso, but her hands and feet were gigantic, like a dramatic afterthought, extra turns added in a game of Hangman. Her tiny office seemed like a prank that had been pulled on her.

"When did you call?" Nita asked.

"I've tried every night this week. Around six, I guess."

"We unplug the phone during dinner. Am I in trouble?"

"No, no. Nothing like that. I just need to talk to them about something." She held out a business card. "Can you ask them to call me?"

Nita sensed she was lying about Nita not being in trouble. She stared at the card, almost hidden by Miss Taylor's huge, slablike thumb. Taking it seemed like signing her own arrest warrant.

Miss Taylor, seeing Nita's hesitation, added, "Oh. Do they not speak English?"

Nita saw an opening. "Not super well. You can tell me what it's about and I'll tell them." Miss Taylor raised an eyebrow, so Nita hedged. "Or you can tell me when you want to meet with them, and I'll make sure that they come. But I should be there too. So I can translate."

"Well, let's see." With one hand on the door frame, Miss Taylor swung her long body in and out of her office, swiping a leather-bound planner off her desk. "Do you think they could come in on Monday morning? Maybe eight-thirty?"

"I'll ask."

"And I'll make sure to write you a note for homeroom." Miss Taylor wrote something down. She looked up at Nita with an expectant, self-satisfied smile, the look of grown-ups as they bestow a gift and glow with their own benevolence, giving themselves the gift of a child's reaction.

Nita shifted uncomfortably. "Can I go now?"

"Oh, of course. Let me know what they say."

Nita was still part of the first wave of kids to leave. The others had lingered at their desks and lockers, while she had been eager to get home. She'd been thinking of Wolf all day. She worried her parents would make him disappear as capriciously as they had produced him.

Wolf sat at the bottom of the brick school steps.

He was covered in dirt, snout to tail. He waited with the same troubling, ancient patience as he had that morning. She stopped in surprise, then walked down to meet him. "What are you doing here?" she murmured, rubbing his head.

The other kids rushed to see the dog, gathering around, chattering excitedly, each trying to get Wolf's attention. "Is he friendly? Can I pet him? Does he bite? Hi, Doggie! Hi!" He looked confused and stumbled backward. He didn't snarl or growl or snap, which the kids would have understood. Instead, he raised his back hackles like a cat, and looked to Nita with panic and warning in his eyes. In a loud voice, she told the other kids to step back. She pulled Wolf away by the collar. They groaned in disappointment and yelled things after her, calling her selfish and mean for not letting them play with the cute dog.

He trotted contentedly beside her all the way home, a far cry from that morning on the leash. She considered him warily. "I wish you could talk," she said aloud. He turned to her voice with interest, then stopped to urinate into a bush.

Nita spent the weekend helping her father fill in the huge hole Wolf had dug under the fence and lay concrete blocks around the perimeter. On Monday morning, as Nita waited by the car for her parents, she heard Wolf's nails scratching against the wood as he climbed onto one of the blocks and tried to scramble up the side of the fence. Just the black tip of his nose appeared over the top with each jump and fumbling fall.

THE FACES OF other children kept appearing in the window of Miss Taylor's office — the window faced the hallway, as the room had no external walls. Nita's parents and Miss Taylor seemed oblivious to this, the stuck-out tongues and curious head-tilts, the glee and incipient gossip.

Miss Taylor looked even more like a giant behind her small desk, crammed in with Nita's family, their stout three-some. Nita was almost as tall as her mother, who was only a few inches shorter than her father, all of them proportionally broad, firm-footed. Her parents had each shaken Miss Taylor's hand as they entered. "It's so nice to meet you," she said.

Her father said nothing. Her mother said, "Yes, yes," not yet betraying Nita's lie.

"So. I've asked you here today because some of Nita's teachers — all of her teachers, in fact — think it would be a good idea to skip Nita ahead a few grades. Which is to say, to the high school part of the building. We'll have to do some testing to determine exactly what grade she should go into."

Nita's father rubbed his chin. Her mother said quickly, "Oh. No, thank you."

Miss Taylor looked at Nita. "Can you explain it to them?"

"She doesn't need to explain anything to us," Nita's mother said. Miss Taylor, realizing she'd been duped, shot Nita a disapproving look. Nita shrugged. "We just don't think it's a good idea."

"May I ask why not?"

"She'll be a little girl among women and men."

Nita thought of what she'd heard through the heating vent, her mother insisting that Nita was a little girl as though that had suddenly come into question.

"She can graduate early. She can go to college early," Miss Taylor said.

Nita's mother turned to Nita. "Are you annoying your teachers? Is that why they want to get rid of you?"

Nita rolled her eyes. She knew her mother was joking, but she also knew her dry delivery was going to fly over Miss Taylor's head. Miss Taylor's office was decorated with inspiring messages on yellow construction-paper suns, written in black cursive with big, kid-friendly loops. No irony lived here.

Miss Taylor said, "I don't think you understand. This is an *opportunity*. We think Nita is . . ." She glanced down at Nita, and Nita grinned back at her, knowing she wasn't supposed to hear this. "We think she's very gifted. A genius."

Nita's mother snorted. "Do you know what she did this morning, at breakfast? She noticed there was some writing on the bottom of her milk glass. Just the manufacturer name. So she tilted the glass to read it. While it was still full of milk. Spilled milk all over the table and the floor." She touched Nita's hair affectionately. "My little genius. *Pah.*"

"Aren't you worried about her being bored? Unstimulated? Wasting her potential?"

"Are you bored at school?" Nita's father asked her.

"Yes," Nita said.

"Are your classmates bored?" her mother asked.

"Yes. School is boring."

"No offense, Miss Taylor, but I don't think kids are supposed to find school terribly exciting. That's not really the point, is it? Reading, sums, keep them from killing each other. That's all we're asking for."

"I really think . . ."

"We're her parents, or aren't we?" Her mother stood and her father followed suit. Her voice was self-possessed. "So let's not keep Nita from class any longer. Enough of this nonsense.

She'll not be a high-schooler at twelve." She guided Nita out the door by the shoulder without saying goodbye to the gawping Miss Taylor.

They walked Nita to her homeroom. The meeting had lasted less than ten minutes. "Now, Nita," her mother said, "you're to keep this to yourself, all right? Don't go bragging to your friends. And don't think you can start slacking off. All this tells us is there's no reason you shouldn't be acing all your courses."

Nita had seen the teenagers on the other side of the linking hallway, their hulking flannel forms and sullen, craggy faces, their discontent as alarming as that of peasants on the cusp of revolution. They bore no resemblance to the sexy teenagers she watched on TV.

All the same, whenever she watched *Doogie Howser, M.D* reruns, Wolf's head across her lap, Nita felt a twinge. She'd pledged since the age of three to become a doctor, like her father. As the blond wunderkind performed surgery on-screen, Wolf seemed to understand Nita's murky jealousy better than she did. He jumped up and rushed the television, knocking it from the stand with a savage toss of his head. The bubble-shaped Zenith exploded into shards and a brief symphony of sparks.

THE TURN HAPPENED around puberty. She was speeding up, or everyone else was slowing down. Her body became a hindrance. She couldn't believe how long it took to write something out, her mind sparking ahead of her wrist, the close-up tedium of each pencil stroke. She could see every answer on an exam at once, the sheet overlaid with answers as clearly as a photograph, as though seeing forward in time. How slowly she talked, how slowly everyone talked, their jaws opening and closing, their heads dipping to the right as impulses dawdled on the way from their ears to their brains to their smacking lips.

Her body could do one task while her mind did several others. She could be talking to friends, placating them, saying what was expected, pretending to study with them, pretending to lose at games that were absent any challenge, while mentally constructing her science fair entry, turning its problems over in her head. She found that everything, even art class, even sports, even conversations, could be approached like an algebra problem. Broken down into components and reconstituted to the desired result. She was valedictorian, captain of the field hockey team and the debate team and the mathletes. She could have been more, if she weren't limited by corporeality, if she could only divide her brain among a thousand bodies, an army of soulless golems lurching toward collective perfection. If she could only outsource eating and sleeping. A torrent of thought, of insight, was trapped inside the mechanical bend of bones, snap of tendons, fragile and unreliable and always, always slow.

NEITHER NITA nor her parents had meant it when they said Nita would be the only one to care for the dog. Her father, especially, had relished the thought of a shaggy body warming his toes in the winter, cooking a secret ration of corned beef for the two of them. But Wolf kept them to their word. When Nita wasn't home, Wolf sat and stared out the window, unmoving. Sometimes he fell asleep sitting up, but he never lay down to rest unless she was there. If Nita's parents approached him, he backed away until trapped in a corner and then pawed at the wall, scratching the wallpaper. At first, he wouldn't eat unless Nita sat on the floor beside his bowl, where he could keep an eye on her at the same time. He never seemed happy, or tired, the slack-jawed panting eagerness Nita had thought was the default for all dogs. The closest he came was a slight, dignified wave of his tail when he first spotted Nita through the window.

"He needs toys," Nita told her parents. "Treats." Something else to love.

They bought a squeaker toy in the shape of a giraffe, and a book for children on dog training. Nita put the giraffe down in front of Wolf in the backyard. He tested it lightly with one paw, and when it squeaked, he jumped and skittered away, looking at Nita as though betrayed.

On the book's advice, she wedged treats into the seams of the giraffe. Cheap nubbins of flour and peanut butter had no effect, so she upped the ante, covering the toy with bits of her father's beef jerky.

Wolf sniffed the changed scent and pounced. He held down the giraffe with both paws and tore it open in one pull of his maw. He dug quickly through the cotton batting until he found its plastic squeaking heart, took it into his mouth, and dropped it at Nita's feet. He sat, waiting, as a soldier for his next command. He followed Nita around as she gathered up the cotton that had been flung across the lawn in the process. She left the jerky to the neighborhood cats and raccoons.

The dog-training book seemed to be for an entirely different species from Wolf. It emphasized all the wrong things. She taught him the parlor-trick commands so quickly it was satisfying to neither of them. But his aversion to anyone but Nita, his sleepless days and joyless silence, his bottomless, demonic energy—the book had no advice for this.

If his walks were too short, or if she just let him out into the yard instead, she would turn in her desk chair while doing homework and find Wolf lying on her bed, staring at her with a glinting intensity that made her lizard brain nervous. If she dared to skip a walk entirely, Wolf would quietly and efficiently destroy something. Never anything of her parents', never anything expensive. A school project. The commemorative T-shirt from her first year at Forevermore. A book with dirty passages in it that she'd stolen from the library. Somehow Wolf seemed to know what mattered to Nita and Nita alone.

She had only herself to blame. She should have taken him for a longer walk. She should have paid him more attention.

The first time she went to a school dance, Wolf jumped out an open window, tearing through the mesh screen and wearing its frame around his middle as he ran down the block.

They climbed into her long-suffering bed each night, and he stared directly into her eyes, nipped harmlessly at her clothes, gave a few restrained, tremulous licks, shuddered with pleasure as she scratched his neck — acts of worship, total immersion in her being. He lived uneasily, and only Nita gave him peace. Nobody loved Nita like this. Not her parents, nor her school friends, girls who had been quick with declarations of forever when they were young but now seemed to nod along to what Nita said and probably talked about her behind her back.

She woke in the night drenched in sweat, pinned by Wolf's heft, dog hair already past her mouth and compressing in her throat, a crushing, stultifying embrace. She envied other dog owners, sometimes, the only other people wandering the suburban streets in the early morning. The ones with friendly dogs, emanating love in all directions, like a hazy corona of light. But sometimes she pitied them, that they would never know the focused, scorching beam of another creature's obsession.

EACH GRADUATE at her high school had a mandatory five-minute meeting with the guidance counselor in the autumn of senior year. The counselor on this side of the walkway was more battle-worn than Miss Taylor, her posture defeated and her eyes hollow, health- and social-services pamphlets instead of paper suns. "So," she said, uninterested, almost sarcastic, "what are you planning to do with your life, Nita?"

"I'm going to become a doctor."

The pitch of her interest, and one of her eyebrows, raised a fraction of an inch. "Really? Why? You hate people."

Nita's mouth fell open. That seemed like something a counselor wouldn't be allowed to say to a student. "I don't hate people!"

The counselor shrugged. "My mistake. Well, you have a plan. Let me know if you need help with your applications, et cetera."

"I don't hate people," Nita repeated, still stunned. "I once—" She stopped. She'd shuffled this memory in with other things forcibly half remembered: walking in on her parents having sex, dropping a heavy book on the head of another toddler at day care because she wanted to see what would happen. "I once saved four other girls at summer camp. We were stranded and almost died. I saved everyone."

"Is that why you want to be a doctor? To feel like that again?"

Nita continued to gape. "I've always wanted to be a doctor. My father's a doctor. It's a good career. Isn't that what your job is supposed to be? To direct us to good careers?"

"Nita." The counselor sat forward in her chair. She blinked, bleary-eyed. "You don't need my help. You know that."

NITA LIVED at home while she attended college. She was still the one who took care of Wolf, but she was busier, staying late on campus most days. He hadn't mellowed with age, as the vet had assured them he would. The only change was a break in his silence. He howled despondently at the ceiling when Nita was gone all day.

She came home one night to find her parents watching TV in the living room. Wolf was outside, they said; he wouldn't eat his dinner and they couldn't take his cries anymore. They'd deal with the complaints from the neighbors tomorrow. Nita slid open the back door and called out Wolf's name, expecting to hear him bounding toward her in the dark. When she didn't hear anything, she worried he'd escaped and gone looking for her again. She stepped outside barefoot, onto the wet grass. She continued to call Wolf.

As her eyes adjusted to the blue dimness of evening becoming night, she realized one of the neighbor's cats was in the middle of the lawn, poised mid-run. The slim gray tabby watched her with yellow eyes. Cats never came into their yard anymore. Each one had met Wolf and not returned. This tabby Nita knew to be particularly brave, sometimes strolling languidly along the top points of the fence, staring down at Wolf as he snarled and jumped.

Nita and the cat looked each other in the eye, and then the cat lay down, facing Nita, its tail drifting back and forth serenely. Nita's heart lurched. "Wolf," she cried. "Wolf!"

She walked around the corner of the house and there he was, huddled against the foundation. She knelt beside him and lifted his head, heavier now, onto her lap. His body was still warm but his mouth had cooled. His tongue lolled from his loosened jaw. His eyes stayed mercifully shut. She lowered her face and murmured his name into his fur, which smelled as it always had, of wet dog.

She went back in the house to get her parents. When her father saw the heap that had been Wolf, he said, "He looks like he's just sleeping."

A savage voice inside Nita disagreed. Wolf had slept lightly, tensely, ready for flight, nostrils twitching and tracking Nita. The body in the yard looked defeated as Wolf never had. It looked like any dog, one she couldn't have picked out from a lineup as hers. A German shepherd with typical markings, a black cape and a black snout on tan, with none of Wolf's madness. She said nothing.

Nita and her father carried Wolf inside. Nita sat on the

floor beside Wolf, petting him absentmindedly as she had when he was alive. Her father called the vet and learned that cremation was $700. He called several other vets and discovered that theirs was the only one within a hundred miles who cremated animals. He called Harjeet and suggested he contribute to the cost, as Wolf had been his dog too. Harjeet laughed and hung up. Her father proposed burying Wolf in the backyard; her mother feared he would be dug up by another animal.

Her father called the vet again and consented to the $700. Did they want an autopsy as well, for an additional $300? Her father ranted into the receiver that even in death that dog cost a fortune. Nita intervened, taking the phone, and said an autopsy wasn't necessary. Animals were allowed to die mysterious, unquestioned deaths, as in nature, as though there were no unfairness to be exposed.

That night, as she lay in her ludicrously small bed, a bed she'd outgrown many years ago but hadn't asked to replace, scarcely wide enough for her and Wolf, with her feet hanging off the end, she felt a sudden rush of relief. For the first time in seven years, the room wasn't oppressively hot, and she wasn't penned in between Wolf's powerful form and the wall. She considered the possibility of sleeping in, without being pounced upon at dawn. A day not defined by monotonous walks, every day the same, the simplicity and relentlessness of Wolf's demands. She was free.

The guilt of this thought finally cracked her open, and she wept in gulping sobs for hours. She cried herself to sleep, she cried again upon waking, she cried until her throat was hoarse and her eyes felt pressurized, as though they'd burst out of her head.

In the morning, her mother came in and sat at the edge of the bed. "I thought I should wake you," she said. "Since you're used to Wolf doing it." When Nita didn't respond, she added, "You should leave soon to make it to class on time." And finally: "My love, it was just a dog."

Wolf was still on the floor of the living room, covered now with an old floral tablecloth. Nita touched one hand to the flowered lump before leaving. Her father took Wolf to the crematory while she was on campus. They kept his ashes in an unceremonious cardboard box in the basement. Nita felt nothing for the box.

The air in the house changed, moved more easily. Her parents could finally relax in their own home. Nita grieved privately, every moment she was alone: on the city bus, in the bathroom, in bed. She saw the tabby in the yard more and more, a living reminder that she was the only one who mourned Wolf's absence. She didn't move out until she started medical school, where she met Sadiq, who was funny and gentle, the last in a series of nice, inoffensive suitors.

She knew a kind of man existed who would love her as Wolf had. Who would hunt her every moment, carve her name into his arm, clutch her in his sleep with the same crushing force. Who would die without her. If Nita died, Sadiq would remarry, rebuild over the ruins until his first love was forgotten. As it should be. Nita resigned herself to never being loved like that again.

And some part of her grieved until they handed her Evan, laid him upon her chest in his first blanket, and she saw the bottomless void of need open up once more.

2

AFTER THE ACCIDENT, Nita tried out alternative versions of her story on strangers, people she wouldn't see again. Seat neighbors on airplanes, and later, other mothers at hotel pools who were eager to commiserate. As an adult, her appearance belied her personality. She'd inherited her neutral expression and hooded eyes from her father, the face of a kind but not especially attentive listener. Her short, narrow waist was hidden by heavy breasts and broad hips, an inviting, maternal body. People were always trying to talk to Nita. Slow her down, get in her way.

Nita had a friend from med school who'd gone into emergency medicine and burned out from the stress, who just couldn't weather another twenty-four-hour shift or watch another teenager die. Sometimes Nita told this story as though it were her own: a revelation in a hospital parking lot, sobbing against a guardrail. Her listeners liked this story, but Nita didn't like the fallout. It made her sound weak, an open heart for them to fill with their confidences.

More often, Nita told a story adapted from a scenario in a textbook: she was an internist in private practice on a routine visit to a patient in the hospital. She didn't wear her white coat, not wanting to be confused with hospital staff or asked to consult on other patients. In a sweater and jeans, her hair pulled in a low ponytail, she sat beside the patient in the visitor's chair and held her hand. The patient's boyfriend walked in and mistook Nita for the lover he'd long suspected his girlfriend had. The boyfriend, unbeknownst to Nita and the hospital administration, was the one who'd put the patient there in the first place. He picked up his girlfriend's breakfast tray and beat Nita across the face until an orderly came in and pulled him off. Ever since, Nita has had consciousness-splitting migraines that prevent her from practicing medicine.

The flaw in this story is that Nita would never sit by a patient's bedside and hold her hand. Nita abhorred non-diagnostic touching of any kind. She *was* an internist in private practice, when the accident happened, the newest and youngest of forty doctors in a physician-owned multi-specialty clinic, an all-in-one house.

The real story, the one she was forced to tell friends, family, and colleagues, was that an employee of the linen service that the clinic used put a carton of sterilized gowns on a high, narrow shelf, a spot where they didn't usually go, and didn't notice the carton tipping forward as he closed and secured the closet door. The real story: Nita was the next person to open the closet, and the carton landed on her head.

Mundane. Cartoonish. Without the whiff of life-ending tragedy she was trying to convey. Sometimes a faint curl at the edges of her listener's mouth, as though they were picturing Nita sprawled on the floor, animated birds and stars circling her head.

The doctor who examined Nita thought she had a mild concussion, told her to take the afternoon off and monitor herself. He was skeptical when she later told him about the migraines. A dry hangover, a cleaving pain behind her eyes and a sensitivity to sound and light. Something she could work through if she had to, like a strobe light in a noisy room. He was even more skeptical when Nita said she thought her personality had changed as a result of a traumatic brain injury. He ordered all the tests she requested and they came back clean. "Some doctors can't resist giving themselves fanciful diagnoses," he said, speaking in general terms to soften the insult, which Nita recognized as a physician's trick. "Maybe the migraines are just a coincidence."

She read her chart. The standard phrasing, "Patient claims headaches began with blunt trauma from falling box," caused a bubble of anger to pop in her gut. She didn't *claim* anything. What happened was what happened.

SADIQ WOULDN'T BACK her up. She seemed the same to him, he said. If anything, they got along better these days. He liked having her home so much. He even threw this out: "I'm a doctor too."

"A cardiologist!" she shouted. "Not neuro."

"Well, what did the neurologist say?"

Nita stormed off. She slept off her migraine in the bathtub. When she woke in the evening, she called her father and had the same argument, except she shouted, "You're an anesthesiologist!" She told her father about being unable to carry a teacup on a saucer; it rattled too much. "Shaky hands," she said. "Tell me that's not a neurological symptom."

"Weren't you always like that? I thought that's why you didn't consider surgical. Your mother's hands are shaky, and nothing fell on her head," her father said. She could hear the TV on in the background.

"I was never interested in surgical. My speech is different too," Nita continued. "Slower. Can't you hear it?"

"You mean slurred? No, you sound fine."

"No. Slower. People used to complain about how I talked too fast, remember?"

"Then isn't that a good thing?"

Sharply, Nita asked, "Good thing for whom?"

Her father paused. "What did the neurologist say?"

NITA KEPT a log of all the changes that no one else noticed:

Television. Before the accident, she had grown to hate it. She would sit beside Sadiq on the couch, her leg twitching, her mind reeling with everything else she could be doing. The figures on the screen seemed to say such inane, obvious things. So did real people, of course, but TV shows seemed worse for the contrivance—someone wrote this dialogue, other people approved it, other people memorized it, millions of dollars were spent. Now, alone in her bedroom in the day, Nita watched daytime soaps on the small second TV. She found them comforting, the light and color palette of the cheap sets, the rhythm of the overenunciated voices, the stories that demanded little from her.

Her changed gait. She walked softer, slower, rolling her feet, no longer her mother's little elephant.

Her favorite Vietnamese deli. She'd only ever had the banh mi sandwich. It was so good she'd never felt the need to order anything else. She'd brought her colleagues there and insisted they order the banh mi as well, and held a small, secret scorn for the ones who ordered pho or another sandwich, who chose to miss out.

The first time she went back there after the accident, when she got to the front of the line, the sight of the menu boards stopped her. Four white placards, printed in small text with square photographs of each dish. The items were numbered one to seventy-two. *Seventy-two*. Nita felt dazed, paralyzed, unable to parse this huge array, even to separate the English and the Vietnamese, like she'd forgotten how to read. Which of these seventy-two items did she want?

SADIQ'S MOTHER CAME to visit after Nita's injury. Nita had always found her mother-in-law irritating, her visits endless, but this time, it was a relief to have someone else around. The cooking Nita had hated — cheap, fatty cuts of meats swimming in oil, lentils overcooked to paste, corrosive with salt and chili peppers — now tasted homey and comforting.

Nita woke from a nap — that was another thing for the log, naps — and followed the sound of voices to the living room. Sadiq and his mother were beside each other on the sofa, their backs to Nita. They kept talking. They hadn't heard her come down the hallway. She realized they were talking about her. She leaned weightlessly against the wall to listen.

"She thinks they missed something on the MRI. I think she's just relaxed for the first time in her life, from not working. You know she used to record everything we ate? Not just what *she* ate—what *I* ate as well. To make sure we were getting enough macronutrients. Even on vacation. She finally gave it a rest."

"She told me she liked my lamb!" Sadiq's mother said.

"She let me pick the movie last night."

Nita let him pick the movie all the time! Didn't she? Except when he picked something stupid, or he took too long, scrolling through screen after screen of listings, seemingly paralyzed. Like she'd been at the deli.

"And"—Sadiq got excited, turning more toward his mother, pulling his legs up on the couch like a child—"she even . . . I probably shouldn't be telling you this, but . . ."

"I'm your mother! What can't you tell me?"

Sadiq paused, rolling something around in his mind. Nita remembered, dimly, that those silences used to infuriate her, especially during an argument; she'd wanted to shake him and say, *What? What is it? Spit it out!* "You know Nita's never wanted kids."

His mother gasped.

Sadiq stared into the middle distance. "I wasn't sure. Or —no. I wanted kids, definitely. But Nita had this . . . rock-solid argument against them. Why nobody should have kids. Overpopulation and finances and all kinds of stuff. She does this thing where she talks really fast, and she doesn't take a breath, and everything she says has this airtight logic that just . . . that doesn't let you in. Makes you feel stupid."

"And now?"

"She said she's thinking about it."

Sadiq's mother let out a shout of joy and hugged Sadiq around the neck.

WORST OF ALL, her brain, its exquisite machinery. Had she been that dead-set against children? Or had she just wanted to win the argument against Sadiq, who hadn't been able to articulate why he wanted them, who wanted to upend their life and flood it with unknowns without a plan, a specific reason for doing so? Did she not want a baby, viscerally, or was it just the more defensible position? She'd once felt so certain about everything, that she knew what was best for her and for Sadiq and for her smoking, overeating, motorcycle-riding, aggravatingly noncompliant patients.

She still had her near-photographic memory, but it was harder to make decisions, big and small, banh mi and baby. It was harder to sort through all that information, networks expanding in infinite fractals out from the center of her mind. When she started seeing patients again, she did what she was supposed to do: she gave them the most likely explanation for their symptoms and sent them on their way. But she wanted to tell each patient every possible scenario, the most improbable causes, the way each disease might progress. She could see it all at once, all the branches of their lives splitting and splitting again, terminating in a thousand different deaths, in three days, in fifty years. She struggled to shift between patients. She had twenty minutes, sometimes fifteen, to examine, diagnose, and write her notes.

When it became too much, the thin, bright blade of a migraine sliced through the chaos. She admitted to herself, without telling Sadiq, that she might need to change careers. Perhaps she could research or teach.

One morning, she noticed she'd left a suitcase in the car, after a trip to a conference two months earlier. It had sat nestled on the floor of the backseat, full of dirty laundry, while she'd wondered vaguely what had happened to this or that shirt or sweater. She sighed and dragged it into the house.

She opened the suitcase and the first thing she saw was a mostly empty birth-control-pill pack. No. She'd been on birth control for seven years and had never missed a single pill. Had she seriously forgotten for two straight months? Impossible.

She bit the inside of her mouth nervously. Her teeth felt fuzzy on her tongue; she hadn't brushed them that morning. She might not have brushed them the night before either.

3

NITA HEADED to the far corner of her backyard that housed the stacked wooden frames of her beehive. She put on her bee-keeping suit in the shed and lit the smoker. The view from behind a widow's veil. The bees landed on Nita's hat and nylon-covered arms, too light to feel, their antennae twitching cautiously. She cooed a greeting as she approached the colony, unconsciously trying to harmonize with the held tone of their buzzing, to soothe as she stole.

In the shed, Nita crushed the comb she'd taken into a jar. She duct-taped that jar upside down on top of another jar with a layer of mesh between them, on a sunny corner of the work table. The honey flowed with meditative slowness. She wanted to sit on the floor and watch it ooze, trapping the amber light through the dusty square window in the shed door, stare into its center until her thoughts passed away. She wanted to sit naked in the bathtub and pour fresh, warm honey over herself until she was a sticky golden statue.

Six months earlier, Nita had gone to her first meeting of the local beekeepers' society, at the home of Jeanne and Simon, the British couple who headed the society and wrote the obsessive but charmingly self-aware newsletter. They showed off the hives they kept on their three-acre vineyard, located in the hills between sprawling mansion estates and unconquered fields of bramble, roosters crowing in the distance. Nita had loved the smell of their smoker, filled with pine needles, and felt curiously unafraid as the confused bees poured out.

In Jeanne and Simon's living room, drinking their wine, Nita described the dimensions of her backyard, and her plans to start a hive behind the shed. A gruff, widowed retiree in the corner, who also kept a large number of colonies on a large tract of land, said, "That's too small. You'll be giving up most of your yard to the bees. Your kids will have nowhere to play."

"Nonsense!" Simon had crowed. "That's plenty of room. And your kids can get into beekeeping when they're just a little bit older. Lots of families do it together." He and Jeanne were childless. "We'll help you get set up and pick your gear."

Bees as a species were passing from the earth unexplained, but hers were orderly, unmysterious, a society that functioned under rules and roles, with Nita as god above all.

NITA REMOVED HER SUIT, left the shed, and returned to the house. She passed by Sadiq on the computer in the living room, several windows open across the immense monitor: basketball scores, a medical paper, the *Wall Street Journal*, Twitter, a tech blog review of a new phone. Nita wondered if he just added porn to the matrix, or if it got to be full-screen. Did he keep one eye on the real-time stock values as he jacked off?

"I have a late tee-off today," Sadiq said, without looking up. "Will you be okay with the boys?"

Seeing the quotidian masculinity of his interests, laid out across the computer screen like tiles in a mosaic, she felt a kind of despair. This was a man who never liked anything he hadn't been told to like. A man built by and for advertising. "Sure," she said. Of course she'd be fine. Her children ate fresh honey, fresh berries from the runners she'd planted for the bees, elaborate meals from scratch. She made her own cleaning agents and bath products. The hours flew. The hours crawled.

Evan, her older son, burst out of his bedroom door as she passed in the hallway. He'd been waiting for her, coiled like the springs of a trap. "Ahhh-ahhh-ahhh! I am George of the Jungle!"

"Pajama time is over, George," Nita said.

"No!" Evan shouted. "Pajamas all day!"

"Pajamas are for sleeping," Nita said.

"Pajamas are for all day."

"It's time to put on your tee-ball uniform. You wear your uniform to tee ball."

"No, I wear pajamas to tee ball."

"Did you wear pajamas to tee ball last week?"

"Yes, I did!"

"No, you didn't."

"I did! I did, I did, I did!"

Nita often found herself in this position. Evan, four years old and immune to reason, was perhaps the first equal she'd ever had in an argument.

Evan slammed the door to his bedroom and held it shut. Nita pushed down the handle and forced the door open with her shoulder. Evan ran to the corner and faced Nita, his knees bent, ready to sprint past her. She grabbed him by the waist and wrestled him out of his pajamas before he slipped from her grasp, running back into the hallway in his underwear.

"Ahhh-ahhh-ahhh!"

Sadiq had meandered in their direction. "Hey, buddy," he said to Evan, "it's almost time to go. Do you want me to drive you?"

"No! I don't want to go to tee ball. I hate it."

Nita, gathering up his gear, muttered, "Last week, you said it was your favorite thing." Evan had to be run every day, burned out as much as possible. Tee-ball, the pool, the playground, the trampoline gym, just a big, fenced-in field — otherwise there'd be hell to pay. He had Wolf's gift for targeted destruction. So often she'd come upon Evan holding something only Nita loved over his head, the glee in his face as he let it drop.

"Did not! I hate it! You're lying!"

"I can pick you up afterward and we can go for ice cream," Sadiq coaxed.

"I hate it! I want to stay home and play! I want Mom to take me!"

Nita threw his duffel bag of tee-ball crap into the hall-way. She knelt before Evan and grabbed him by the shoulders. "Which one?" she said. "You want to stay home, or you want me to take you? Make sense!"

Evan looked stunned for a moment. He started to cry.

"Nita, he's just a kid," Sadiq said.

She shook Evan lightly. "Evan! Look at me. Do you want to stay home or do you want me to take you to tee ball?"

Evan gasped each word through his tears. "I . . . want . . . you . . . to . . . take . . . me."

"All right then." She picked up Evan and he threw his arms around her neck with abandon, burying his snot-covered face in her hair. There was a slight pinch in her back that she had no time to investigate. She put him down on the dresser that had been his changing table, his long legs hanging off the end, and dressed him like a baby.

Sadiq hovered behind her. "He's only like this when you're around. He's so different when it's just him and me."

"So you've said."

Once dressed, the boy held out his arms to be lifted again.

"Should I carry him to your car?" Sadiq asked.

"Mommy," Evan demanded flatly.

"Let's give Mommy a break, buddy," Sadiq said.

"Mommy!"

Sadiq jumped back. "Should I check on Mati?" he said to Nita.

Couldn't he just *do* something, anything, without asking first? "Mati's fine," Nita said. "He's asleep. I'll wake him up to come with us." She picked up Evan by the armpits and put him down, upright, on the floor. "I have to carry your brother. You have to walk. Go put your shoes on."

"Carry me!"

"Put your shoes on *right now*."

Evan ran away. To put on his shoes, or more likely not. Sadiq said, "Don't you think you're too hard on him?"

Nita recalled when, recently, Evan had knocked a small picture frame off the mantel, cracking the glass. He was home with Sadiq and the so-called mother's helper they'd hired, a high school senior from the neighborhood named Holly. Both Holly and Sadiq had somehow not seen this happen. Evan hid the frame in his toy bin before announcing, casually, "I have something to show Mommy."

"What is it?" Sadiq had asked.

"It's for Mommy only."

She'd yelled, he'd cried. As he must have known only she would yell, that Holly and Sadiq might let him get away with it, comfort him, say it was an accident. The same thing happened when he'd run face-first into the door frame. He wouldn't let Sadiq come anywhere near him, wouldn't allow anyone else to tend to the small cut on the side of his head. "Don't touch me," he'd screamed. "Mommy! Mommy!" Getting shriller and shriller.

Another day, Nita had gone to a job interview for a part-time position in pharmaceutical research. Evan had asked Holly when Nita would be back and she told him three o'clock. Evan nodded, accepting this, and they'd had a fun, normal afternoon.

Evan could recognize numbers at an early age, before anyone had made a conscious effort to teach him. Holly told Nita, later, that when the digital clock rolled over to 3:00, it was like a switch flipped inside him. "Where's Mommy?" he asked.

"She'll be back soon."

"You said three. When the first number is three."

"Yeah, that's what I thought. Maybe she's stuck in traffic."

"Where's Mommy?"

"I told you—she'll be back soon."

"I want Mommy."

"Evan—"

"I. Want. Mommy. Mommy. *Mommy. Where's Mommy?*"

Mommy Mommy Mommy. Exhausting. Maddening. But also—to Nita's truest, darkest self—intoxicating.

She wrangled both boys into the car, tightly gripping one of Evan's wrists until she'd clicked him into place. When the garage door was open, he had a tendency to run down the driveway, barreling into the road, unafraid and unrepentant, no matter how many times she'd scooped him up or pleaded for him to never, ever do that again. Evan banged on the glass with both fists.

Nita settled into the driver's seat. Evan tried to lean forward, reaching for her, while his restraints kept him in place. "Ahhh-ahhh-ahhh!" he yodeled, directly into her ear.

"Evan," Nita said, starting the car. "How many boys are there on your tee-ball team?"

"Eighteen."

"So if I wanted to divide them into groups of six, how many groups would there be?"

"Three."

"If I wanted to give everyone two cookies each, how many cookies would I need?"

Evan swung his legs, bored. "Thirty-six."

"If I wanted to divide them into equal groups of five, how many groups would there be?"

"You can't."

"Why is it called tee ball?"

"I don't know."

"Guess."

A pause, pleasingly brief. "The thing we hit the ball off, it's called a tee."

"Why is the big-boy version called baseball?"

"Because there are bases." Evan considered. "But tee ball has bases too. So that's a stupid name."

Sometimes Nita even envied Evan — his genius was blossoming earlier, he was a boy, and he was growing up in a time, place, and socioeconomic stratum where children were as worshipped and minutely studied as saints.

Nita rounded the corner at the end of their street. "It is a stupid name."

After a few moments of thoughtful silence, Evan said suddenly, cheerfully, "I love you and I hate you, Mommy."

Nita knew what she should say, the talk she could begin, but no one else could hear them. Except Mati, staring peacefully out the window. Mati, who adored everyone, nuzzled anyone, was liberal with his toothless smiles. His eyes were full of slow-dawning delight. Evan, as an infant, had had a frank, discerning stare that made adults feel the absurdity of their cootchie-cooing. Mati slept through the night on schedule and had an oddly neutral smell for a baby — he smelled like baby powder and enclosed rooms, not the sweet-shit animal rankness that Evan had had from birth. Mati should have been the favorite. The good baby. As Sadiq was a good man, her parents were good parents, all this plain-faced, dutiful love.

"I love you and I hate you too," she said. In the rearview mirror, Nita and Evan smiled at each other, their secret smiles.

HOLLY ARRIVED AFTER they came home in the afternoon. Dopey, well-meaning Holly, who came by for a few hours every now and then. When they'd hired her, she'd never changed a diaper, but she'd perkily assured them she'd practiced on dolls in a course at the Red Cross.

Holly played awkwardly with the boys in the grass, chasing Evan around with a stooped back, while Mati turned his head back and forth, giggling and trying to follow their movements. Nita was folding laundry on the screened-in back porch. "How's school going?" she asked Holly, through the mesh.

"Okay, I guess. The SATs are coming up."

Nita paused a moment before speaking, deciding that there was no harm, Holly was no one. "I got fifteen-ninety on mine. There was this boy in my year who got sixteen hundred. God, I hated him. I still remember his name."

"Um, that's nice," Holly said. Evan squealed and cut a sharp left turn to get away from her.

Nita continued, "I was sixth in my class in med school, and I still remember the names of the five people who were ahead of me. I used to recite them, like a mantra."

Holly laughed nervously.

"I'm sure you'll do fine," Nita said.

"Not as well as you, though," Holly said. "Evan? Where'd you go?"

Screams.

Evan appeared from around the corner of the shed, swatting at his face, stumbling, screeching at the top of his lungs. He seemed out of focus, somehow blurred. Nita realized why. He was a walking cloud of bees.

Nita bolted out and across the yard to snatch Evan up. The buzzing had a different frequency than usual, a confused tone. A few of the stings on Evan's face were already starting to swell. Holly ran alongside them as Nita hurried back into the enclosed porch. The bees didn't follow. They remained in a formation centered on the hive with the overall shape of a hand, the palm hidden behind the shed, wavering, tapered fingers of bees extending outward.

"Let me see," Nita said. She examined Evan, who sobbed and howled. To her relief, he had fewer stings than she'd thought, and only on his face, neck, and hands.

"We should go to the ER, right?" Holly said.

"No, I think I can handle it."

Holly had to raise her voice to be heard over Evan's crying. "Really? He looks so messed up."

"It's not as bad as it looks."

"But, like, how do you know?"

Nita stared at Holly. "I'm a doctor."

"I mean, I know, but, like . . ."

"You know what," Nita said. "I need supplies. Can you go to the drugstore and get aloe vera and calamine lotion?"

"Yeah, sure. Of course." After a brief pause, Holly said, "Where are your car keys?"

"What? You're not driving my car. Walk."

"It's just—the nearest drugstore is kind of far, and it'll take me a while."

"Then hurry up! Go!"

Holly, still seeming bewildered, ran out the side gate. Nita brought Evan into the house. She'd just needed to get rid of Holly.

Nita held Evan down while she pulled the skin taut and removed the stingers with tweezers. She let him ice his hands while she iced his face and neck. "It's cold," he whined.

"It has to be cold to bring down the swelling," she said.

"It hurts."

"I know."

Holly returned just under an hour later. She came in the front door, holding a plastic bag in breathless triumph. "I got the stuff," she said. Evan was already calm, cuddled against his mother in an armchair, half asleep. Holly looked around. "Where's Mati?"

Mati.

Nita jumped out of the chair, causing Evan to stir and whine.

Mati sat contentedly where they'd left him in the yard. In the sunlight, his face was flushed but placid. He faced the shed behind which the bees had retreated. As Nita picked him up, he turned to her with a slightly drugged-looking smile. Heatstroke. All his exposed skin — head, arms, and legs — was sunburned, but not terribly so.

Nita carried him inside, a bundle of heat, like a casserole dish straight out of the oven. His diaper was wet. Holly stood at the back door, mouth agape. "He's fine," Nita said hurriedly.

"You left him out there," Holly said, "with the bees."

"The bees didn't bother him. He got a little too much sun, but he's totally fine."

"You just *forgot him?*"

Nita turned away. "Evan needed my attention, and Mati was fine." She would say it over and over again until it got through to the girl. "And look, now I can use the aloe vera you bought."

"You mean you didn't need it for Evan?"

"You were panicking. I needed calm so I could think clearly and take care of Evan." Evan came and stood beside his mother, wrapping one arm around her leg. She put one hand on his head, her other arm holding Mati tightly to her chest. He was starting to doze. "I'm a doctor, and their mother, and I'm telling you, he's fine. Cultures all over the world and for most of human history didn't hover over their children night and day the way we do."

Holly blinked and pressed her thumbs into her eyes. When she removed her hands from her face, she looked the way she often did with the kids, dimwitted and strangely tortured, out of her depth. Nita tried to sound reassuring. "It's okay, Holly. Accidents happen. Everything got a little chaotic, but the boys got out with only a few stings and a sunburn. Normal kid stuff. I'm going to take care of Mati. You can head home."

Holly nodded. Nita carried Mati into his room, Evan trailing quietly, clutching on to her leg as well as he could as she walked. As she changed Mati's diaper and soothed his burns, she could hear the garage door opening, the clacking track and low, mechanical hum. Sadiq was home.

She hummed softly to Mati as his eyelids drooped and fluttered, as she did with the bees. The door connecting the kitchen and the garage clicked open. She heard Holly's and Sadiq's voices murmuring. Sadiq's voice rising. And then the sound of his precious golf clubs clattering as he dropped the bag unceremoniously onto the kitchen tiles.

Mati twitched awake. Nita continued to hum and he settled again.

She reemerged with the children. Holly stood next to Sadiq, her arms crossed, the righteous, smug expression of a kid who's just tattled to Daddy. And Sadiq had taken Holly's words at face value. He trusted this outsider—who knew nothing about babies, bees, medicine, motherhood, anything, who was barely more than a child herself—more than he trusted her.

She pressed one hand to Mati's back as he slept on her shoulder, and squeezed Evan's hand tightly with the other. She kept her chin raised and her gaze level. Sadiq stared back at her, as if he knew something about her that he wished he didn't, something he could never unknow.

CAMP FOREVERMORE

THE GIRLS SET OFF toward the islands, flat slivers and small rises between wisps of low fog. At this distance, it seemed impossible that any of the islands was large enough to accommodate six people at high tide, even more impossible that the largest one contained what might be called a town.

Fifteen minutes in, Siobhan's shoulders started to ache and she noticed her wet hands were forming blisters. Jan's kayak glided with machine smoothness and consistency, like a moving walkway at an airport. Siobhan paused to rest for a few beats and looked behind her. First she saw Nita, paddling with the same kind of clean, methodical strokes, staring straight ahead, not looking down at the paddle the way Siobhan did. Beyond Nita, Siobhan could see the kayaks of other groups, that unmistakable neon against the gray-green, gray-brown, and gray-blue of water, land, and sky. Some of them were singing and chatting, distant girl voices like the nattering of birds. Jan's group worked in silence. The larger group, all the girls of Forevermore, was beginning to dissipate and spread in different directions. Siobhan found the sight alarming. She wanted to corral them back together.

She started paddling again, a little faster to make up for her break. She started thinking about the night to come. It was amazing to her that they didn't have toothbrushes or pajamas. Toothbrushing, bathing, and rules of civility would be suspended. She hoped she would share a tent with Dina and Jan, while Isabel would be foisted off on Nita and Andee.

"Count off!" Jan yelled.

"One," answered Nita.

"Two," said Andee.

"Three," squeaked Isabel. So the girl could talk.

"Four," said Dina.

Siobhan said, "Five."

"All right!" Jan called. "Keep it up, sisters!" Her strokes sped up just slightly, with no change in her posture, no visible exertion, the distance between her kayak and theirs growing just enough for them to notice.

THEY SLOWED in the shallows of an island about the size of a closet, a peak of rock jutting just slightly out of the sea. They locked their kayaks together using their paddles and stayed in the boats, eating the snacks Jan passed around. Standard camp issue: two dry oatmeal cookies and an individual tin of peaches. Jan told them about sea otter families that hold hands as they sleep in order to stay together.

Jan glanced at her sports watch and announced, "We're making incredible time, sisters." She slurped the packing water from her can of peaches. "You're such fast paddlers!"

Siobhan wanted to comment that the speed hadn't been up to them. They'd been following Jan. And Siobhan, in fact, wouldn't mind slowing down. Her hands were red across the base of her fingers. She'd put on her woolen gloves, but they'd gotten soaked immediately and were worse than useless. The lessons the day before had involved practicing on dry land first, and a lot of drifting around and chatting while the instructor was busy with someone else. The relentlessness of the morning's journey, kayaking strictly as a mode of transport, like they were hurrying to catch a plane, had not been fun at all.

As Siobhan considered whether or not to speak up—she didn't want to give Nita the satisfaction—Jan added, "We'll probably be at Lumpen before lunchtime." Siobhan relaxed. A whole afternoon to set up camp and play on the beach in the sunshine.

"I wonder . . ." Jan said, working something out aloud. "You were promised a full day of kayaking. Calling three hours plus breaks a full day was a stretch to begin with, and now it'll probably only be two and a bit. Maybe we should change our destination and camp somewhere else, so you can have the real experience, like we used to." Jan nodded to herself, deciding. "We'll go to the big island."

"But that's cheating," Nita said. "We're supposed to rough it somewhere with no people and stuff. That's the whole point."

"Yeah," Siobhan jumped in, begrudgingly grateful to Nita. "They have a motel and a restaurant and a ferry and —everything."

"Don't worry—it's a very big island," Jan said. "Lots of funny little nooks and crannies. I know lots of places we can camp that are miles and miles from anyone, where no one would ever stumble upon us." Jan turned her attention to Isabel. All the others had wolfed down their snacks, their breakfast of limp toast and reconstituted egg burned off long ago, but Isabel was gnawing wetly on her first cookie like her teeth couldn't quite break through. "What do you say, Isabel? Up for a little extra paddling?"

Isabel nodded with a grim expression, as though she'd been

asked to weather an unavoidable storm and there was nothing to be done about it. *You can say no*, Siobhan thought, trying to communicate telepathically with Isabel. *Tell Jan you're tired.*

THEY HAD LUNCH on Lumpen Island. The sun was a faded, silvery circle behind the clouds and fog, so faint Siobhan could stare right at it. They dragged their kayaks up the rocky shore. Jan tied all the boats together, and anchored her larger one to a loop she'd embedded in the rocks.

The rocks and sand gave way to moss and dirt as they walked away from the water, and a few thin black spruce that looked surprised to be there. Jan spread a tarp around where the sand ended, the border between beach and woods, and they sat down to picnic.

While Jan handed out their ham-and-cheese sandwiches, Andee leapt to her feet, pointing out at the water. "Oh my God," she said. "Look! It's a seal!"

Siobhan couldn't see anything. "Where? Where?"

"Right there." Andee's finger jabbed at the air.

"I don't see it," Nita said.

"Right *there!*"

They were all standing now. Siobhan caught a flash of movement, a ripple, maybe a dark, slick head popping up and vanishing under again. "Was that it? I think I saw it!"

"I don't see it!" Nita repeated, getting frustrated.

"There it goes again," said Andee.

"I saw it that time!" Dina said. "I think. Maybe."

"Is that it?" Isabel asked.

"*Where?*" Nita demanded.

"It's gone now," Isabel answered.

"Take your sandwiches, sisters," Jan said. "You can keep looking while you eat."

After the seal, they ate in silence, studying the water, hoping something equally magical would appear. Jan put a plastic container of baby carrots and a bag of chips in the center of the tarp. She tore the bag carefully, opening it up into a single, flat piece, then folding the edges into a bowl to hold the chips. She seemed startled that the girls were impressed by this trick and wanted to know how she did it.

Siobhan felt a rush of fondness for Lumpen Island, for the ground beneath her and the tarp keeping her butt dry. Potato chips had never tasted so good, so oily and salty. She felt sated. Sleepy, accomplished, an afternoon feeling.

"I like your hair," she ventured, to Dina.

"Thanks," Dina said. "I like your fleece."

Nita turned away from Andee as she ate her sandwich. The seal seemed to have created a rift between them, and Siobhan tried not to feel good about it.

When it was time to leave, Siobhan rose reluctantly. Jan waded out to the tops of her tall boots to help each girl clear the shoreline. The paddling felt twice as hard. Stiffness settled into Siobhan's neck and shoulders. She started perspiring immediately, hot in her head and cold through her core, where her long-sleeved T-shirt sopped up the sweat under her fleece. She looked back at Lumpen as it receded behind them, at what could have been.

THEY COULD SEE the big island from Lumpen, but for a long time, they didn't seem to be getting any closer. When the details of the land finally became clear, trees and sheer cliffs and high, abrupt edges, Siobhan tried to speed up — the end was in sight! — but her short, frantic, uneven strokes had the opposite effect. It didn't matter: Jan was also slowing, her vigorous straight path becoming a series of large, swooping S-shapes as they traced the coastline. Birds began to pass overhead, gulls and terns with white-dipped wings that were unfamiliar to Siobhan.

It took forever for Jan to find the right spot for them to go ashore. Finally, as they rounded a corner and saw a crescent of white-gray sand and a relatively shallow slope, the whole beach only about five meters long, she turned inland. Even Jan seemed weary and beaten down. She didn't say anything as she coasted into shallower waters and ran her kayak aground. When they'd arrived at Lumpen, there'd been lots of hearty yelling, warnings and instructions. This time, the girls were left to guess at what they should do, following blindly like ducklings. Andee had trouble with the turn. She overshot the beach and had to turn completely around to rejoin the group.

Jan helped them, one by one, out of the kayaks again. She was panting, out of breath. The girls leapt out of the boats as though they were on fire, rushing out of the water, abandoning the job of pulling the kayaks onto land to Jan. She dragged them one at a time up the shore, leaving them scattered haphazardly on the beach, their neon tips pointing in every direction. It was more work, after that, to gather them together so they could be tied. The girls watched, seeing the defeated curve of Jan's back, listening to her labored breathing. They knew they should help, but they were too tired. And anyway, she was the grown-up, and they were only kids.

Once Jan had knotted her own kayak into the anchor, she turned around and looked east, toward the mainland, the direction from which they'd come. Siobhan followed her gaze. The sun was firmly on the other side of the sky, well below its zenith.

Jan opened her mouth to address the girls and no sound came out. She coughed and cleared her throat. "Whew. Good job, sisters." Her voice was raspy, drained of its cheery determination. "It's getting late and we still have lots to do."

Jan nailed in the posts and pitched the two tents. The girls hovered nearby, holding poles, handing them to Jan when prompted, like field nurses. "Are we going to have dinner soon?" Andee asked.

"It's not even four o'clock," Jan answered.

"But I'm hungry."

"I'm hungry too," Nita said.

"I thought you wanted to rough it," Jan said. "This is roughing it."

Siobhan was taken aback. Jan was tough, not mean.

"Do you girls remember what kindling is?"

"Small, dry sticks and twigs," Nita volunteered.

Jan put her hand on Nita's shoulder. "Right. You girls are going to gather some kindling for our fire, sticking as close to the beach as you can, and I'll head into the woods to find some larger fuelwood."

"You're going to leave us alone?" Siobhan said, incredulous.

"I won't be long, I promise."

"But aren't there cougars? And bears?" Dina said.

"Should we hang the food in a tree or something?" Nita said.

"We'll do that before bed. Nobody has seen a cougar or a bear down on this part of the island," Jan said. *But it's an island,* Siobhan thought. *It's not like the cougars and bears can leave.* "Just make lots of noise, like little girls do."

When Jan reached the edge of the trees, she turned around and waved at the girls, who hadn't moved. They must have looked frightened, because she added, "Be brave, sisters! That's what Forevermore is all about!"

THE GIRLS WANDERED, gathering bits of wood. Some kind of prickly bramble grew thick on the ground, poking out from the woods and running almost all the way to the water. It was obviously too supple and alive to burn, the vines a mix of green and pinkish brown, so tangled and abundant Siobhan felt like she could see it growing, lengthening and knotting around itself.

Siobhan followed Dina away from the others. She glanced at the spot where Jan had entered the woods as they passed. There was no obvious path. She had just stepped between two trees with her machete in hand and disappeared. Siobhan stuffed her pockets with scraps of driftwood and fallen twigs. Dina scanned the ground intently, her head tipped forward, apparently finding nothing. She tossed her long bangs out of her eyes.

"What if Jan doesn't come back?" Dina said.

Siobhan stopped and stared at the other girl, who continued with the pretense of searching, her gaze at their feet.

"What if she gets lost? Or hurt? Or eaten by a cougar?"

"She said there's no cougars on this part of the island," Siobhan said.

"It's an *island,*" Dina said. Siobhan didn't admit that she'd had the same thought. After a moment, Dina continued, "She's old. Like, ninety."

"She's not ninety."

"I heard her say she first came to Forevermore in 1934. That's like a zillion years ago."

"Sixty. That's exactly sixty years ago."

"Okay, so that would make her what? Seventy?"

"Between sixty-nine and seventy-two. If Forevermore was for girls the same ages then as it is now." Siobhan was unnerved that Dina couldn't figure that out for herself. She didn't want a stupid best friend.

"Okay, so that's, like, really old. She could just keel over and die for no reason."

"People don't die for no reason."

"Yes, they do," Dina insisted. "My grandpa did."

"No, he didn't. He died of something."

"No, my mom said he just died for no reason."

"They didn't want to tell you the reason."

Dina's head jerked up. Siobhan remembered when she'd told her kindergarten best friend that there was no Santa Claus, and how that had been the end of that friendship too.

Without any outside signal, the girls regrouped by the kayaks. They dumped their finds into a pile, and then they sat down and sorted them by size, as Jan had instructed. When they were finished, the wood arranged in a gradient from small to large along the sand, there was nothing left to do but stare into one another's worried faces.

"We should make noise," Siobhan said. "To keep the bears and cougars away."

"We could sing a song," Dina said. "Or play tag?"

"I'm too tired," Nita said.

"Me too," Andee said, stepping sideways, closer to Nita. Apparently they had made up.

"I can teach you guys a clapping game," Dina said.

"*Okay*," Nita said, in a grudging voice. "I *guess*." For some reason, they all turned to Isabel for the final vote of approval. Isabel nodded. The girls sat in a cross-legged circle and played Dina's game, chanting its singsong rhymes at the top of their lungs, a parody of carefree fun as, somewhere, a cougar stalked, and the sun continued to cross the sky.

WHEN JAN FINALLY RETURNED, the girls could tell something had gone wrong. She had an armful of downed wood, as promised, but her machete was missing, and her pants were streaked with something dark, with a tear low on the right leg. "Whew," Jan said, her voice even hoarser than before. "The woods have changed since the last time I was here." She flung her arms open and the wood tumbled out, clunking loudly as the branches struck one another and the ground, like she'd dropped a bunch of anvils in a cartoon.

Jan kneeled beside the wood, her hands on her knees. "Oh,

boy. Whew," she repeated. She wiped the sweat from her forehead with her sleeve. Underneath her reddened cheeks, her face was ashen.

"What happened?" Nita said. Andee crossed her arms, eyeing Jan suspiciously, like she was an imposter.

"Were you attacked by a cougar?" Dina asked.

Jan laughed, throwing her head back, showing her teeth. She was missing some in the back. It was the first time they'd heard her laugh, and it didn't sound at all the way Siobhan would have expected. A witchy cackle, almost hysterical. "No cougar," she said, catching her breath. "I just tripped on some of those darn vines." As if remembering this was supposed to be an educational trip, she added, "They aren't native to this area. They came over from Europe, and now they're taking over."

"That's called an 'invasive species,'" Nita supplied.

"Where's your machete?" Siobhan asked.

"What?" Jan fumbled at her belt. "Oh, drat. I guess I lost it."

They carried the wood and supply bags up from the beach, at Jan's request, and reconstructed their kindling gradient on the harder dirt ground near the tents. The light was falling, the sun spread like a thin layer of jam across the horizon.

Jan explained what she was doing as the dryer lint she'd brought caught the flame from her lighter, then the matchstick-size shreds, the pencil-size twigs, and finally the branches she'd snapped into shorter lengths over her knee. She described the pyramid-shaped structure she'd built and how the fire would burn over time. She didn't seem to notice that the girls were standing an odd distance away, where they could hear her but were beyond arm's reach. Something, they thought, had changed about Jan. She was talking too fast, and each of her sentences ended with a wheeze, a hummingbird flutter of an inhale-exhale, before she barreled on again. Her face, lit from below by the growing firelight, had a skeletal quality, her lips drawn into her mouth, her eyes sunken in their sockets.

The girls perked up once the food came out. They wrapped baking potatoes in tinfoil and shoved them near the fire. Jan whittled the ends of five twigs to points with a small foldable knife, bemoaning the loss of her machete, and the girls roasted hot dogs and marshmallows. Jan showed them her secret technique for making s'mores, wedging a square of chocolate into the marshmallow itself. Siobhan looked across the fire and saw a smudge of chocolate on the side of Nita's face. Jan drank from a battered tin cup of fire-boiled tea, made from plants she'd picked up on her walk. She showed the girls its ingredients — dandelion, pine needles, rosehips, all the edible delights the forest had provided.

Darkness freed the stars and made everything more than a few feet from the fire disappear. Whenever there was a lull in their talk and laughter, they could hear the water lapping against the shore. Jan asked if the girls could point out any constellations. Nita sketched out the Big Dipper with her finger. Andee said the stars around it looked like something, and Jan said, "Very good. That's Ursa Major." Siobhan was annoyed that that counted as an answer, but more annoyed that she couldn't draw any lines between the scattershot lights of the sky, or remember any of the other times someone had tried to explain to her the heroes and creatures that were supposedly there.

The potatoes took so long that they were the last things the girls ate. Jan split them open with her knife, and steam rose from the dry, fragrant flesh. While they stuffed their faces, Andee expressing disbelief that it tasted so good without butter or sour cream, Siobhan noticed Jan pulling up her pant leg. Jan turned her leg this way and that, examining her scraped shin.

Jan caught Siobhan looking and smiled at her, dropping her pant leg back down over what had appeared, for a moment, to be dried blood and mud matted in hair.

Jan declared it was time for bed, and the girls let out a collective whine of disappointment. "Ohhhhh." Sleeping bags were unfurled, the fire doused, food bag hung, flashlights clicked on and off. Siobhan got her wish, squeezing in beside Jan and Dina. As if Dina had forgotten their conversation while gathering kindling until now, her bad feelings temporarily assuaged by hand-clapping and marshmallows, Dina gave Siobhan a look of pure hate as she rolled away from her in her sleeping bag. Siobhan wished she were bunking with Isabel, whose shyness now seemed mysterious, even comforting.

SIOBHAN COULDN'T SLEEP. The outside was noisy: waves, crickets, and an unidentified rustling. Dina snored. Each time Jan or Dina moved in their sleep, their sleeping bags rubbed against each other or the walls of the tent with a grating, plastic-friction sound. Siobhan fingered the heart-shaped zipper pull on her jacket, trying to soothe herself with its smooth, metallic texture.

At Forevermore, the girls weren't allowed to have watches, so Siobhan had no idea what time it was. It seemed like hours passed as she lay there, completely awake. She knew that in the morning she'd be irritable and have that dehydrated, cotton-in-the-brain feeling she got after sleepovers, from not getting enough sleep, and then she'd have to paddle all the way back.

A new sound made Siobhan jump. A low, agonized moan. *Ghost*, Siobhan thought. *There's a ghost!* Her hand flopped inside her sleeping bag until it closed around the flashlight she'd kept at hand for exactly this reason. She hesitated about turning it on, not wanting to wake Jan and Dina. She knew how this went in TV movies. Only she would be able to hear the ghost, and everyone would laugh at her.

When she heard the moan a second time, she clicked on the flashlight, still held down near her thigh. She slowly lifted her arm out of the sleeping bag and pointed the light in the direction of the sound.

The beam caught Jan right in the face. The next moan was interrupted as Jan woke with a start, a moment of choked silence. "Wha — what?" Jan said.

Siobhan tipped her light sideways, so it illuminated Jan's sleeping bag instead of her face. "You were making a weird sound," she explained weakly. Realizing the noise had been coming from Jan did nothing to calm Siobhan. In the circular face cutout of Jan's mummy-style sleeping bag, Jan looked more ghastly than any monster Siobhan could have imagined. Her skin was a waxy yellow-white, her open eyes bulging and burning with catlike intensity. "Jan?" Siobhan whispered. "Are you okay?"

Jan took a long time to answer. She wheezed, a ragged, painful-sounding inhale, before saying, finally, "Yes. Don't worry. Everything's fine. Turn off your light." Dina's snoring had continued unabated.

Siobhan clicked off her flashlight. She scooched lower in her sleeping bag and tried to erase the sight of Jan's altered face. She knew something was wrong, but she didn't know how to contradict an adult who said everything was fine.

Jan's breathing settled down after a few minutes. Siobhan was starting to think Jan had gone back to sleep when Jan said softly, "Are you having trouble sleeping, Siobhan?"

"Yes," Siobhan replied.

"Is something on your mind?"

Too many things. She asked Jan something she'd been wondering since she'd first heard that Jan had been around since the camp's inception. "What was Forevermore like when you were a camper?"

"Oh, it was wonderful."

"Was it different than it is now?"

"Yes, a little."

"How?"

"We had horses. They got rid of those. And real bows and arrows. They hadn't invented the safety ones you girls will be using next week, during the archery course. And I think the trees were thicker, and there were more songbirds about—heavens, they were *loud*—but it might have just seemed that way because I was younger."

Jan was whispering excitedly, with the exuberance of someone talking about their favorite thing in the world. Siobhan started to relax. "That sounds really cool."

"Some of the changes were for the better, though. For example, at least four of you wouldn't have been at Forevermore back then."

"What do you mean?"

"Well. I assume you're Catholic, right?"

"Yeah."

"Forevermore was only for white Protestant girls when it started. So you wouldn't have been allowed to come, and neither would Nita, Dina, or Isabel. I'm not sure about Andee. There were other camps for Catholic girls—you could've gone to one of those."

Siobhan thought about this. And what would have happened to Nita, Dina, or Isabel? She was too tired to dwell on it further. "Was the song the same?"

"Yes. The camp anthem has lasted all this time. I've heard it sung by hundreds of girls. We used to have more songs, though."

"What kind of songs?"

"Other songs about camp, and about being a girl, and some about God. They'd sound pretty silly today."

Siobhan had an idea, a way to test whether or not Jan was truly okay. "Can you sing one for me?"

After a pause, Jan said, "I'm not supposed to do that."

"I won't tell anyone."

Another pause. "Okay," Jan said. "We used to sing this one on hikes." She cleared her throat, coughing just a little, and began to sing in a quiet, rumbly voice. *"Onward, Christian soldiers, marching as to war,/With the cross of Jesus going on before."*

Without meaning to, Siobhan dozed, slipping under and half waking, sinking completely as the hymn wound to a close, leaving Jan alone in the conscious world.

KAYLA (ANDEE)

1

THE DAY KAYLA and Andee's father left, three years before Andee went to Forevermore, he said only, "Well, I'm going now." He took only the folding knife he carried in his pocket, his wallet, and the clothes on his back. Kayla understood this as a fundamental difference between men and women: men could leave, women had to stay.

In the kitchen, their mother tore one of the cabinet doors off its hinges, less out of anger than that she momentarily forgot her own strength and the door's flimsiness. Their parents had referred to their house as "the shithole," but Kayla thought it was actually quite lovely, a shotgun cottage on its own patch of grass outside of Waco, cornflower-blue with shutters, the ground overtaken by mustard flowers, dandelions, and morning glories. The two girls had slept on the veranda off their parents' back bedroom, ordered to bed before the sun had set, listening to the cicadas and watching the trailing flight of dandelion seeds. Kayla remembered it as the nicest place they ever lived.

Two days later, their mother had packed the car. From the backseat, Andee asked, "Where are we going?" Beside her big sister, Kayla sucked on the ear of a stuffed rabbit, its once-white fur soiled and sticky.

Their mother pulled out onto the main road before answering, drove full-tilt over a gouged-out spot in the asphalt, causing the girls to bounce off the seat. "I have friends all over the country — did you know that? We used to live on a farm together in California. Now they're all over the place. Sea to fucking shining sea, and down in Mexico too. Your daddy never thought too kindly of my friends, but he's gone now, so we're going to go see them. Isn't that great?"

Kayla nodded, as she sensed she was supposed to. Andee insisted, "But where are we *going?*"

They went first to Austin. In Austin, their mother's friend gave Kayla a ukulele. He taught Kayla how to play on his acoustic guitar over several weeks. She understood these lessons to be transactional: she learned to play in exchange for sitting on his lap while he lifted her hair to his nose, closed his fist around thick locks of it, stroked her chin, and told her she had "big blue kitten eyes." Andee wouldn't sit on his lap, so she didn't get presents. Then one night, Kayla woke to find their mother had carried her out to the car while she slept. Only her sister, her sleeping bag, and the ukulele were there. Her clothes and toys, such as they'd been, had been left behind.

They drove for seventeen hours, out of Texas, through Arkansas, across Tennessee. Kayla spent the time listing everything she'd lost: "My bunny. My nightgown with the ice cream cones and the lacy shoulders. My yellow socks. My yellow sweater. My blue socks. My blue T-shirt. My penguin T-shirt . . ."

"We'll get you new stuff, honey," their mother said.

They stopped at a food stand and their mother bought three hard rolls with ham and butter. She passed two back to the girls. The ham smelled like dirty shoes, so Kayla gave hers to Andee. Andee stuffed the whole thing quickly into her mouth like she feared Kayla would change her mind.

In Knoxville, Kayla, Andee, and their mother shared the guest room of a relative of a friend — or a friend of a relative, some string of connections — a sour-faced, retired teacher named Marianne. Again, Kayla took lessons, this time in the kitchen while Andee ran off somewhere, outside the apartment building, free on the streets.

"Your mother is a sinner," Marianne said, during one of their first mornings together. "If you don't accept Jesus into your heart, you'll go to Hell along with her."

"How do I do that?"

"Well, first, you have to say it. Say you accept Jesus."

"I accept Jesus."

Marianne pulled Kayla's thumb out of her mouth. "Stop that. It's a filthy habit."

Kayla sat on her hands, the only way she could stop herself. "What makes my mom a sinner?"

"It is the fate of women to tempt men. It's our curse, from the beginning of time, and why the Lord punishes us with blood and the pain of bearing children. You understand what I mean, don't you?"

Kayla didn't, but she nodded along anyway.

"You can atone for this sin, the uncleanliness of your body, the *obscenity* of it. Or you can embrace the devil and flaunt it, use it for worldly gain. That's what your mother does."

Their mother didn't come home that night. Marianne cooked them fried potatoes and onions, with a piece of cornbread and a glass of milk each. The onions were undercooked, still sharp, and the milk had taken on the flavor of fridge mold. Kayla gave most of her meal to Andee. Andee finished every speck of potato and drop of milk, and put the cornbread in her pockets. "You have to stop being such a princess," she said. "What if Mom doesn't come back? What if Marianne stops feeding us?"

"Why would Marianne stop feeding us?"

Three months in Knoxville before their mother hurried them out of the apartment, down the outside stairs, screaming, "Judgmental bitch!" over her shoulder.

They got back in the car and crossed northwest. Andee pointed out animals as they passed through South Dakota and Wyoming: Sheep! Antelope! Pheasants! Rabbits! Geese! Eagles! The pert, surrendering flags of white-tailed deer as they leapt across the highway. Plump wild turkeys, lazy and oblivious in the middle of the road. Hundreds upon hundreds of cows.

"You did not see an eagle," their mother said.

"Did so!"

"Well, how about that!"

A motel room in Billings, Montana. Their mother vanished for two days and a night. The girls kept the curtains drawn and the TV on the whole time, blaring through cartoons, daytime talk shows, sitcoms, crime dramas, infomercials, cartoons again. They paced and dozed. Andee gathered up the change their mother had left on the radiator and bought them some chips from the vending machine around the corner.

Their door faced the parking lot. In the late afternoon on the second day, the handle started to rattle. Andee opened it, thinking their mother was having trouble with her key. A man stood there, hunched over where the doorknob had been. He straightened up, looking surprised to see them. "Oh, hello," he said. "I didn't think anyone was in there. Thought the TV had been left on." He leaned in, looking over Andee's shoulder. Kayla sat on one of the twin beds in her unicorn pajamas, her face stained with cheese-puff dust. "You girls alone?"

"No," Andee said. "Our daddy's in the bathroom."

"That so." The man was wearing a jacket that was too big for him, a nice one, tan leather and sheepskin, his spindly, scarecrow body sticking straight through it like a toothpick through a grape. "Mind if I come in and wait for him, then?"

"Daddy said not to let anybody in," Andee said.

He looked directly at Andee, as if for the first time. "Well, you tell your daddy that he's going to be charged for an extra day." Knowingly, he added, "Tell your mama too."

Andee locked the door behind him, then dragged a chair across the room to wedge it under the doorknob. Kayla marveled at her ability to lie, quickly and confidently, right into a grown-up's face.

When they were back in the car, driving south, Kayla could see something had turned in Andee, gone dark. Kayla tried to revive her by pointing out the critters along the roadside, drinking in the creeks. But she didn't know their names the way Andee did. "Bird," she said.

NINE MONTHS IN Denver: the first time since Texas that the girls enrolled in a school. Andee caught up to the rest of her third grade class like she'd never left. Downstairs in first grade, Kayla found herself staring at the clock all day, black numbers on white under a dome of glass. A red triangle for the second hand, ticking with rigid, reassuring regularity. Assuring Kayla that the minute would end. The hour. The day. Their time in this place.

A basement apartment in Ontario, Oregon. In each new place, Kayla followed Andee blankly around the neighborhood, into corner stores, to parks, to fountains busted open in the summertime, to libraries with air-conditioning, baseball games in makeshift dust bowls, soccer on proper fields made municipal green in the spring. Kayla felt like she was waiting out these outings the way she waited out the school day, eager for them to be over even though nothing better waited on the other side. She watched from windows and behind bushes as Andee took the abuse shouted at her by neighborhood kids, usually older, until they were impressed by her refusal to leave, by the way this eight- and then nine-year-old girl stood there squeezing her fists on the sidewalk, on the edges of games. They always let her hang out with them in the end.

A house full of people—including a large number of children—in south Seattle. This seemed, in a more concrete way, to be their mother's destination. The adults here seemed happy to see her, surrounded her with hugs. The food was good, served out of tureens and stew pots, the kitchen and dining room chaotic during meals, people everywhere. Andee and Kayla rolled their sleeping bags out onto the floor of a bedroom shared with five or six other girls, while their mother bunked with several other adults. There was a treasure trove of hand-me-down clothes. Kayla picked through to find things she liked: a white peasant blouse, a pair of jeans that was only a little bit too big, a gingham shirtdress, a soft pink cardigan. Andee took a fleece-lined hoodie, several pairs of men's work socks. She took lots of clothes, indiscriminately, anything that fit, for any season, and jammed them into the bottom of her sleeping bag, the same place she kept a stash of food.

Families came and went, older children ran away. Charlotte, a woman their mother had introduced as "my oldest friend in the world," was one of the only dependable fixtures in the house, the one who answered the beige wall-mounted phone in the kitchen and cajoled everyone into stirring and chopping, in turn. Charlotte had greeted them effusively when they'd first arrived, hugging Andee and Kayla, kissing their cheeks with her brightly lipsticked mouth. But Kayla had gradually become aware of Charlotte staring at her whenever they were together, that she was visibly startled when Kayla walked into a room. More than once, Charlotte told her, "You look just like your mother when we were kids." And though she smiled as she spoke, something in her voice make Kayla feel inexplicably guilty, as though her very presence stirred up some old enmity, threatened a tenuous peace.

Near the end of third grade, Kayla was startled out of her schoolroom stupor when she heard Andee's name over the PA during the morning announcements. Andee had won a national essay contest. When Kayla tried to congratulate her sister that afternoon, Andee muttered, "It's no big deal. Probably won't even happen." Kayla wasn't sure what Andee was referring to—*what* probably wouldn't even happen—but she could tell Andee was straining against hope, trying desperately not to be disappointed again. She saw Andee carefully forging their mother's signature on a raft of documents, more at one time than they'd ever needed to before.

That summer, Andee vanished for more than a week. In the overstuffed, ever-shifting house, only Kayla and her mother seemed to notice, and only Kayla seemed to care.

"Andee will come back on her own in time," their mother said. "Do you know who she went with?"

Kayla was confused: Why would Andee run away? Andee had adapted so well to the current iteration of their lives. She liked their new school, had shown up in the middle of the year and still gotten decent grades, she'd won that contest. When someone had picked a fight with her on the playground, she'd soundly knocked him on his ass. Kayla roamed the house looking for clues. Andee's sleeping bag and her cache of clothing were gone.

Kayla finally found an early draft of Andee's prize-winning essay in a notebook. It was a fictionalized version of their endless road trip with their mother, somehow sadder and more vivid than it had been as Kayla had been living it. She cried for the two little girls in the story. The first-person narrator was so unlike Andee, needy and desperate and ragged, an orphan from a fairy tale, while Kayla thought of her sister like a weed, in the best way—thriving and taking over anywhere, a flowering shoot that could bust through concrete. And the sister was just a baby, a drooling prop, a burden, younger than Kayla had been. Kayla wanted to believe this was a calculation on Andee's part—she'd made them more pitiable to improve her odds of winning—and not how Andee really felt, how Andee really saw them. The Andee in the essay was alone in the world. The draft ended with a half-sentence that seemed copied from somewhere, a prompt on a form: "What going to Camp Forevermore would mean to me," and then blank lines.

When Andee returned, their mother was away again. Charlotte had to fetch Andee from somewhere less than a day's drive away, posing as an aunt, as she did in many situations, for many of the kids. Andee no longer had her sleeping bag. She slept wrapped in a knitted blanket covered in dog fur that she'd found elsewhere in the house.

On her first night back, Andee gave Kayla a friendship bracelet made of yarn, saying she didn't want it anymore. Kayla tied it tightly around her wrist and admired it for a long moment. She curled up beside her sister and whispered, "I was afraid you were gone forever."

Andee said, "What if I was? What would you do?"

"I'd miss you."

"But what would you *do?* You know you can't count on Mom," Andee said. "You can't count on anybody. What would you do?"

Kayla blinked at this, confused.

"Forget it," Andee said.

One night, around Kayla's eleventh birthday, she and Andee went to bed before everyone else. A rare moment when it was just the two of them, listening to each other breathe, the adult voices and laughter through the walls.

Kayla nodded.

Sally, watching their conversation, said, "Come on, now. Let's go. I'm starving."

"See you Sunday," Eric said.

SALLY AND ERIC broke up soon afterward, but Kayla continued to go to the church every Sunday. She met Eric around the corner and he drove her in his messy station wagon. Heaped in the back were a couple of guitars, a large gas canister, blankets, a lot of garbage. "Sorry about the old jalopy," he said, with another wink. He called her "cupcake" and "sweetheart" and hugged her as greeting and farewell, sometimes kissing the top of her head.

The church was a converted warehouse with modern stained-glass windows, a 1970s-style Jesus made of tangram shapes in primary colors. It was Kayla's job to set up the folding-chair pews while the musical devotion group rehearsed in the early morning. Eric wrote a lot of the songs himself, or at least, set simplified Bible verses to a verse-chorus-verse-bridge-chorus structure over a I-IV-V chord progression. He had a country-music voice, a soulful twang Kayla knew was affected — his speaking voice had the clipped dullness of a northerner — but nevertheless made her feel at home, recalled her faded memory of the cornflower house.

After the service, Kayla followed Eric to the office he shared with the youth pastor, one of the former administrative offices at the back of the warehouse. A banner of Matthew 19:14 hung across the back wall: JESUS SAID, "LET THE LITTLE CHILDREN COME TO ME, AND DO NOT HINDER THEM, FOR THE KINGDOM OF HEAVEN BELONGS TO SUCH AS THESE." Beside a small desk, there were large beanbag chairs in a corner, a shelf full of children's Bibles and Christian storybooks, always-stocked jars of jellybeans and cheese straws.

They cleaned, polished, and restrung Kayla's ukulele. He

let her play one of his guitars as well, and over several months, seasons—the cold rain, warm rain, and mild sun of the Pacific Northwest—he taught her the names of the chords, how to strum and how to pick, how to play his songs and other Christian rock classics, how to transpose his lessons to her ukulele. If she finished setting up early, Eric let her practice alone in his office. The luxury of privacy was new to her.

One afternoon, he asked her, "Did you go to Bible school as a kid?"

"Nope." Marianne's mix of reading, arithmetic, and hellfire didn't seem like it would count.

"How are you finding Pastor Mike's sermons?"

Kayla toyed idly with one of the tuning pegs. "Good."

Eric put his hand over Kayla's, stilling it. "You can tell me the truth."

"They're boring, I guess. Or confusing. I don't really know what he's talking about."

"Have you tried reading the Bible I gave you?"

"Yes. I liked the—the beginning. The first couple pages. I've read them a bunch of times. But then it gets too hard."

"Mmm, I could see that. Would you be offended if I suggested something a little easier?" He grabbed the first volume of the children's illustrated Bible from the shelf. "I know you're too big for this, but it might clear things up for you."

Kayla looked at the cover, an illustration of a white dove with an olive leaf in its beak flying across a stormy sea. She touched the picture, feeling a strange kinship with the bird. She liked that Eric treated her like a child. It seemed to her that no one had. "Would you read it to me?" she asked.

Eric looked surprised and then pleased. More than pleased: lit with joy. "I'd be honored to," he said.

They curled up together in one of the beanbag chairs. Kayla made herself as small as she could as she picked from a fistful of jellybeans and leaned into Eric's chest, feeling his voice rumble through his rib cage. The Jesus in the pictures reminded her a lot of Eric: his scrabbly brown beard, his warm brown eyes, how he didn't care if she got crumbs or tears on his shirt. They worked through all twelve volumes this way, as a dependable coda to her guitar lessons. She knew she couldn't tell anyone else about the beanbag chair. They wouldn't understand. They'd ruin it somehow, make it dirty.

Eric was special not because he didn't lust after Kayla, but because he resisted. Kayla knew she was living temptation. She was a daughter of Eve. She accepted this as her trial from God, finally understood Marianne's warning. But Eric was strong. Sweaty and flushed from the heat trap of the vinyl, they ignored his erection pressing between them, his voice trailing off if she forgot where she was and slipped her thumb in her mouth, teeth to nail and the salt of her own skin.

Her favorite song, not written by Eric, was a modern ballad called "Jesus, Lover of my Soul." At first, she just liked the melody, which had the tenderness and devotion of a love song, and how well it transposed to solo ukulele. Then, the longer she played it, the more she could *feel* the lyrics, feel the total surrender to the will of God, the release of her earthly plans and desires, their pettiness and unimportance. What mattered was what He wanted, not what Kayla wanted. It transformed the experience of her life so far. A life inflicted upon her by others. What held her, helpless in its thrall, wasn't the power of her mother, her mother's friends, Andee, teachers, and men, men everywhere staring at her, always men — it was the plan of the Lord. She felt absolved of the past and the future. Better things would come if she remained passive and pious, if she believed.

AS THEY LAY beside each other on Sally's pull-out sofa bed, Kayla asked, "Andee? Aren't you afraid of going to Hell?"

Andee took so long to answer that Kayla had thought she'd

fallen asleep. "Whoever made Hell is an asshole," she said, "and I'm not afraid of assholes."

THE INEVITABLE DAY CAME. Sally, screaming: "I am done with you! Never again! I'm going to work, and when I get back, you and your fucking freeloading kids better be out of here, or I'll call the cops."

Andee and Kayla didn't help their mother. They watched as she threw things into her battered, distended suitcase. "We don't have a car," Andee said.

"We'll take the bus."

Andee asked, "Where are we going?"

"Rosarito. Mexico. I have friends there." She abruptly turned and grinned with that fierce, alarming fire. "Doesn't that sound great? Warm and sunny. Margaritas and carnitas on the beach."

Andee and Kayla exchanged a look. "I don't want to go," Kayla said. "I like it here."

"Well, that's too bad, honey, because you can't stay. Sally won't let you."

"Maybe she would," Andee said, "if you weren't here. Just long enough for us to get our own place."

Their mother laughed. Just once, sharp and mean. "Right. And how are you going to do that?"

"We'll get jobs," Andee said.

The suitcase slammed shut. "You know what? You go ahead and try. You girls have never appreciated how fucking hard it is to—to just *live*. You've always been uptight, ungrateful little bitches, getting us thrown out of every good situation that ever came along. See how you do without me. You *see*."

And then she was gone.

SALLY LET THEM stay but told them they'd have to start paying rent—a small amount, well below market rate for even their shared sofa bed. Andee missed the last few weeks of her senior year, but she got her diploma anyway; Kayla dropped out, relieved that she'd never have to step into a classroom again.

Andee found a job at a bookstore. Kayla worked as a server for a couple of years until, shortly after she turned eighteen, her church bought the coffee shop next door. She became a barista and technically one of three dozen part-owners, through service. On top of her full-time job at the café, she cleaned the church offices and bathrooms, raked leaves and pulled weeds, counted the collection money, played on the musical devotion team, watched children in the nursery. She liked the cohesiveness this gave her life: everything for the church.

Eric was "called" to their sister parish in Eugene. He came to Sally's to say goodbye when only Kayla was home. He mashed his face against hers in something like a kiss, his fingers digging into her shoulder and under the strap of her tank top. She fought her way out of his grip. He allowed himself to be shoved back and started to weep, tears running down his pitiful face. "Forgive me," he cried.

"The Lord will forgive you," Kayla said.

SALLY MOVED and signed her lease over to Andee and Kayla. Andee took the bedroom and Kayla stayed on the sofa bed, their sleep uncontaminated by the breath of the other for the first time. Andee was promoted to assistant manager, had an amicable group of friends and lovers. Kayla had the church. They paid their bills, were kind to each other, kept the apartment neat enough. Such things were still possible. These years had the quality of peacetime after war. A new appreciation for silence, order, each day's similarity to the last.

On her rare evenings off, Kayla did what she thought of as another service for the church, unassigned. An evangelical effort.

The café had a nondescript name, nondescript couches and tables, inoffensive local art (fruit still-lifes painted by the woman who played the piano on the musical devotion team), a microphone and a stool in a corner, nothing to indicate its affiliation with the church.

On these evenings, Kayla sat on the stool in the corner and played devotional songs, singing in her high, delicate voice. Even amplified, she was frequently drowned out by the steam-train exhalations of the espresso machine.

As adults, she and Andee had their mother's thin, dry blond hair, broad forehead, and prominent brow. Andee cut hers into a fashionable, unflattering pixie cut that made her face look hard and square, Neanderthal ridges of bone. Kayla let hers grow uncontrolled, broken at the ends and frizzing at the hairline. She pulled it into a bun when she played, a twist wound tight, a golden halo reflecting the café's ceiling pot lights as she bobbed her head gently to a song, the face of an ancient Nordic priestess. She embraced the new-old-fashioned style of the moment, dresses from Goodwill that buttoned high, narrow through the body and sleeves with no stretch, flowing below the waist. The cotton was thinned with age and skimmed over her as though substanceless; she was covered neck to shin but somehow naked, eye-catchingly vulnerable.

Church members recognized her from the devotional team, where she was up on the platform at the start of service each Sunday, and they clapped politely between songs. But she didn't play for them. She played for the other customers, drinking their lattes and clacking away at their laptops, the ones who wore some visible sadness or loneliness. A hole to be filled by God. They were distracted by the sight and sound of Kayla, stopped to listen in spite of themselves. Even some of those who laughed at first, who rolled their eyes, mockingly covered their ears. They could go silent, succumb. Music could be their way in, as it had been hers.

"Praise him with the sounding of the trumpet," she sang. "Praise him with the harp and lyre. Praise him with tambourine and dancing, praise him with the strings and pipe. Praise him with the clash of cymbals."

She looked up and saw a man sitting at the table closest to her, his eyes closed and his shoulders relaxed, possibly asleep. His hands were folded neatly on the table in front of him. As she transitioned to the final chords of the song, his eyes opened. They were lighter than hers, blue, fragments of sky in a sunken face. He looked well preserved, a pink flush and an artificial smoothness to his cheeks, the way the very wealthy age. She smiled at him as she sang, radiated Jesus's love and welcome.

He approached her as she tucked her ukulele into its bag. He stood with his hands clasped behind his back, like someone considering a painting. "You have a lovely voice," he said. "May I buy you a cup of tea?"

Kayla had never been good at rebuffing customers' advances. She took their business cards, scribbled numbers, made the coffees they ordered for her and then dumped them down the sink. She sat at the man's table with her ukulele in her lap while he bought her a mug of peppermint tea. He hadn't asked her what kind she wanted. She hated peppermint tea, thought it tasted like toothpaste. She took a sip and continued to smile agreeably.

"My name is Walter Groff," he said. He spoke with the extreme formality and mid-Atlantic accent that Kayla associated with old movies.

"Kayla."

"Are you part of the church next door?"

"Yes," she said, eager. "Would you like to know more about us?"

"I should say so. I own both buildings."

Kayla's face fell. She looked around the café for a church

authority, but she recognized only the Wednesday-night Coping with Divorce group.

"My family has owned this land for a long time. It seems we're leasing it to you and your church for a song."

"It's not *my* church. I mean, it is my church, only in the sense that it's the church where I . . . I'm really not the one to talk to about this."

"My understanding is that the church is collectively owned by all of its members. Doesn't that make it yours?"

"No—the church isn't—just the café, and not everyone, and it's . . . I don't really know the details. The legal details."

Walter seemed amused. "Don't look so nervous, my dear. This is only one part of the giant mess my father left behind. When he passed away, we discovered our money was tied up in whimsical land holdings all over the country, with no apparent pattern or plan. I've spent my life trying to make them useful. This area is a particular thorn in my side—why it hasn't been developed to its full and very valuable potential."

"Maybe," Kayla ventured, "your father saw the good that we do."

"He wasn't religious."

"You don't have to be religious to appreciate our church. Maybe he was . . . sympathetic. And generous."

Walter laughed. A prim, controlled laugh that would fit inside a teacup. "Unlikely. Drunk and forgetful, more like. He probably forgot he owned it by the time the boom started."

Kayla felt a small, internal quiver, like a needle wavering on a dial. "So what are you going to do?"

"About your church? I haven't decided yet. There are a lot of vacant warehouses in this stretch—those are being converted or coming down. I'll deal with the occupied ones on a case-by-case basis."

"How could we convince you?"

Walter cleared his throat. He gazed down at the table and fiddled with the paper napkin he'd used to carry her tea. His ramrod-straight posture wilted just slightly. He shifted, all at once, from intimidating to awkward, almost boyish. "Would you have dinner with me?"

She took another sip of her peppermint tea. It tasted even worse now that it had cooled.

THEY WALKED TOGETHER down the industrial road, past the church, to a restaurant Kayla was certain hadn't been there before. The restaurant had no sign, but was brightly lit from within, a beacon in the dark from a distance. As they got closer, Kayla could see a crowd of people clustered outside its doors.

Walter guided her inside. The restaurant retained the cavernous space and exposed ductwork of a former factory. Like Kayla's church, but to different effect. Chandeliers hung far above their heads, distant as stars.

Once they were seated, she said, "You own this too."

She ordered the steak he was having, even though she didn't like red meat, the tang of blood and the violent way it shredded. What arrived seemed to be something else entirely, like butter in the guise of beef. The wine, the chocolate mousse, even the salads—everything had the same otherworldly, unexpected richness, delicious but somehow wrong, sick-making.

Walter complained about his life. Walter's father had squandered his own father's money on decades of bad guesses in real estate speculation, selling too soon or holding on too long. Whole developments had been left unfinished and unconnected out in the desert, modern-day ghost towns. Their family had gone from exceedingly wealthy to merely wealthy to the sham appearance of wealth, and were only now recovering, now that Walter had dug out a few gems from the wreckage. On top of that, his mother's end-of-life care was bleeding him dry. At the age of seventy-nine, she had prepaid for five years in an expensive retirement community in southern California, predicting she would live to the same age her mother had. She was now ninety-four and still refusing to move. She wanted to die watching deer skitter across the golf course, skirt the koi ponds.

Kayla tried to be sympathetic.

At the end of the meal, out on the sidewalk, Walter asked if he could give her a ride home. A town car appeared from even farther down the road, where shuttered, unconverted warehouses still held the memory of industry.

In the car, he said, "I hope you'll consider me a friend, and that I can see you next time I'm in town." He gazed at her fondly, as though she were a photograph of a place he'd once visited. He hadn't touched her.

He didn't mention the future of the church, so she didn't either. The evening had not been unpleasant, and it wouldn't be unpleasant to repeat it.

3

"I CAN'T REMEMBER the last time we were both home for dinner," Andee said. They were opening cans of beans and tomatoes and dumping them into a pot for chili. "Usually at least one of us is at work."

Kayla made a noncommittal noise. She hadn't told Andee about her friendship with Walter, the dinners — sometimes weeks apart — that had been happening for almost a year. There wasn't anything to tell, she reasoned. He still hadn't done anything untoward. It was just dinner. He'd tried to give her presents, jewelry and clothes in branded boxes, but she'd gently rebuffed them and he'd stopped. And no one at the church had mentioned any changes to their lease. "This is nice," Kayla said.

Kayla was afraid that Andee would accuse her of being a hypocrite, even though she hadn't said a word about Andee's ungodly habits, the men and women who passed through her bedroom. She knew she should be more concerned with her sister's eternal soul. The first priority of every member of her church was to get their friends and family to join, and Kayla had no friends outside the church and no family other than Andee. Andee could get hit by a truck tomorrow and they would never get to meet in the Kingdom of God. But Kayla also knew she should lead by example, rather than pass judgment. Let her light shine upon others so that they may see her deeds. And Kayla felt—this thought seemed blasphemous, prideful, yet true all the same—that Andee was, in her way, indestructible. If she were hit by a truck, she'd survive. She'd survive anything. There was plenty of time yet to bring Andee into the fold.

As the chili simmered, Andee read at the table and Kayla practiced the songs for that week on her ukulele. A light summer rain pattered softly at the window. Perhaps unconsciously, Andee started humming along.

The door buzzer went off. They both jumped. "Expecting someone?" Kayla said.

"No."

Neither stood. They peered past the connected living room, as if someone were going to bust through the apartment door. "Should we just wait for them to go away?" Kayla asked.

Andee started to answer when the buzzer rang again, longer and more insistent. Andee went over and pushed the intercom button. "Hello? Who is it?"

"Girls! It's Mom!"

Kayla had never thought she and her sister looked that

much alike before this moment, when she saw her own horror mirrored back.

The door buzzed aggressively a third time.

Andee reached for the door-release button and then withdrew her hand. "Fuck. What should we do?"

Kayla thought: *We should've moved, so she couldn't find us.* She thought: *Honor thy mother and thy father, so that you may live long in the land the Lord your God is giving you.*

"Let her in," Kayla whispered, still hoping Andee wouldn't.

Andee pressed the door release.

They listened to her climb the stairs. Andee opened the door before she could knock. She was here. In their apartment.

"Hello, girls! Miss me?" She kissed them each on both cheeks, something Kayla could not recall her doing before. They received the kisses and made no gesture in return. Their mother wore a strapless dress, blue with orange flowers, despite the rain, and sneakers without socks. "Is Sally around?"

"Sally doesn't live here anymore," Andee said. She'd left the door hanging open.

"It's just us," Kayla said.

Their mother sat on the couch and put her sneakers up on the coffee table. She rested her hands on her flower-patterned belly and looked up at them expectantly. "Nice setup you have here. What's that delicious smell?"

Andee shut the door slowly, glancing out into the hallway as if something there could save them. Kayla said, "Dinner."

"What are we having?"

Andee stepped toward the couch and stood over their mother. "How long are you staying?"

"I just got here." She dropped her feet from the coffee table with a thud that made them both wince. "If you recall, I kept you clothed and fed and safe with a roof over your heads for most of your goddamn lives. I'd think you could spare me some dinner."

Andee swallowed. "Just dinner. And then you — you go on your way."

"You're going to kick me out in the middle of the night? With nowhere to sleep? Your own mother?"

They had seen this happen so many times. Their mother had friends all over the country.

"YOU'RE QUIET TONIGHT," Walter said. They waited on the sidewalk for his town car to arrive.

Kayla was underdressed, a thin sweater over her dress on a night that called for a jacket, the first turn of autumn. "Have you ever been married?" Kayla asked.

"Yes. Twice." Walter glanced at Kayla before adding, "Both happy."

"You were a widower twice?"

"No. Twice divorced. We were happy for many years, the marriage ran its course, we ended it on friendly terms. Twice. It's the best anyone can hope for, really."

To Kayla, a happy marriage was briefly interrupted by death and ended with a reunion in Heaven, but she didn't say that. "Any children?"

"No, thank God."

The car pulled up, and they slipped into its warmth and dark anonymity, as into black water on a moonless night. She'd prayed over this decision. For it was a decision; she was going to make something happen, not submit mindlessly to the desire of another, and if it was a sin, she had to take responsibility for it.

Walter looked out the window, a circle of orange light passing over his face from each streetlight, between longer stretches of darkness.

She'd decided, ultimately, that Jesus would forgive her if everything she did was in service of a holy union. If she learned to love Walter, as she often thought she could, and became his wife, gave him everything that a wife ought to give.

She reached out and squeezed Walter lightly on the forearm. *Hello,* her hand said. *I'm here!* He turned to her. His expression was quizzical. She raised her hand to his chin. "Do you love me?" she asked.

Walter spoke carefully. "I enjoy being around you. Quite a lot."

"I think you should kiss me."

She felt him leaning away from her touch. He said, "You don't owe me anything."

Kissing Walter seemed logistically difficult, coming at him sideways in the close quarters of the car as he resisted. So she took his hand and placed it inside the neck of her dress, just to the left of her sternum, against her heart. He let out a hissing breath as though he'd been punctured.

"Your skin is so soft," he said.

They stared at his hand as if it were an independent creature, both waiting to see what it would do.

LATER THAT NIGHT, choosing her moment, she asked again. "Walter, do you love me?"

"Yes," he said. "Yes, I love you. I love you so much."

KAYLA WOKE UP cold on the sofa bed. Andee was gone and the blanket they shared was heaped on the floor. Kayla's thumb was past the threshold of her lips. It took her a few minutes to remember where she was, how old she was, that she hadn't regressed or fallen through time in the night.

She sat up and assessed the room. Her mother was banging around in the kitchen. The bathroom door was closed and light leaked out from under it. Presumably Andee was inside. Kayla went into the bedroom to get a shirt from their now three-way-shared closet. She noticed a new cigarette burn in the bed, a singed hole that went all the way through the sheet, down to the mattress. At least the beddings hadn't caught fire, she thought.

Kayla followed the smell of something else burning, back to the kitchen. "I'm making pancakes," her mother called, standing over the stove.

The pancakes weren't causing the smell. Kayla put on the oven mitts and pulled a cast-iron pan of blackened bacon out of the oven. "Thanks, but I don't have time. I have to go to work."

Her mother's mouth curled downward in distaste. "Andee said the same thing. I try to do something nice and you two just don't have *time* for me. For your poor old mother who made this nice breakfast that's going to go to waste."

The lower half of the smoke detector hung on its cord from the ceiling, where their mother had pulled it out. Kayla coughed and waved an oven mitt over the smoking remains of the bacon. She was amazed that her mother was able to ignore it, blithely flipping a pancake two feet away. "Thank you," Kayla said again. "If you put some pancakes in the fridge, I can eat them later."

Andee flew out of the bathroom. She was fully dressed, in her bookstore uniform, but her hair was sopping wet, dripping down her back. "Where is it?" she demanded.

Their mother continued to poke at the side of her pancake. "What?"

"You know what. The jar."

"I took it to the change-counting machine at the grocery store for you. What's the sense in keeping a jar of pennies and nickels under the bathroom sink?"

Andee didn't bother arguing about the contents of the jar. "What did you do with the money?"

"I bought stuff to make my girls breakfast."

"And?"

"What do you mean, 'and'?"

Andee was shouting now. "Where's the rest of the money?"

She shrugged. "I owed a friend." She slid the first pancake onto a platter at her elbow. "Why are you getting all worked up? You two big shots, always running around, in and out of here at all hours. Can't spare a little bit of change for the woman who raised and protected you. Nickels and pennies, that's all it was. Barely covered the bacon."

Andee had a little money, Kayla knew, in a bank account. Everything Kayla made went either to their shared expenses or back to the church, directly into the collection plate or, when it was her turn, toward the cost of the food and supplies for the recruitment picnics. Kayla felt this was more than fair — more than just her Christian duty, she knew the church would take care of her if something happened, if she needed it. Better than a savings account. The Lord provided through the sharing and good works of men.

The jar was a silly thing between the two of them, years of small change filling a one-gallon pickle jar Kayla had taken home from the café. They meant to do something fun with it, someday, together, joking about things the jar could never cover: a jet, a boat, a trip to Paris.

Kayla went to Andee, meaning to comfort her, but Andee jerked away before Kayla could touch her. She entered the kitchenette and picked up the platter with both hands. Kayla had time to remember where it had come from — a hand-me-down from another parishioner, gifted shortly after Sally left and they first needed to furnish the place — before Andee hurled it to the floor. The dish shattered at their mother's feet, the lone pancake lolling like a tongue. Their mother didn't flinch, didn't have the involuntary, autonomous reaction to a loud sound that almost anyone would, her senses selectively dead.

• • •

KAYLA HAD WAITED and waited, submitted in every way she could think of. Abject. Compliant. Couldn't Walter see what a good wife she'd be? Still he hadn't asked, hadn't even feinted toward it. Until, finally, she pulled away from him for the first time, sat up in the bed of his riverfront hotel room, and said, quietly, evenly, "You're never going to marry me."

"Hmm?" Walter was slow to come out of the fog, the plea-sure-fugue.

Her chin lowered to her chest, her hands limp in her lap. "All I can do now is pray for forgiveness."

Walter pulled himself up on his elbows. "Say again? You want to get married?"

"We *have* to get married, and soon. Or I can't keep doing this."

He held very still, as though she were a skittish animal, primed to flee. He beheld her for a long moment, her trem-bling lip, the blond hair down almost to her waist. "You can see," he said, slowly, "how I would feel trapped."

"I'm not trying to trap you."

"I don't think you understand what you're saying." He nudged her arm in a fumbling, jocular gesture. "What if we went away together for a bit? On a trip? Would you like that?"

She shook her head. "You don't get it. I should go."

"No, wait." He sat up. "Listen. I'm not as rich as you think I am." He gestured around the room. The open partition to the bathtub, the fireplace, the view of the Willamette. "This isn't how I live. I can afford to spoil you like this when I visit, but I couldn't do it all the time. It wouldn't be what you expect."

"I'm not—"

"Let me finish." He took her hands. "I know you're not some gold digger who wants to get in and wait for me to die. I'm not accusing you of that. And you know I'm still paying alimony to two other women. You know my family will protect the money this time, that they'll keep it from you once I'm gone. There'll be a prenup and they'll defend it until you're dead too. You must know all of that. God knows you've listened to me talk about them enough. I'm trying to tell you that I don't have the energy for you. To treat you the way you deserve to be treated. What we have now, that's all I can manage." He paused. "I've thought about it. What it would be like to have you with me all the time. In my house. To take care of me. It's cruel. It's too cruel."

They were both exposed to the waist, two feet of empty bedding between them. She felt embarrassed to look at him and vulnerable in her nudity, in a way she never had before. *Perhaps*, she thought, *I never loved him until now.*

She said, "Shouldn't that be for me to decide?" When he started to speak again, she interrupted. "I want this. For lots of reasons. Please trust me."

She drew his head down to rest on her shoulder. He let out a shuddering breath and she felt him relax, the surprisingly heavy weight of his skull. Her blood pulsing, her skin warm and young as life itself.

"I'M ENGAGED," Kayla announced.

"To who?" their mother shouted. "You're still a fucking *baby!*"

Andee, as though she'd been waiting, as though this clinched it, said, "I'm going to Alaska."

WALTER SIGNED a one-hundred-year lease to the church.

4

WALTER HAD A COLD. Walter's cold turned into pneumonia, and his age showed in a way it never had before. He'd always been thin, debonair and sharp-cheeked, straight lines in a tailored suit. Now his skin rested unimpeded against the bones of his eye sockets and hung loosely from his cheeks. His eyes seemed to bulge out of his skull. His wrists and ankles, which might have before been described as delicate, dancer-like, had the sheared-bone look of a corpse.

Sitting on the examination table, Walter stared straight ahead as though he couldn't see Kayla or the doctor, his body swaying slightly, dreamily, a reed in a faint breeze.

"Shouldn't we go to the hospital?" Kayla said.

"At this point, no," the doctor said. "His symptoms are relatively mild. Pneumonia can be serious at his age, but I'd just keep an eye on him for now."

So Kayla took Walter home and tucked him into bed, even as she was convinced he was dying.

She was out of time.

On the tray she usually used to bring him breakfast and the newspaper, she placed a glass of water and her Bible.

Kayla didn't love her new church, though she was trying. It had seemed similar to her old church on paper, when they'd first moved to Sherman Oaks to be near Walter's now-deceased mother. Part of the same new evangelical movement, that same upstart feeling, informal, brightly colored, almost commercial. The pastor was married with children but he looked extremely young, baby-faced, like a boy in his father's suit. He wore a headset mic and paced as he delivered his sermons, asked them rhetorical questions, spoke with the blunted, rangy anger of a teenager. There was no ambiguity to his sermons, no room for Kayla's thoughts and compromises. No gaps for God. There was right and wrong, and so much was wrong. And the choir and the musical devotion band were full. Kayla could sing along with everyone else, she could lift her hands. It somehow wasn't the same. She felt lonely for Walter, who never came with her. She felt muted rather than buoyed by the other congregants. Her voice would disappear and she would mouth along without realizing it.

She put down the tray and took Walter's temperature. He was still running a fever. As she helped him sit up, she saw what she took to be a shadow before realizing it was an imprint of his body in sweat. She rocked him in her arms and hummed. His body stayed tense, resistant, as though she were a stranger. He moaned.

"Walter," she whispered. "I'm going to baptize you. Do you understand?"

"Why?"

"So we can be together forever."

He turned into her neck and moaned again, a bovine lowing. "I want to be together now."

"We are. I'm right here."

"Hold my hand." She twined her fingers with his and squeezed. He said, "I'm afraid."

She remembered her own baptism in Portland. They set aside a Saturday once every few months for adult converts, and together they dragged a freestanding steel tub out from storage. Her breath knocked out of her by the force of the water and Pastor Mike's hand on her head. She was submerged long enough for thought and the end of thought, for the Kayla she had been to drown, mortal fear snaking through her belly and up out of her burbling lungs, released. Her first gasping breath after rebirth. The clarity. The ecstasy. The hollers of those standing by in witness.

She whispered into the top of Walter's head. "It's time to get right with God. Are you ready?"

His neck lolled forward.

"I need you to say yes." She rubbed his back. She felt the muscles beginning to give.

Weakly, he assented. "Yes."

She reached across to the tray with one hand, without releasing him from her embrace. She took the glass of water. "Walter Groff, do you reject Satan? Do you repent for your sins? Do you accept Jesus as your personal Lord and Savior, as the one true God?" When he didn't respond, she added, "Walter?"

"What do I do?"

"You just say yes."

"Yes."

She poured a trickle of water into the part of his hair, once, twice, three times. The water ran down his forehead, parted at his brow into multiple streams, passed over his eyelids, dripped, rejoined in the crevices alongside his nose. His parched mouth opened slightly, welcoming in the moisture. The water split again at his chin, running down his neck into the collar of his pajama top, joining the damp silhouette on the bed. "I baptize you in the name of Jesus Christ."

She wiped the water from his eyes. She kissed him in the center of his forehead. She unbuttoned his wet pajamas, used them to dry his head, and tossed them aside. She took off her clothes and wrapped her body around his and the comforter around them both, on the dry side of the bed, and held him for what she thought would be the last time.

In the morning, his fever had broken.

TO KAYLA, the message was unequivocal. God had returned Walter to her. There was only one person left whose eternal torment she couldn't bear.

She called the last number she had for Andee.

"I thought you were in Alaska."

"I was. I'm in Wyoming now."

"Can I come visit you?"

"Not easily. We just lost commercial air service."

The cold glass screen of her phone against her cheek, Kayla

tried to picture Andee's face, to connect it to this impatient, distrustful stranger. "Do you remember," Kayla said, "when we drove through Wyoming with Mom? You were amazed by all the animals."

A moment of dead air, and then Andee's voice became familiar again. "I still am. I'm a ranch hand now. At least, for the rest of the spring and summer." She paused, laughed at nothing. "I can pick you up if you can get yourself to Buffalo."

ANDEE PARKED HER TRUCK at the farmhouse. The two sisters walked along the highway together and recounted the last few years. A man who worked at the bookstore in Portland with Andee had been going to Alaska to work in a mining camp, and once Andee knew Kayla was leaving, she asked to tag along in his truck. They needed bodies. She ended up in the camp kitchen — fourteen-hour days, seven days a week in the summer, the initial adrenaline of the midnight sun and then the slow creep of madness, demented by the light. Enough money that Andee didn't work at all come winter. She took a cabin, split her own wood, hauled her own water and propane, borrowed a snowmobile when necessary. She fell in love with a naturalist guide for tourists, on the same seasonal schedule, who seemed like the only other woman for a thousand miles. Magical winters spent in their shared cabin, the short days occupied with the work of staying alive, the endless night for talking, fucking, and heavy, restorative sleep. Lying out on the ice of the frozen river together, beneath the silent symphony of the Northern Lights. Huskies drawing one another into song from opposite banks.

Then a miserable winter spent trapped together. Falling out of love. A miner who was leaving, returning south to work on a ranch managed by a former boss, and Andee caught another ride.

"What are you going to do when the season is over?" Kayla asked.

"Not sure yet. I heard about a job in Yellowstone that sounds pretty all right."

Kayla told her story. Andee stopped walking. She looked at Kayla as though drawing from a deep well of sadness. "I always hoped for more for you," she said.

"What do you mean?" Kayla thought of all the material comforts of their home in Sherman Oaks. "I have a great life. And I just witnessed a miracle."

They walked under the big sky, the livestock close to the road, brought in from the hills for the springtime lambing and calving, dull eyes and open faces watching as the sisters passed. Some freshly sheared lambs huddled naked around a trough, deer and turkeys skipping in to steal bites of feed. Now that Kayla was here, she found it hard to get around to the reason she'd come. Andee had aged, from time and hard-weather work, but Kayla still could not accept that she would ever die.

The highway forked and they followed the curve to the northwest. A small roadside chapel came into view, the size of a closet. Another sign from God, a reprimand to Kayla. "Let's get out of the sun for a second," Kayla said.

They ducked under the archway into the cool shade of the chapel. Just walls, a roof, and a painted crucifix. "Do you mind if I say a quick prayer?" Kayla said. Andee shrugged.

Kayla took Andee's hand. She couldn't remember the last time she'd held her sister's hand, if she ever had. Kayla shut her eyes. "Lord, thank you for my husband, for bringing us together and then granting us a little more time together on this earth. Thank you for Eric—through him, I first came to know you. Thank you for my home church and that they may sing your praises for another century. Thank you for my sister. Thank you for all the people who took us into their homes while we were growing up. And bless and keep our mother, wherever she may be."

When Kayla opened her eyes, Andee's head was titled back, tears running from the corners of her eyes to her up-turned ears. Her face pointed up, Kayla thought, toward the Lord in Heaven.

CAMP FOREVERMORE

SIOBHAN WAS AWOKEN the next morning by her full bladder. Daylight showed through the nylon of the tent. She was surprised that Jan hadn't woken them, as the cabin counselors had, with clapping and merry shouts.

Siobhan became aware of a sickly sweet, mammalian smell that made her worried that she'd wet her sleeping bag. Her eyes still bleary with sleep, she stumbled as she stepped over Dina, accidentally kicking the other girl in the back, and Dina squealed in waking and protest. Siobhan unzipped the flap and sat at the entrance with her legs sticking out to put her shoes back on. She hobbled away from the tents to squat behind a tree.

As she pulled her pants up, she heard Dina screaming.

Siobhan sprinted back. The other three girls rushed out of their tent. Dina stood in her socks by the flat, scorched spot where their fire had been, her mouth wide and blaring like a siren. Nita shoved her feet into her sneakers. She grabbed Dina by the shoulders, shaking her and yelling her name. "What is it? What? Why are you screaming?"

Siobhan ducked her head back into the tent. Jan was still there, lying flat on her back. Bundled tightly, mostly hidden by her yellow sleeping bag, she looked like an enormous caterpillar. Her eyes were open and staring up at the pitched apex of the tent. The wildness that Siobhan had seen in them the night before was gone. A faint blue stained Jan's temples, the color of veins or an old bruise.

Siobhan knelt at the threshold of the tent, unwilling to go closer. "Jan?" Jan didn't move or blink. Her jaw hung loosely open. Not like she was surprised, but like a dentist had just said, *Open wide!*

Siobhan waited. Part of her believed that Jan would cough, flutter her eyes, sit upright, apologize for scaring them. Dina's screaming died down outside. She could hear the other girls talking. Andee said, "Did you try to wake her up?"

When Siobhan reemerged, Nita asked, "Well?"

Siobhan found she didn't have the air in her lungs to speak. She just shook her head.

"I did it!" Dina yelped.

They turned to her.

Dina was crying and hiccupping, barely able to get out the words. "I talked about her dying and then she did. I *cursed* her."

Siobhan felt a flash of annoyance. Now, she thought, is not the time for this babyish nonsense. The annoyance was a relief, a way of galvanizing around a different emotion, something other than the terror that hovered like movement at the edge of her vision.

Nita put her arm around Dina's neck and guided her roughly so that the five girls stood together in a circle, in front of the tents and Jan. Isabel had her arms crossed, shivering as she rubbed her upper arms.

"What do we do?" Andee said.

"We need to get help," Siobhan said.

"Right," Nita said. "We should start kayaking back to Forevermore."

"What? No," Siobhan said. "We're already on the big island. We just need to walk to town and find a phone."

Nita gestured around them, at the enclosed beach and the pathless woods. "And which way is town?"

"We just walk away from the water, and we'll hit a road eventually. Jan had a compass. I think it's . . ." Siobhan hesitated. "I think it's in our tent."

"We know Forevermore is four, five hours away. We know we can make it because we did it yesterday. We don't know how far town is."

"We know it's closer than Forevermore! We're already here!" Siobhan yelled.

"Don't you remember what Jan said? She said we'd camp somewhere that was miles from anyone, and no one would ever stumble upon us. But if we get in the boats, we just keep paddling east and we'll be back to the mainland!"

"We didn't get here in a straight line," Siobhan said. "The route was complicated. I'm sure there was a good reason. Rocks and . . . stuff. Water that's not safe." The inherent safety of land over water seemed obvious to Siobhan. Her incredulity made the words jumble in her mouth, made her sputter, like having to argue that the sky was blue as it hung above them, plain to see.

"There's a map of the islands in Jan's bag," Nita argued.

"But we don't know where on the big island we are!"

"Exactly!"

Dina was still sniffling. Through her tears, she said, "They'll notice when we don't come back today. They'll come looking for us. Maybe we should just stay here."

"But nobody knows we're here," Andee said, with dawning horror. "They think we're on Lumpen."

Nita rubbed her forehead. "We could go back to Lumpen and wait there. Or half of us could wait on Lumpen in case rescuers come, and the other half could continue on to Forevermore in case they don't."

"No," Siobhan said. "We're not splitting up. That's the worst thing we could do."

"Why?" Dina asked.

"It . . ." Again, Siobhan felt stymied by the obviousness of what she wanted to say. Why did Dina have to be so stupid? "It just is!"

"Guys," Isabel said, very softly, like she didn't want to wake a dangerous animal. "Look."

The girls turned in the direction Isabel pointed, toward the water. Nothing immediately appeared to be amiss. The bland slapping of the waves on the shore, the dull-colored water and rocky sand, the overcast morning, the thorny vines. "What?" Andee said.

"The kayaks," Isabel said.

The pile of boulders held no sign of the anchor loop that Jan had jammed in the day before. Off in the distance, static at the horizon as though teetering over the edge of the world, far enough to look unaffected by the motion of the waves, a sliver of red was tethered to a bundle of neon green. The kayaks had sorted themselves into their most buoyant arrangement.

Dina's crying escalated again, piercing as a newborn's. Siobhan looked around and took stock of the supply bags: two by the tents, one in the tent with Jan, one tied between the trees. "There were water jugs and stuff in Jan's kayak," Siobhan said, "and the first-aid kit."

"We should go after them," Nita said.

"What? How?" Siobhan said.

"We should swim after them. Quickly, while we can still see them."

"Are you crazy? The water is freezing cold. And look how far away they are."

"We need those kayaks! You know we do! The longer we spend talking about it, the farther away they get!"

"And then what? We're going to pull them back to land?"

"We can jump in and paddle them back!"

"The paddles are still here," Isabel said.

"So we'll swim out holding the paddles, and—and . . ." Nita stomped her foot. "I don't care what you do, but I'm going."

"Nita," Siobhan said. The other girl looked agitated, keyed up for a fight. "Nita, you'll drown. Or freeze. Okay?"

Then Nita was crying too. Not like Dina was—angry, defiant tears seemed to escape under their own power and Nita shoved them away by the cuffs of her sweatshirt. "What happened to Jan?"

"I don't know," Siobhan said. Watching Nita cry stung her eyes. Before she realized it, Siobhan was crying too. She tried to sound brave. "I guess she was sick."

"Maybe that cut on her leg got infected? Or there was something poisonous in her tea?" Nita suggested, almost reflexively.

"Can that kill you in one night?" Andee asked.

Siobhan tried to think of things that killed people quickly. What part of you, if it failed, immediately meant the end? "Or, like, her heart? A heart attack? Or her brain?"

"An aneurysm," Nita said.

"Maybe she was sick and she didn't tell us," Isabel said. They'd never heard Isabel use full sentences before this conversation. She still spoke in a tiny, breathy whisper, but there was something solid underneath, a surprising conviction.

"Why do adults do that?" Dina wailed.

"Maybe that's why she wanted to do the trip this year, even though she's not a counselor," Isabel continued. "Maybe she knew it would be her last chance."

Siobhan doubted this, from what she knew about grown-ups. It seemed unlikely Jan would intentionally spend her last days with a bunch of unfamiliar children. How could anyone, even Jan, like Forevermore that much? Why wouldn't she do adult stuff? Drink and smoke cigarettes and stay up late and go to nightclubs and travel anywhere in the world she wanted?

Nita blew her nose into her pinched fingers and wiped her hand on her sweatshirt. "Well," she said, "I guess we have no choice but to try and walk to town. Which way should we go?"

Four pairs of eyes rested on Siobhan, and one stared blankly into infinity inside the tent. Siobhan didn't want to be the leader; she just didn't want to get back into the kayaks. "We should eat breakfast first," she declared. "Before we set out. And — see what supplies we have left."

Lowering the food bag took on a serious, ceremonial air, like lowering a flag to half-mast. They each took a turn at puzzling over the pulley-winch system, before Nita climbed the tree and yanked the whole setup down. "If Nita can do it, a bear could have," Siobhan said under her breath. She was criticizing the arrangement, not comparing Nita to a bear, but Andee heard and glowered at her.

"Really?" Andee muttered, watching Nita shimmy down the tree. "You're going to keep being a bitch? Now?"

No one had ever called Siobhan a bitch before. Her legs wavered underneath her and then steadied, like she'd just caught a medicine ball in gym class.

Nita rooted around the food bag. "More camp food. One pouch of instant oatmeal, one pouch of instant hot cocoa. Six wrapped PB and Js, six cookie packets, six cans of fruit cocktail —"

"We should write this down," Siobhan said.

"Why?" Nita asked.

"I don't know." It was something they would have done in an adventure book. Take inventory.

Nita continued, "There's two leftover hot dogs from last night, half a bag of marshmallows. Two big bottles of water."

"Oh, good—so they weren't all in the kayak," Dina said.

"And this." Nita took out a drawstring cloth bag. She opened it and the girls gathered in closer. There was a bag of trail mix, a package of gummy bears, and a single candy bar. "Jan's secret stash, I guess." Nita plucked something out of the cloth bag and held it up for the others to see. It was a Ziploc bag rolled up around a white twist of paper.

"What is that?" Siobhan said.

"Seriously?" Andee said.

Siobhan guessed that Dina and Isabel didn't know either, from the looks on their faces, but they were smart enough to keep their mouths shut.

"It's a joint," Andee said, exasperated. "Pot. Weed. Marijuana. *Drugs.*" She added another synonym each time Siobhan failed to rearrange her confused expression.

"Jan wouldn't do drugs," Siobhan said firmly. Teenagers with greasy hair, the ones who shoved Siobhan and stole her beloved frog-shaped wallet last summer, while she was waiting to be picked up outside the amusement park—*they* did drugs. The basement-dwelling uncle her family visited briefly on Christmas morning every year, because he wouldn't leave his dark, dank house. Not straight-laced, tough-love Jan, singing the camp song louder than anyone, with the force of the hundreds of girls she'd heard in the past. *And I shall love my si-is-ters . . .* She'd never sing it again, Siobhan realized. She shuddered.

Andee rolled her eyes. "Clearly she did."

"She's dead," Siobhan said.

"So?"

Isabel murmured, "So you shouldn't say bad things about a dead person." Andee looked chastened. Once again, Isabel had the last word. Siobhan noticed that Isabel's gaze and attention kept drifting, her head cocking to sounds, as though she were expecting a visitor.

Nita tucked the weed back into the cloth bag. "So, oatmeal?"

At the fire pit, Siobhan was able to recite highlights from Jan's lecture on how to build a fire, but when she looked down at the remains of the previous fire, and the remaining fuel-wood—in the cold morning light, the branches looked larger and damper, like they'd swollen with absorbed night moisture and dew—she had no idea how to act upon it. Nita listened to Siobhan's faltering recitation, and then said, "We'll need her lighter and starter."

"Where are they?" said Dina.

"In her bag," Siobhan said. "In the tent." After a pause, she added, "I'll get it."

Siobhan dashed in and out of the tent as quickly as she could, grabbing Jan's bag and a bundle of her own things, trying not to look. She almost crashed into Isabel, who had trailed behind her as stealthily as a shadow. "I just wanted to see her," Isabel said.

"I don't," Siobhan said, hurrying past.

Nita got a faint glow to appear at the center of last night's woodpile and the girls sighed with outsize relief. Siobhan thought of a scene in the last book she'd read before leaving home, where some children find a dead fairy, a winged woman the size of a fist, and bring her back to life. Nita and Andee fanned the glow gently to flames. Dina poured water into Jan's pitted metal pot before asking how they were supposed to suspend it over the fire. Siobhan stuck a long branch through the pot handle, and she and Nita held it up on either end. Andee swapped in for Siobhan when her arms got tired.

They scraped the oatmeal into the camp-issue, disposable foam bowls. Andee was the first to lick her bowl clean, pushing her whole face into the bowl, then they all did. What went unspoken was how much work this meager meal had been, how strangely draining, even for Isabel and Dina, who had done nothing but stand to the side, looking anxious.

"We should get walking," Nita said.

Dina was staring into the fire. She still wasn't wearing shoes or a jacket. She hadn't gone back to the tent, and her socks must have been soaked through. "I don't want to put out the fire."

Nita was rooting through Jan's bag. "Where's her compass?"

Siobhan didn't want to say, but it couldn't be avoided. "She wore it around her neck."

"We need it," Nita said carefully. Not volunteering.

"I'll get it," Isabel said.

They turned to her, surprised. Tiny, pocket-size Isabel. Nita said, "Can you get her watch too?"

"You don't have to," Siobhan said quickly. Lifting the compass over Jan's head was bad enough, but to get the watch, Isabel would have to unzip the sleeping bag, undo the clasp around Jan's cold wrist, and run off with it while Jan watched, as a mannequin watches. Grave-robbing.

"I can do it," Isabel said.

"And my stuff," Dina added, her voice falling, uncertain. "My sleeping bag, and my dry bag, and my jacket, and my shoes."

Isabel nodded.

As they waited for Isabel, they stared silently at their feet, ashamed and apprehensive. They listened to Isabel scrabbling around inside the tent, trying to interpret the soft, small sounds. When she emerged, she had everything. She had even rolled up Dina's sleeping bag and stuffed it back into its carrier.

Thanking Isabel seemed insufficient, so no one said any-thing. They turned their attention to the problem of carrying everything, how to consolidate and divide the tents, sleeping bags, dry bags, and food bag between them. The larger bags had cross-body straps that were not made for long-distance carrying, and they were so loose around the girls' bodies that they'd have to knot them. "Do we need the tents and sleeping bags?" Dina asked. "Is it really going to take more than a day to walk to town?"

"Probably not," Siobhan said. "But . . . just in case?"

"But they're so heavy. All of this is so heavy."

"We can't leave her," Isabel said suddenly.

"What?"

"Jan. We can't just leave her."

"Why not?" Andee demanded.

Isabel had a strange, vacant expression. "Someone has to stay with her."

"She's dead," Andee said harshly. "She doesn't care."

"She might get eaten by a bear," Dina whispered.

"Crows, more likely," Nita said, peering up at the sky.

"Don't joke about that!" Siobhan snapped.

"I wasn't joking."

"Someone has to stay with her," Isabel repeated. "She can't be alone, in case . . . I'll stay with her. You guys go."

"No," Siobhan said. She repeated it louder. "No. No, no, no. We are not splitting up. We are not leaving anyone behind."

"We need you to help carry stuff," Nita said.

Isabel gave her a weary look and offered up her palms, as though to remind them of her toddlerlike stature. "I'll wait here in case someone from Forevermore comes to look for us. Maybe someone knows about this spot, or they'll see the kay-aks and figure it out. And if not, when you guys get to town, you can send help for me and Jan."

"Jan's dead!" Andee insisted, a waver in her voice like she

might cry. Siobhan felt it too, the urge to start crying again, furious with Isabel: Why was she doing this?

"That way you'll only have to carry one tent," Isabel went on, like she hadn't heard. "You can all fit in one."

"What if we're gone all night?" Siobhan said. "Are you going to sleep . . . in the tent . . . with Jan?"

"If I have to," Isabel said.

"Isabel makes a good point," Nita said. "If someone finds her, she can tell them which way we went. Or if we get to town first, we can tell them where Isabel is."

"And Jan," Isabel added.

"Jan's *dead*." Andee seemed unable to say anything else. "What is wrong with you?"

"We'll leave you some of the food and one of the water bottles," Nita said, already pulling packets out of the food bag, making decisions. Leaving Isabel one sandwich, one cookie pack, and all the heavy cans of fruit cocktail. "We should get going. It's getting later and later."

"You saw her," Siobhan said. Isabel stared at her feet through her eyelashes.

"Sometimes people look dead and they're really not," Nita said. "I read about it in one of my dad's books. That's why doctors are the ones who have to make the call."

"What if we wait a little longer?" Siobhan said. "If we spend one more day here, and Jan doesn't wake up, will you come with us?"

"We'll run out of food if we do that," Nita said. "We only have enough for today."

"Shut up!" Siobhan was crying again, and again it had caught her unawares. In the past, she'd been able to feel tears before they came, as pressure welling up in her chest and throat, but this was a new kind of crying, connected to a different, more immediate source, a part of her body she could not feel. "Just shut up, Nita!"

"I'll show you," Andee said. "I'll prove it." She reached into the food supply bag and pulled out Jan's closed switchblade. She turned and ducked into the tent.

The other girls huddled behind her at the open flap. Andee knelt beside Jan's sleeping bag. Dina covered her face with her hands.

"What are you *doing?*" Isabel cried. "Stop it! Stop it!"

Andee flipped open the knife. She wavered for only a moment, her face looking slightly ill, green-tinted, but no less determined. She plunged the knife into the sleeping bag, low, about where Jan's feet would be. Isabel shrieked.

A horrified silence followed. Even Andee, Siobhan thought, had hoped that Jan would cry out, awake and alive and bellowing. None of them could quite believe the human form in front of them wouldn't react to being stabbed. Jan stayed silent and unmoving, her pried-open expression unchanged.

Andee sat back on her heels. She opened her fist and the knife tumbled to the floor of the tent. A small dark spot bloomed on Jan's sleeping bag. "There," Andee said, a quaver in her voice. "There, see?"

In the entrance to the tent, Isabel sank to her knees. "I'm not leaving Jan," she said. "I don't want to be out in the woods without her."

Nita became the third one to kneel. She put her hands on Isabel's shoulders from behind and murmured into Isabel's ear, but Siobhan could still hear her. "It's okay. You stay here. We'll be really quick. We'll walk to town and get help. We'll tell them where you and Jan are. Maybe you're right. Maybe they'll get Jan to a hospital and she'll be okay."

Isabel nodded without looking back. Nita lowered her chin to one shoulder and spoke in a low voice to Siobhan and Dina. "Let's go."

ISABEL

1

ISABEL AND VICTOR drive south toward Santa Cruz from their home in the suburbs of northern California. Victor's apricot-colored surfboard is lashed to the roof rack. Ash from a distant forest fire drifts down like black snow.

Isabel reaches across the gearshift to touch the back of Victor's head. Her hand moves slowly down his body, cupping the back of his neck, fingers trailing over his shoulder and forearm, landing on his upper thigh with a friendly squeeze. She draws her hand back. She feels sated, as though she leeched a substance out of Victor through her fingertips, into her bloodstream: a mild, warming high. Her eyelids are heavy.

Over the dashboard, across the horizon, the red glow of sunrise or the fire itself. In the early-morning haze, the cliffs on all sides—lush ridges in daylight—look flattened and beige, like hills of sand.

Victor wonders aloud if he should take one highway or another. He talks about the weather conditions, technical jargon about tides, winds, and surfing technique that Isabel indulges but doesn't absorb. His voice eddies pleasantly around her sleepy mind.

They exit the highway and drive through a small coastal town. Surf shops, bike rentals, gelato, handmade crafts. Nothing is open yet. Their car descends a steep incline toward the beach, through a damp layer of fog. The spectacle of sunrise ends. The sun becomes a sizzling, perfectly round yolk, hanging low across a canyon between the hills to the east.

They park across the street from the boardwalk. A carousel and an arcade with walls of pink sandstone, also closed. Hot dogs, deep-fried seafood, ice cream, funnel cakes, closed. The smell of stagnant cooking oil and rotten fish.

Victor changes. Isabel sculpts a mound of sand into a backrest, spreads a blanket in front. She has a stack of books and magazines and a travel mug of milky hot tea. The beach is chilly and desolate, the colors of the boardwalk storefronts washed out by years of salt, sun, and wind. Isabel wraps another blanket around herself, though she's already dressed in layers of synthetic and wool. She looks away as Victor wades out and rides. The waves crash over hidden trenches like curls of cold butter. They seem enormous and violent to Isabel, a house-size monster storming the shore. It's better not to watch.

Good, strong waves. Yet the beach is empty, no other surfers, no kites or kayaks, no wanderers or addicts. An hour or so passes. Isabel checks her phone periodically even though the result is always the same: no service.

The wind ruffles her pages forward. Her eye catches a phrase that ruins a twist in the novel she's reading. She ties her hat into her hair. It blows off her head anyway, whipping behind her, still attached to her hair, yanking at her skull. The second time, it pulls completely free, rolls playfully across the sand, grounding and then lilting upward again like a stone skipping across a pond. She chases it. Her hair blows around her face and into her mouth.

She catches her hat where it comes to rest in a divot in the sand, the edges still flickering. She seizes it with both hands. She looks up. The empty ocean stretches away. Where's Victor?

The surface of the water is reflective silver, making it hard to focus her eyes. She looks for his orange surfboard. She looks for his black wetsuit. His slick of wet hair. His tan face. His hand. A shape. Anything. She looks back at her blanket, thinking maybe he's come out to meet her. The wind has knocked over her tea, leaving a spot of wet sand.

She calls out, inquiring, *Victor?*

She stands still, listening. The ocean roars like the white noise of a television, turned all the way up. The rustling of leaves somewhere. Louder, longer: *Victor!*

She feels acutely alone. The ocean draws waves from its depths reflexively. It howls and crashes to the same rhythm as before. It doesn't care about Isabel and Victor.

Her heart is thudding but she stands still. Is he just out too far to see? She pictures herself running frantically along the water's edge. She sees herself wading in, diving down, kicking up the sand at the bottom, searching pointlessly. She can see more from here, at a distance. She grew up by the ocean. She knows not to trust its pull. She cups her hands around her mouth and yells his name as loudly as she can.

She calls his name three times in a row, broken into its syllables. *Vic-tor!* It sounds like the word and not the name, the one who gets the spoils.

She can't help it. She runs. She goes back to her spot on the sand, checks her phone, and of course, no service. Who would she call, if she could?

She runs. She runs. He must be farther along the beach somewhere, he must've decided it was too dangerous and went in search of calmer waters. He's *somewhere*. The ocean is vast but not infinite.

She waits. She's covered in sand for some reason. When did that happen? Her calves are wet and the sand sticks. Sand in her mouth, her eyes. Sand weighs down her feet.

She waits.

She pulls out her phone and starts running again, up the beach, away from the water. One bar flickers in and out, then disappears. When she reaches the boardwalk, she sees someone inside the beachfront café. She bangs on the glass door. The employee, a drowsy young man in a white apron, gestures at the CLOSED sign. She bangs again with both fists. I need help, she cries. It's an emergency!

Is it? Is it yet?

He reluctantly turns the lock and opens the door a crack, to hear what Isabel's yelling about. His manager, a middle-aged woman in a brown patterned dress with glasses on a chain, counting cash as she assembles the float for the day, says, Oh, for God's sake, let her in.

Isabel calls 911 on the café phone. She stands by the door with the receiver against her ear, still scanning the ocean. The young man in the apron hovers nearby, faintly regretful. He wants to help.

IN A FUNDAMENTAL WAY, Isabel believes nothing bad has happened to Victor. He's safely out of view. Even as the police arrive, and then the coast guard, and a small rescue boat putters back and forth from where she saw him go in. She has a conversation with the woman in the brown dress, on a loop. Isabel says, He's a strong swimmer, he's an experienced surfer, he knows his limits, he knows the water, he knows this beach. The woman says, I'm sure he's okay. Isabel says, He's okay. They go back and forth: He's okay, he's okay, he's okay.

The hours stretch into years of possible lives. Isabel thinks about how mad she'll be when it turns out to have been nothing at all. Victor came out of the water far down the beach, judged that the water had turned, and is hiking back. He paddled his board into calmer waters, to lie flat on his back and doze, not realizing he's out of sight.

The woman in the brown dress asks Isabel if she'd like something to eat. Isabel starts allowing for the possibility of a small injury, a twisted ankle—he's clinging to his board, out too deep, waiting for rescue.

The woman in the brown dress says Isabel really should eat something. The light is changing. The sea is beginning to calm. The beach has filled with people, gawkers and onlookers and those determined to enjoy themselves. The arcade lights up. The carousel plays its mocking tune. Serious injury, then: Isabel imagines Victor's life as a paraplegic. She would nurse him through the early days, the relearning, the physical therapy. They'd cry together. When he went back to work, his co-workers would applaud. He'd join a wheelchair basketball league.

FIVE MILES DOWN the beach, outside the wind tunnel made by the shape of the backing hills, nine-year-old June builds a sand castle at the water's edge. Her parents are far up the beach. Her little sister, Emma, who is hot and bored, sits between them underneath an umbrella and sucks on a freezer pop.

June thinks she might be out of her parents' sight. Or almost. A girl shape in a purple swimsuit. She feels a frisson of naughtiness. Lately, being alone feels exciting instead of scary. Or rather, it feels scary *and* exciting. Even though she doesn't do anything bad, it's just the idea that she could. The realization that her mother doesn't know everything.

pened, then this happened, then this happened. Mr. Greeley ran drama as a multi-grade class during the school year and a club in the summer, with at least two shows that bookended the school year.

Isabel's best friend at the time, Marcy, was Mrs. Webb in *Our Town* in the fall of their sophomore year. Marcy described the play's folksy dialogue and school-friendly inoffensiveness and Isabel felt bored just thinking about it. She waited until closing night to go because Marcy promised to take her to the cast party afterward. As the curtains opened, Isabel folded a paper crane from her program, sitting with her legs tucked up on the wooden folding chair. She'd come alone and sat in the second row, in the section of the audience for parents and the supportive old ladies who came to everything.

As the lights came down and the curtains parted, Isabel felt momentarily disoriented. She'd been in recitals and Christmas showcases in elementary school, when everyone had to be, but at fifteen, she'd never been in the audience of a live show before. The darkness swallowed up the auditorium, the school, the night beyond. Nothing existed but the stage, the world shrunk to its conspicuously shallow dimensions.

Elliott Mars, a junior, played the Stage Manager. He strode out and began the opening speech of *Our Town,* mapping out each building in Grover's Corners. He was pale and absurdly tall, six feet four without any of the other trappings of manhood.

Elliott was hypnotic to watch. He looked out over the invisible town with nostalgia and fondness, his voice casual. He navigated among objects that weren't there with ease. You believed they were there because he did. He noted the passage of time with such quiet wonder that Isabel felt it slipping away. She felt herself age, she felt the regrets she didn't yet have.

At the end, as a parade of sweaty teenagers dripped stage makeup, grasped each other's hands, and bowed, the parents leapt up for a roaring, standing ovation. Isabel stayed in her seat. Stricken. She hadn't realized how much she'd been crying until the lights went up. The other kids had been fine, decent. In a moment, Isabel would recover herself and go out into the hall to congratulate Marcy and tell her she'd been great. She would make a point of mumbling a similar sentiment to the senior who played Emily, whose revelations about life and death — however hammily played — were primarily what had made Isabel bawl.

There was nothing that could be said to Elliott. Isabel was impressed that her peers had achieved the bare minimum — they could brave a crowd and remember their lines and enunciate clearly and mime shucking peas and holding umbrellas, something Isabel could never do. But their competence only highlighted Elliott's radiance. His unselfconscious grace, expressive from his eyebrows to the tips of his fingers. He alone made Grover's Corners real. He could act.

Isabel hovered near Marcy at the cast party at the drama teacher's house, worried someone would ask what she was doing there. Marcy was ignoring her, busy reliving the high of the performance with her castmates, dwelling on some hilarious near-disaster in the wings. Isabel looked around for Elliott. She spotted him talking to the drama teacher and his wife. Out of costume, everyone had reverted back to their T-shirts and plaids. Elliott wore a maroon button-up and dark jeans. He and the two adults appeared cut out from another scene and pasted into this one. The after-party of a Broadway show, cocktails instead of store-brand cola cans. Everyone seemed small and provincial beside him.

Isabel noticed a cluster of more familiar kids in the corner. Her people: misshapen nerds in unflattering black turtlenecks. The stagehands, the set builders, the tech team, everyone who needed the art credit or extracurricular but couldn't or wouldn't act. She could do that.

ISABEL WATCHED the next play from the distorted broad angle of the wings. She was so distractedly in love with Elliott that she couldn't enjoy this show — *Harvey* — the way she had the last one. The kids had more trouble with comedy, or the teacher had more trouble directing them. The audience was confused by the pauses and the broad gestures, a constant game of *Was that a joke?*

Elliott, of course, was Elwood. The drama teacher was probably picking shows that played to Elliott's strengths — his ability to make seen the unseen. The way he stared a man-size imaginary rabbit creature in the eyes, communed with it, and placed a hat on its head, the creature was as clearly and effortlessly in the room as Elliott was. Elliott made Harvey more compelling than the other solid, real actors.

Isabel had mooned and planned all year. She thought about Elliott every night to soothe herself to sleep. His eyes, an ordinary blue when she saw him elsewhere at school, darkened onstage, became stormy, almost indigo. His soft-looking, feminine mouth, on a sharply defined jawline. His wavy brown hair, coiffed high off his forehead. After a while, though, the details became muted, and the words to describe them fell away. He was simply perfect. Each and every thing about him, perfect.

She had never spoken to Elliott, but the cast party would be her chance. She would tell him he'd been great, and he would know, from the way she said it, that she *really* appreciated his talent, really *saw* him, apart from and above the gushing compliments and congratulations that had to be bestowed on everyone else. And then! Then the summer romance of her dreams.

The drama teacher's wife came from money, and they had no children. Their house was intimidating and sophisticated, many small rooms divided on a large swath of land, heavily decorated with fragile things. The teenagers clumped in the

Greeleys' living room with a case of soda and generic, family-size bags of chips. Isabel waited until Elliott was alone. She broke away from her sullen, skulking group — wearing their inferiority in the hunch of their shoulders — and strode up to him.

"Hi," she said.

"Hi."

She craned her neck to talk to him. He gazed down at her without moving his head, leaving it completely up to her to bridge the extraordinary height difference. "You were great tonight," she said.

"Thanks." He started scanning the room for someone else.

She stepped closer, which meant tilting her head back even farther or talking to his sternum. "No, I mean, *really* great."

He looked at her again with a flicker of annoyance. "Thanks," he repeated.

Isabel left the party and walked home. She forgot Marcy's mother was supposed to drive her. She slipped out stealthily, on ghost feet, like a stagehand: a black shape on a black lawn through a black night.

As the party wrapped up, Marcy started looking for Isabel. She asked everyone if they had seen her. Kids who didn't know Isabel pretended to look for her, using it as a pretext to open every door in their teacher's house, poke through the closets and drawers as though she could be hiding there.

The drama teacher's wife had the sense to call Isabel's house and confirm that Isabel had made it home all right, and that she and her husband weren't liable for the disappearance of a minor. Somehow this fact didn't circulate. By Monday morning, people who weren't at the party were asking if that missing girl had been found.

GABE IANESCO, a junior and fellow backstage lackey, had been cured of a speech impediment as a child. It left behind a peculiar hesitancy to the way he talked. He would pause before speaking, stare hard at the auditor to make sure he had their full attention, screw up his mouth in preparation, half open his mouth, close it again, and only then would he begin. He had smooth, olive skin and symmetrical features that would have been attractive on someone else. His small, round head on his thin neck bobbled unnervingly. He drove a red salt-ruined subcompact that he called a "chick magnet" without irony. Almost everything that came out of his mouth was a lie. Everyone knew it. He was a creep and a loser. The lowest of the low.

It was nothing to Gabe, upon hearing about the missing girl, to brag that he'd taken her out to the backseat of his car. He told the potheads at the wooded edge of the parking lot, who sometimes let him come around and spin his tales while they smoked, like their personal court jester. He told his lab partners in biology and chemistry and his drill partners in PE, who were stuck by his side for an hour at a time. He told anyone unfortunate enough to be in the same block of lockers as his. He added new lewd details upon each retelling.

No one believed him, of course. Not exactly. But the story began to splinter and spread, each piece more believable than the whole. Maybe *someone* had sex at the cast party. In the drama teacher's house? A shut-up bedroom somewhere. A handjob in a closet. The drama teacher's house was near a deserted field, and a car had been seen parked on the field from a distance. Had Gabe disappeared from the party too? Nobody could remember. Nobody paid him much attention. Maybe it wasn't Gabe, but was it Isabel?

The aura around Isabel changed, a whiff of scandal, a muttered *slut* from people who had never noticed her before.

MEANWHILE, ISABEL had had a lot of time to think, walking home from the party, and then lying awake in her bed, on the same pink flowered sheets she'd had as long as she could remember, so threadbare they were ephemerally soft and almost translucent. She'd spent a long school year watching Elliott work. Before and after drama, when everyone else stood around chatting and swinging their legs off the edge of the stage, or frantically copying homework for other classes, Elliott paced and practiced lines. She'd overheard enough conversations to know that this didn't endear him to anyone, this weird, pretentious giant in his somber grown-up clothes and talk of *method* and *Broadway*. Elliott's mother drove him to auditions sometimes hours away, where he would be told he wasn't a cute child anymore, but he'd have to fill out to play a teenager. His actual, in-progress pubescence was too off-putting. So now he drank whey-protein shakes and took evening dance classes.

Isabel had taken to reading biographies of geniuses and novels about vampires without realizing what they had in common. Her attraction to Elliott had taken on a new shade: she envied him. She envied his passion, his talent, his single-mindedness, as she envied the great men of the past and the bloodlust of night creatures. She didn't love anything the way he loved acting. She worked hard for her B-minuses, but not that hard. She bummed around the mall with Marcy, went to school, listened to music and read books and watched TV and masturbated. She was fifteen.

There was the surface pain of being rejected by Elliott, sharp and indulgent, something out of a sad song. She wasn't pretty enough. Or cool enough. She could cry about that. And then there was a deeper pain, more like fear. From the way he had stared straight through her. She'd felt, for the first time, how ordinary she was. Saw in a flash of intuition the ordinary life before her, the ordinary, banal adulthood. Without beauty or meaning or fame. Her life in the audience.

It only made her want him more.

REHEARSALS BEGAN on the fall show. Marcy quit drama altogether, unwilling to give up her summer, and the backstage kids weren't needed for the first month. Isabel had a part-time job at the concession stand on the beach, pulling hot dogs from the filthy water of the steamer and dispensing runny soft-serve. She spent her days off at the beach too, lying on the water output pipe at low tide with a book or a magazine over her face until her arms got tired or she fell asleep. Sometimes Marcy joined her and they'd lie on the grassy knoll above the beach instead — the sand itself was impassable, full of rocks and glass and garbage — and suntan in their bikinis. Isabel had been a normal-size girl until about age eight, as tall as her peers, and then she got stuck there while they all shot past. Her body had stayed more or less the same, no more than the slight slant of a man's chest. She could still wear children's clothes. Marcy had breasts, stray hair sticking out the side of her bikini bottoms, the flesh on her thighs and bottom taking on an alien weight. They complained about their bodies halfheartedly, drugged by the sun, the silvery waves.

When Isabel was called into drama club, she considered following Marcy's lead and not going. It had been a relief not to think about Elliott. But she worried that not facing the leers would come across as an admission of guilt, confirmation that something *had* happened the night of the cast party.

So she worked on the floor of the auditorium with the rest of the crew, cutting cardboard with X-ACTO blades and painting scrap wood and donated furniture. The school seemed different, the rooms mostly closed, the halls silent. The summer-school classes were quieter. The adults renting out the gym for who-knew-what were very quiet, sitting in circles or neat rows of folding chairs when Isabel peeked through the glass.

By the end of July, when the tech team moved to the box and the catwalk to practice cues, the auditorium was sweltering. The crew worked in the dark whenever possible, sluggish and agitated, fighting over the one good paintbrush, hitting the wrong switch with an elbow, falling asleep. People started leaving early, arriving late with a Slurpee in hand, not showing up at all.

Elliott was the last to leave every day, insisting on one more run-through. His scene partners were often absent, so he pulled a standing fan onstage with him. The blades split and distorted his voice when he leaned in. Some of the newer people thought he was being intentionally funny; the rest knew better.

Mr. Greeley raged at their laziness, their unreliability. But even he got tired of waiting for Elliott to finish. It unnerved the teacher to see Elliott waiting outside the locked school doors when he arrived, drinking from a massive to-go coffee cup that couldn't be good for a seventeen-year-old. Breaking several district rules, he gave Elliott a key to the auditorium's outside door, which was accessed through the utility closet they were using to store props.

Isabel regularly contrived to be the second-to-last to leave, to feel that same surge in her heart as she had at *Our Town* as she watched Elliott and the fan alone onstage. On one such afternoon, just the two of them in the auditorium, the unthinkable happened: Elliott called out into the darkness. "Isabel? Is that you?"

Normally, she would have yelped, "Hi! Yes!" but she'd been, just a moment before, completely engrossed in his monologue. She instead stepped out of the shadows without a word, making herself visible in the shaft of light coming from the school hallway, beyond a crack in the auditorium door.

Elliott knew her name.

He squatted on the balls of his feet at the edge of the stage. "I knew I wasn't alone."

She didn't trust herself to speak. She'd ruin this somehow.

"Do you mind coming up here and practicing with me? It would be so much easier if I just had a face to look at."

He reached out a hand. Her heart was going to explode. She took his hand and he yanked her onstage. She gulped, looking around helplessly. "What do you want me to do?"

"Just stand there."

He restarted his monologue. Isabel was conscious of her hands, her tongue in her mouth. Should she cross her arms? Let them hang by her sides? Should she look him in the eyes? She couldn't do that. She bent and unbent her knees, locking and unlocking them. Had standing always been this complicated?

Elliott stopped midsentence. Midline. "Hey, can I ask you something?"

She almost said, *Of course.* "Sure."

He paused. "Well. That thing with Gabe? At the cast party? That didn't really happen, right?"

Isabel had had this conversation what felt like a million times. Every other time, she blurted out, sometimes yelled, "Of course not! God!" This time, she had another one of those brief, sad, adult feelings, an intuition she could not have explained in words. She said, "Not exactly."

FOR THE NEXT WEEK, Elliott talked and Isabel listened, like she was a priest or a therapist. They stayed in the auditorium for hours after everyone had left. They ran lines, or he did, Isabel's face alternately blank, nervous, rapt. They sat in the theater seats in the dark and he talked about the future he dreamed of, the theater schools in New York or secondarily Los Angeles or tertiarily Toronto. The full houses, the artsy workshops. Caught up in this reverie, the boundlessness of summer, the closeness of their breath in the unlit auditorium, he kissed her. They kissed.

He ruined it immediately. "Look, can we keep this a secret?"

Her stomach dropped. The vein of self-hatred that had been dug the night of the cast party was still fresh, easily accessed. Its depths continued to surprise her.

"I mean, you of all people know how people at this school talk. I don't want to make this whole thing worse for you."

"I don't care," she said.

"And I don't want it to distract from the show. It's kind of barely hanging together as it is."

The show? she thought. Who cared about the show?

"And" — he looked away from her now — "I'm actually not supposed to date. Because, like, my grades aren't that great, since I'm always at acting class and dance class and auditions and stuff. So I promised my mom I wouldn't do anything else to distract me from school."

When would she ever talk to his mother? How would that even come up? He was ashamed of her, plain and simple. Who could blame him? She saw her worthlessness clearly now. She wondered how she could have missed it all these years.

ELLIOTT HAD CAUGHT Isabel at a moment in her development as an animal where her skin was perpetually pricked and lit and full of fire. A caress on the shoulder made her shudder. A kiss on the neck felt like death. She came from his distracted kisses, the faint, inexpert rubbing of his hand through her jeans. She would never need less, never be more receptive or willing than this.

They kissed and fumbled in the theater seats. Every moment felt precious, high-stakes. Every time she thought it might be the last. After a week, when that new, dark intuition sensed he was getting bored, she pulled him wordlessly into the prop closet and dropped to her knees. After a month, he asked her if she had a condom. She didn't then, but she did the next time, and — without discussing it with Marcy, as they'd always promised they would — she let him lift her tiny body against the wall, crush her, fill her with a deep, lancing pleasure that made her want to weep.

THE LAST TIME, it was just too hot. August was drawing to a close. Isabel felt dizzy, addled, trapped in her body, claustrophobic in the closet. They peeled their sticky skin apart and turned away from each other, dressing in silence.

Her back to him, she said, "Hey, so. I was thinking. When school starts, we won't be able to use the auditorium anymore."

Elliott didn't answer. She glanced over her shoulder. The muscles of his back flexed as his shirt dropped over them. The whey protein converted to new flesh like lumps of clay on a wire frame. Meatlike striation and stretch marks. This final obliteration of childhood, the body expanding to destroy itself from within. She stopped looking, focused on her own buttons and clasps as his clicked and rustled behind her.

"Let's just see how things go, okay?" he said, at last.

School started. Isabel watched opening night from the catwalk, with a girl who chewed gum and breathed through her mouth at the same time. Elliott's costume was unconvincing. He walked with a defeated slump, mumbled and cried out in anguish as needed, but no one involved in the production had the skill to make this suddenly movie-star-handsome young man into Willy Loman. In their perch, the girl said to Isabel, "Was Elliott always that hot?"

"Yes," Isabel said.

Isabel knew every line of *Death of a Salesman* inside and out. She watched the audience instead. They were captivated as they'd never been at *Our Town* and *Harvey*. At the end, instead of a cheering crowd with a sobbing, Isabel-size hole in the middle, everyone was in tears. Even though, having seen each scene countless times, Isabel thought it was one of Elliott's weaker performances. That night, he'd been greedy. He drew the eye when he shouldn't. He undermined the other actors.

The next day, at school, the inscrutable hive mind buzzed about Elliott. The scale tipped, his blossoming good looks finally outweighing his weirdness. Over the week, hovering invisibly above them like a god, Isabel watched the demographic of the audience shift. It went from mostly parents, teachers, and those sweet old ladies, with a couple of patchy rows of students in the back, to the inverse. It was like watching the tide roll out, teenage bodies advancing forward, overtaking the empty seats, a shrinking coastline of grown-ups.

All at once, and from no traceable beginning, Elliott was popular. Elliott was cool. Even more inexplicably, drama was cool. Everyone had to see the show, not because they enjoyed it, but because they were afraid of missing out. People were already excited about the next one, the infinity of a whole school year away.

Elliott didn't talk to Isabel at school. He didn't talk to her before or after each show, as he hadn't at rehearsals until everyone else was gone. She hadn't considered until it was too late that she had no means of communicating with him at all. She didn't even have his phone number. When they crossed paths in the halls at school, she begged with her eyes for the slightest acknowledgment, a flicker of recognition, anything. Even shame. Disgust. Some proof that it had happened.

She didn't tell anyone. No one would believe her now. Not even Marcy, who she saw less and less, who was upset with Isabel for being distant and moody through the last part of summer, tired of her sideways complaints about Mr. Greeley and the other theater techs. "If you hate drama so much, then quit," Marcy had said finally. "I'm sorry I got you into it."

At the end of the run, the drama teacher hosted the cast party, as he always had. This time, cast and crew brought their friends, their friends' friends, kids that tagged along on the way. Kids came in through the back door in the kitchen. Through the garage. The French doors in the study that led to the side garden. The unlatched window in the bathroom. Kids streamed in from all sides, faster than they could be identified and escorted out, with the force of an ocean against bailing buckets. Mr. Greeley and his wife ran around the house helplessly, running to the sound of a crash, or broken glass, closing and locking a door that reopened as soon as they were out of sight, grabbing the beer and cooler bottles that appeared in kids' hands as though out of thin air. The teacher let it go on too long, thinking he could reason with them, that he had a close, long-established relationship with these kids, he knew they were mostly good, and he was a *cool* teacher, a young one, who cared and believed in them—

That was the last cast party.

ONE MORNING, as Isabel walked to her locker between first and second periods, she spotted Elliott leaning back against the radiator at the end of a busy hallway. She continued on her trajectory. Through a gap in students passing back and forth, lining the walls, she saw a girl sitting on the radiator, behind Elliott, with her arms around his neck. She nuzzled in the nook of his collarbone.

Isabel walked closer than she needed to, passing her locker and turning into the stairwell by the end of the hall. Her first thought was: *Well, that makes sense.*

Such was the consensus. Mira and Elliott made so much sense everyone wondered how they'd never thought of it before; their coupledom held the satisfaction of solving a riddle.

Mira was the tallest girl in school, for starters, five-ten bare-foot and five-eleven in the lace-up boots she wore most of the time. Like Elliott, she was exquisitely pretty but unapproach-ably weird. Despite her height, she looked fragile, fine-boned, her long arms and legs the circumference of broomsticks, her mouth a tiny rosebud, her face angelically pale. She spaced out of conversations and class, preferring to draw, sometimes abstract doodles and sometimes near photo-realistic sketches of what was in front of her. She was a satellite friend of one group of girls, as Mira seemed to like clothes and talking about them, but they wearied of her sudden silences and disappear-ances. They accused her of thinking she was superior, floating above the sweaty masses, keeping her hands clean. She just floated away from the accusation. She was untouchable.

Together, embracing against the radiator, Elliott and Mira looked like normal teenagers. Smiling, a little shy, caught up in each other.

THE DESTRUCTION of his home had only slightly damp-ened Mr. Greeley's enthusiasm. The class worked on a quickie midyear production of *A Christmas Carol*.

Isabel was last to leave, besides the teacher, on a cold after-noon in early December. She felt woozy from spray-painting food for the feast scene. She went out through the prop closet door, trying not to think about everything that had happened there. She let it slam locked behind her. The winter sun set against the fast-encroaching night, an orange blossom on black.

Elliott sat on the railing outside the door, staring out.

Isabel stopped in her tracks. Before Mira, she had schemed and wished for a meeting just like this. Now she just wanted to skulk past, unseen.

He turned his head lazily in her direction. "Hey, Isabel. I was waiting for you."

Isabel couldn't process this statement.

He jumped down from the railing. "Do you need to be someplace? Can you go for a walk with me?"

Her voice finally emerged. "Okay," she croaked.

They walked together. No one saw them. The school campus was deserted. They crossed the parking lot, past the edge of the woods where the stoners would have been, along the road, farther down toward the overpass. Elliott didn't speak, so Isabel didn't try. They walked west, into a sun that blinded but offered no warmth. Isabel shivered in her thin coat. She wished, wistfully, that Elliott would put his arm around her.

He led Isabel off the path, through some low scrub, the weeds that survive frost, down to a gap between the pillars of a pedestrian bridge. Hidden there, pressed against the mossy brick, freezing, they embraced, Elliott drawing Isabel into a kiss. His hands wove inside her clothes and she felt as if their glorious and terrible summer had never ended.

Afterward, she felt even colder than before. Darkness had fallen in full. Isabel became conscious of the roar of cars in the near distance and the occasional footsteps above their heads. She asked in a whisper, "What about Mira?"

Elliott took a while to answer. "This has nothing to do with Mira." He started scrambling up the hillside without her.

IT HAPPENED a few more times that month. Twice more under the bridge. Once under the outdoor bleachers of the football field, a frozen metal ledge digging into her back. Once in a gully in the woods that edged the parking lot, the icy creek rushing just past their feet.

It seemed unreal that this was going on in the early dark before she went home for dinner with her parents. Even as a young child, she'd been aware that her parents adored her, and that they didn't know her at all; somehow she'd known not to believe them when they told her she was the smartest, sweetest, most beautiful girl in the world. They'd bought her clothes that were too large, the size on the tag for an average-size child her age, in what they said was her favorite color—it wasn't, but she didn't correct them. When she'd returned from Forevermore, she felt it was her job to reassure and comfort them, to downplay the grisliest details, and not the other way around.

Now they stared at her across the table with those well-meaning, puzzled expressions, as she struggled to smile for them, to humor them as she always had. She still had to wake up and go to school, walk the fluorescent-lit halls, absorb the trivia she was supposed to be learning, listen to the juvenile concerns of her peers, when all the while she was committing an adult sin.

Ebenezer Scrooge brought down the house.

SHORTLY BEFORE CHRISTMAS, out shopping for presents for her family, Isabel stood at a mall kiosk that sold goldfish in filterless, cube-shaped tanks. She stared into their bulging, empty eyes and tried to justify buying one for her mother. When she looked up, she found herself staring into another set of bulging, soulless eyes: Gabe's.

He was standing on the other side of the kiosk grinning at her. A place to lay her rage. A target nobody would care about. Everything was his fault; nothing was his fault. Gabe winked and then walked away, almost vanishing into the Christmas-shopping crowds. Without a plan, Isabel followed him. She stalked him all the way to his car in the parking lot, the red paint growing patches of rust that looked like a fungal disease.

Gabe appeared to be looking around for someone else when he spotted her. A flash of fear crossed his face before his bravado returned, his big, leering smile. He opened his mouth to say something but Isabel cut him off. "Stop telling people I slept with you, you creep."

She watched him turn this over in his mind. It had been so

long that he'd forgotten. "Oh, yeah," he said, the light coming on. "At the cast party last year, right?" His smile widened at the memory. "It was just a goof. Nobody believed me anyway." He opened his arms and made a welcoming gesture with his hands. "We could go make it true."

As Isabel sputtered, clenching her fists, Gabe waved at someone behind her. The boy was unmistakably related to Gabe, with the same features and small head, the same olive skin, even the same bowl haircut. He was a hair taller and had large, round glasses like Isabel's. He walked right past Isabel as though she weren't there. "Okay," he said to Gabe, dully. "I'm ready to go."

"This is my cousin Eugene," Gabe said. Eugene got into the unlocked car without speaking or even turning in Isabel's direction. "Want to come with us? We're going to watch *Die Hard* at my house."

Isabel stared at Gabe incredulously. In what world would she say yes?

For an instant, she saw herself from the outside. From far above, she and Gabe the size of cockroaches, and just as important. She felt the urge to self-destruct, to grind them both out beneath her shoe. She felt a remote curiosity about Gabe, what life he could possibly live outside of school.

Without agreeing out loud, she opened his backseat door and climbed in. She left the door open. She crossed her arms and threw Gabe a hard, challenging look, straight in the eyes. Eugene continued to face forward, uninterested.

Gabe put one hand on the roof of the car and leaned in, his brow furrowing. He thought better of whatever he was going to say. His expression brightened and he slammed Isabel's door shut, walking around to the driver's side.

Garbage filled the floor of the backseat, mostly school papers and fast-food bags and drink containers. Isabel didn't listen as Gabe nattered on and Eugene stayed stone silent. She was busy trying to keep her pants clean and dig out a space with the tip of her boot.

When they pulled into Gabe's parents' carport, Isabel realized Gabe had been bragging about something the whole way there. He kept talking as they got out of the car. "Even have my own entrance. So my parents have no idea when I come and go."

He led them through a door at the back of the carport, directly into a large basement bedroom. An L-shaped black leather couch dominated the space, packed tightly with an unmade bed, an empty aquarium, and a computer desk. The leather was cracked and worn, flaking off at the seams, and the rank smell of sweat and unwashed sheets filled the room. A pyramid of empty energy-drink cans stood against one wall. Two haphazard holes, each the size of a fist, had been cut high up on the wall across from the couch. Gabe noticed Isabel looking at them. "I'm wiring in a speaker system," he explained.

She drifted over to the aquarium. "What happened to your fish?"

Gabe shrugged. "They died."

Eugene flopped down on the couch. He stared at the blank wall. "I thought we were watching a movie," he said in his deadpan voice.

Gabe fiddled with a hacked-together machine on a shelf, which appeared to consist of a VHS camcorder, an overhead projector, and a thick mess of wires and glass plates. Isabel sat beside Eugene, who continued to ignore her. The couch sighed and squeaked beneath her. Eventually Bruce Willis appeared on the wall, fuzzy and overstretched. "I rigged the projector up myself," Gabe said. He produced three cans of energy drink from a mini-fridge under the desk. In spite of herself, Isabel was a little impressed by the separate entrance, the mini-fridge, the couch, the faint, slimy resemblance to her idea of a grown-up apartment. Nobody she knew had a bedroom like that.

"No, you didn't," Eugene said, taking the can from Gabe without looking, without any more movement than was strictly necessary. "I did."

Gabe sat on the other side of Isabel, trapping her between them. His sidelong glances revealed disbelief that she was there at all.

Twenty minutes into the movie, with another squeak of the couch, Gabe lunged. He tried to kiss Isabel on the cheek. She turned her head and caught him on the mouth. Their eyes stayed open. She watched his eyebrows jump up his forehead. A perverse note of glee sang through her, black laughter bubbling up. She felt powerful. The mother of chaos. They leaned toward each other, their arms hanging limply at their sides, not touching anywhere else. A foot away, Eugene watched the movie and sipped at his drink. He got up to go to the bathroom, returned, and sat down in the exact spot he'd left.

Isabel drew away. She reveled in Gabe's dumbfounded expression for a moment longer, and then stood up and walked out. Nobody would believe him anyway.

CHRISTMAS BREAK ROLLED ON. In the dead space between Christmas and New Year's, Isabel met up with Marcy. They had hot chocolate in a café that had fake snow sprayed in the window corners, shiny red paper trees spinning idly on strings.

Isabel knew Elliott and Mira hung out in this café, and masochistically hoped to see them there. She got half her wish. Mira had a large corner table to herself, her tea cold and forgotten. Art supplies covered the table: a drafting board, papercutting knife blades, pencil crayons. She worked at something in a sketchbook, concentrating so intently her mouth hung slack.

Marcy had a gift for Isabel, a childish-looking bracelet she'd made from fishing wire and beads. Isabel had nothing for Marcy.

"I have to tell you something," she began.

"About why you've been so weird all semester?" Marcy asked, looking around.

"Yes."

Marcy put her chin in her hand, in mock interest. "Okay. Explain it to me."

"I was seeing this older guy."

"Oh my God!" Marcy shrieked. Other patrons turned to look at her and she drew Isabel down, their heads nearer to each other and the table. "*What* older guy? Who is he?"

"You don't know him." This felt true. "And we were . . . sleeping together. And I know we promised to tell each other but I just couldn't. I didn't know how."

Marcy covered her mouth with her hands. "Oh my God," she said again, muffled. "Was it . . ." She lowered her hands. "How was it?"

Isabel didn't have the words to answer. The euphoria and terror of falling. "It was . . . nice." They mulled over that for a second. "But then he stopped calling. He just kind of disappeared, and I think he had a girlfriend, and—and . . ." She felt tears welling up. They felt soothing, luscious, like her eyes were full of grit to be washed away. "And I loved him so much."

Marcy held Isabel's hands across the table. This version felt no less real than what had actually happened. "You idiot," Marcy said affectionately. "Why didn't you tell me?"

"I don't know. I wish I had." Isabel let her eyes wander to the corner. Mira hadn't noticed them. She seemed scarcely aware of anything beyond her sketchpad.

After a pause, Marcy said, "He sounds like an asshole."

Isabel let free a laugh. "Yeah."

ISABEL REMAINED HYPERAWARE of Elliott until he graduated. She knew his class schedule; she knew beyond sight whether or not he was in a room. They were never alone again, after December.

In the spring, she went on a single strange date with Gabe. They went to the community pool on a Sunday afternoon, one lane filled with seniors with paddleboards, the rest with young children. They acted unabashedly like those children, Gabe standing a head above the line for the rope swing and the slide. They hogged the pool noodles and the water guns. They chased each other. Their screams and giggles melted into the din of higher-pitched ones, echoing off the high glass ceilings. He kissed her primly goodbye outside in the daylight. He tasted of chlorine. He asked her out again a few days later at school, in the mad scrum of people trying to leave at the end of the day. When she said no and kept walking, he seemed neither hurt nor surprised. Or that was how she chose to remember it.

3

THE SECOND ONE had no name.

Isabel had just moved into an apartment with three other girls. They came as a set: the three had been best friends in the dorms their first year, fallen in love with a four-bedroom walk-up, and recruited Isabel through a Craigslist ad.

The stairs were winter-thaw rotten and the whole building was sinking — the wood floors warped and wavy as a stormy sea, frozen in time — but the apartment was large and beautiful. Iron railings and one exposed brick wall, floor-to-ceiling back windows, an open kitchen. Cheap crap was everywhere. Four-dollar necklaces, ten-dollar shoes with cardboard soles, thin, fraying clothes from H&M and Forever 21. It overflowed their closets and secondhand IKEA wardrobes, broken slats and chipped particleboard. Their kitchen was comparatively spare, a communal set of five pots and pans, mismatched dishes in acrylic and soft plastic.

The three girls, Zoe, Lisa, and Kelly, were pretty enough on their own, but exceptionally pretty together. One blonde, one brunette, one redhead. A sampler effect, like a wine flight or a box of chocolates. They were kind to Isabel, and good roommates, but none of them tried to pierce the veil of her exclusion. Isabel had entered a brooding phase, sighing and rolling her eyes a lot. She was five feet and one hundred pounds, and had no discernible muscle mass, a jiggling layer of fat between her yellow-ivory skin and her weak bird bones. Round silver glasses covered most of her face and she wore aggressively dowdy clothing—wide, pleated slacks, oversize cardigans, scarves. Layers of flowing, shapeless fabric enveloped her petite frame. She looked owlish and ageless, like a child dressed as an old woman or an old woman dressed as a child. Her roommates were better at keeping whatever private darkness they carried to themselves.

The evening of their housewarming party, Isabel sat on the couch, reading, as her roommates appeared at the doors of their rooms in different outfits to solicit one another's opinions. Isabel said little more than "That's nice" and "That one's nice too." She hadn't been helpful with the party preparations either; the other girls had done the lion's share of the cleaning, prepped snacks, Jell-O shots, and a candy-sweet, vile-smelling punch. The playlist they'd put together was already booming from Kelly's speakers.

The girls settled on their clothes and congregated in Lisa's bedroom to do their makeup. Isabel gave up her pretense of uninterest and joined them, sitting on the end of Lisa's bed.

Kelly and Lisa went for a girlish, natural look in pink and peach, while Zoe — less successfully — chose a dark-red lip and smoky eye. They offered to do Isabel's, but didn't push.

Isabel saw herself as an observer. She liked the alchemy of their makeup, envied their hopeful coloration and refined profiles, but was afraid to admit — so publicly, on her *face* — that she wanted attention too. It felt too late, or like hypocrisy. Her life in the audience.

AS THE PARTY reached its peak, an uncountable number of people shoulder to shoulder in their living room, kitchen and bedrooms, and on their fire escape, Isabel found herself pinned near the front door by a continuous stream of ingress and egress. Tiny, invisible, at risk of being trampled.

Isabel listened to a group of boys plot their seduction of her roommates. Legally men, she supposed, but still chubby or stringy, overeager, their bodies glowing with the heat of unfinished, half-grown creatures. They saw Zoe, Lisa, and Kelly as unattainable because they were inseparable. The girls couldn't be divided, so they couldn't be conquered. They discussed the rumor that the three had stayed celibate all through what the boys had perceived — though not experienced — as an orgiastic first year in the dorms. A fog of body spray clung to them and nauseated Isabel. She was standing almost within their circle, backed up against a wall, but they talked over her head without noticing.

One of these boys watched Zoe's back with his eyes narrowed, an expression both pensive and predatory. He took a deep swig of his drink and then started mock-dancing, his movements as big and stupid as he could manage in the tight space. No one else was dancing. He danced his way through the crowd until he was behind Zoe, his arms up, his pelvis out, leaning into her, wiggling against her clownishly.

Another took the opportunity to try to talk to Kelly, delivering a long, low speech. In response, Kelly laughed, gentle and dismissive. She turned and she and Lisa converged, as though magnetically drawn, on Zoe. Kelly and Lisa danced, surrounded Zoe, wedging expertly between her and the boy. With a dribble of fake laughter, he returned to his group. They stunk of failure now, on top of the body spray. Isabel decided to get some air.

Outside, their stairwell was filled with people smoking and chatting. Under the din of voices, she heard the wood creaking as it swayed. She hurried to the bottom, not wanting to be there when it collapsed.

It had rained earlier that day, clearing up just in time for their party, leaving an inviting cool and a shine to the streets. She'd chugged one cup of punch and nursed another, and the sobering air filled her lungs, loosed the stuffing in her head. Isabel thought: *I'll just walk around the block and come back.* Two blocks away, she thought: *Maybe I'll get something to eat, then go back.* Four blocks and she accepted that she'd just ditched the party.

She found a major road closed off. There was a festival on, as there was always a festival on in this city, an art film being shown on an outdoor screen. People sat on blankets and camping chairs in the center of the intersection. Isabel stood and watched. Scored to a fun world-pop soundtrack was a long clip of live baby chicks falling down a metal flue and being ground to their deaths by high-speed blades.

Isabel stayed through a series of seemingly unrelated vignettes, trying to puzzle out a thesis. The film ended before she'd figured anything out. She was at the edge of the crowd, who were oddly quiet as they packed up to leave. Only the sound of chairs being folded, feet shuffling on the ground. A nervous laugh here and there. An old man's voice carried through the near silence: "What in God's name was that?"

As she walked away, a man hurried to her side. He talked quickly, too quickly, as though he needed to say a lot before he ran out of breath. "Excuse me. Are you Thai? I lived in Thailand for two years. I speak Thai."

"No," Isabel said.

"You look just like this Thai pop star. Mai Charoenpura. Have you heard of her?"

"No."

"That's so crazy. *Just* like her."

He was older than the boys currently sweating into their shirt collars in her living room, and he filled out a gray T-shirt and a pair of camo-patterned cargo pants better than they would. His blue eyes shimmered like a gas flame, too bright, too interested. Serial-killer eyes, Isabel thought. She was still just a little, just enough, flattered to be compared to a pop star of any nationality.

She thought: *I'll just walk with him for a little bit.*

"So, you like Stan Wilder?"

"Who?"

"The director. Video artist."

"Oh. I actually just came upon the festival by accident."

"God, lucky you. I'd give anything to discover him all over again."

He was staring at her intently, walking sideways. She kept looking away. This wasn't the first time someone had tried to strike up a conversation with her on the street, but it was one of only a few, and the first time she'd ever responded. She'd seen it happen to Zoe almost every time they went outside. The seeming randomness of the encounter appealed to her, at this point in her life. Like in the movies. The meet-cute and the suspense. Not knowing what comes next.

He talked at some length about the director before circling back to the film they just saw. "You know, it's the second in a trilogy. I don't know *why* they would screen it by itself. You can't truly understand what Wilder is trying to say unless you see all nine hours at once."

"I only saw the last twenty minutes and I have no idea what he's trying to say."

"Exactly!"

Isabel had been mindlessly walking, following him in the opposite direction from her apartment. It was just before midnight, when the bars were full but the streets were empty, everyone settled into wherever they were going to be for the evening.

"You really need to see the whole thing," he said. "At the least the first part, to contextualize the second. What do you say?"

Isabel thought he meant see it *sometime,* in a theater. "Sure."

"Great. We're just around the corner from my apartment. I have the whole thing."

Isabel opened her mouth to object, by instinct. She thought about the conversation she'd listened to at the party, about first year in the dorms, those boys tortured by the idea that people all around them were fucking their brains out while they shuffled from the library to the communal bathroom to their lonely, cell-like rooms. That they were missing out on the prime of their lives, a bacchanal just beyond the wall.

HE LIVED in a squat, painted-brick building surrounded by chain-link fence, a seedy-looking standout on a fancier block. He led her through the front entrance, up three flights of linoleum stairs, and into a studio apartment, just enough room for a single bed in one corner and a stove in another. A fabric scroll written in Asian characters acted as a curtain over the one window. A harsh, uncovered lightbulb hung from the ceiling. There was a shrine of red candles and a golden laughing Buddha on a crowded bedside table.

words: She didn't want this. She wasn't attracted to him. She didn't know what she was doing there. She was afraid.

It wasn't too late. Yet it was. He unbuckled his belt. Like his fingers, his hips were death-white in the dark room. The word "condom" floated to the top of her consciousness, rested dumbly against her palate. Still she lay there, mute, convinced she was inflicting this violence on herself.

HE OFFERED to let her stay the night, suggested they get breakfast in the morning. He lay contentedly back on the pillow and started in on a long anecdote about the best breakfast he'd had in Thailand, a soup of mixed pig entrails and coagulated blood. Isabel numbly reassembled her outfit and left.

When she got back to the apartment, the front stairs were intact. Six strangers were passed out on the sofa and the living room rug. Beer bottles, plastic cups, and glasses covered every surface. The standing lamp was flat on its side, in a pile of broken glass that was once the globe that housed its lightbulb.

She could hear her roommates talking in low, excited voices in Lisa's bedroom. "Isabel?" Lisa called. "Is that you? Come join us!"

Isabel walked stiffly into Lisa's room. Her limbs felt heavy, exhausted. The three girls were sitting on Lisa's bed, side by side with their backs against the headboard. "Where did you go?" Zoe asked.

"Just for a walk."

"Hell of a party, huh?" Lisa said. "Don't worry—we kept everybody out of your bedroom."

Zoe grimaced. "I walked in on Nicole and Calvin in my room."

"Eww!" Kelly squealed.

"Was that before or after Calvin puked off the balcony?" Lisa asked.

"After."

"Ewwww!"

"Were you here when Rodney tried to show everybody his karate moves?" Zoe asked.

"No," Isabel said. She curled up at the end of the bed, perpendicular to her roommates' feet.

"Long story short, Rodney doesn't know karate."

"Is that what happened to our lamp?" Isabel mumbled.

"No. Oh, god, the lamp."

Their voices sounded alert and happy, melodious, an assertion that all was right with the world, like birdsong. Isabel closed her eyes.

ISABEL WOKE UP in the same position, her forehead pressed against the footboard of Lisa's bed. She rolled over and saw that she was alone. Lisa's alarm clock, analog and shaped like a cartoon cat, presumably left over from childhood, revealed that it was past eleven.

She walked out to the living room. The apartment was empty. The smashed lamp was gone, along with all the beer bottles and cups. Clean glasses dripped on the dish rack. The broom leaned against the wall of the kitchen as though pleased with itself. She glanced out the back window and saw several full garbage bags on the porch, the handles tied in neat bows.

Her roommates came up the steps just then, Kelly at the front with a pink cardboard bakery box, Zoe behind her with a tray of coffees. Isabel let them in. "We returned all the bottles and cans," Lisa said.

Kelly raised the box triumphantly. "We used the recycling money to buy croissants!" They bustled inside, the door hanging open as they took off their coats and shoes, passing the warm pink box and cardboard tray to Isabel, filling the apartment with the smell of coffee and butter and kindness and the world outside.

ISABEL WENT TO the student health clinic for the first time, housed in a grand, churchlike building. There were several waiting rooms on several different floors, and it was unclear why you were shunted to one room or another. Isabel was alone in hers. There were only four chairs, upholstered in scratchy, faded blue wool, and a corkboard of colorful posters on morbid topics.

The doctor walked into the room and called to Isabel. Her name tag read DR. NAKIMURA; she was a slight young woman with bobbed black hair, her lab coat hanging to her knees. She seemed shy and awkward as she led Isabel to another room. Isabel wished she and the doctor were less similar, as human beings. Somehow that would have been easier.

Sitting on the paper-covered table, Isabel told Dr. Nakimura what had happened in as few words as possible.

Dr. Nakimura didn't press for details. "Okay," she said. She reached down to a drawer under the table and pulled out a gown. "Undress from the waist down." She walked out. Upon her return, she knocked once and didn't wait for a response. She put a dual pack of Plan B and a pamphlet on the counter.

They reoriented themselves so Dr. Nakimura could take a swab. At the strangest moment, perhaps because the process was taking too long, she broke what had felt like almost ten minutes of silence by asking Isabel how many sexual partners she'd had.

Isabel didn't respond right away. She was focusing her attention elsewhere, beyond this room and the present. "Two," she said finally.

That afternoon, Isabel choked down the first of the huge blue pills and waited. The pamphlet warned of nausea, vomiting, cramping, bleeding, mood swings. Isabel felt nothing. She felt worse that she felt nothing. She wanted to be punished in some way, wanted her body to formally reject what had happened. She would have liked to throw up. To bleed.

Until Dr. Nakimura had asked, she'd never thought of her life that way, defined by Elliott Mars and this guy, whose name she'd forgotten immediately and hadn't asked again. The lesser entries: Gabe, every unrequited crush, passing infatuation, childhood kiss, anonymous pair of hands. Her life as a series of men. What an absurd way to mark the time.

4

OF THE FIVE GIRLS who'd been stranded together, only Isabel and Dina had any contact after Camp Forevermore. When the internet first brought everyone within reach, Isabel got an email from Dina. Her family had moved to the mainland in the intervening years. She suggested they meet up and Isabel agreed, but they never made concrete plans. They each possessed half the story, and if they met up, if they were alone together, they'd have to hear the rest, and relive events they thought they'd moved beyond.

Dina only had access to the version of Isabel that was a table of information — school, program, classes — and she eventually sent another email that said, "Hey, my older brother is taking a class with you this fall. Isn't that a funny coincidence?"

That summer, on a short trip to Toronto, Isabel had gotten on the subway and ended up in the same car as Elliott Mars. He didn't notice her, or he pretended not to, as she slumped down and hid her face behind a book. He looked even more handsome, stubble now grounding his elfin features. Funny coincidence, maybe, or they lived in a country that was geographically huge but psychically, unbearably small.

THE THIRD was Victor Chang.

The Arts building in the center of campus suited the study of the classics and an ancient, lofty idea of education—the entryway had Roman columns over a stone stairwell, and a swath of ivy growing up one wall. White and pink buds had appeared on the surrounding trees, while clumps of snow lived on in the shade. The very cusp of spring.

As soon as Isabel walked through the elaborate entrance, she saw him, and she knew he was Dina's brother.

He sat on one of the bench windowsills of the large, arched windows. The morning light came in at a sharp slant, pooling on the windowsill, giving him a backlit, religious glow. A brand-new copy of *Ulysses* rested against his thigh, cardboard cover and onionskin pages, fat as a Bible. He studied notes in a binder in his lap so intently that Isabel felt free to stare. She leaned against the opposite wall, an equally shiny and unsullied *Ulysses* in her bag. He had tight black curls, Asian features, and a puffy, pockmarked face—the memory of bad acne —with tan skin that made his white T-shirt and teeth seem luminous. He was short and stocky, thickly but solidly built.

She knew he was Dina's brother because she remembered how Dina had looked that second morning of camp, something irresistible in the set of her face and the lines of her body, filling all the girls with desire at once erotic and familial: they wanted her, they belonged to her.

He looked up, startled, directly into Isabel's eyes.

ISABEL MADE a point of sitting next to Victor that first class. Their twenty-person seminar on *Ulysses* began with an ice-breaking exercise about why they were taking the class. Each person either bluffed something about modernism and Joyce or admitted to needing the core credit, feigning passion to impress the professor or dispassion to impress fellow English majors.

Dina's brother introduced himself as Victor, then said something charmingly stupid: he was a computer science student who hadn't had time to read a book in years, and thought he would use one of his electives to get back into it. He saw that this course read a single book over a semester and that sounded perfect. Victor turned in his chair with an airy smile, passing the conversation to the person who should have been next to speak. A snide silence followed instead.

"Well," the professor said, slowly, toying with his suspenders, "we welcome you back to the land of the literate."

A titter of laughter united the English majors, including Isabel, in their expectation that Victor would drop the class, though many of them had chosen it for the same reason. One book, no matter how difficult, had to be relief from the rate at which they'd been swallowing books for their other courses. Three a day, with meals.

The day of the third class, two other students from the seminar happened to be walking down Isabel's street as she left the apartment. She followed them the rest of the way at a polite distance. Bits and pieces of their conversation drifted back to her; they were already talking about *Ulysses*, and about another class in semiotic theory, another in Old English translation, another on Spenser and Milton, as though they weren't going to spend the next ninety minutes and the rest of the day and the rest of their academic careers talking about these things. Isabel felt stupid and exhausted. By the time they reached campus, Isabel understood a little better why so many of her papers had been labeled in red pen "uninspired" or "poorly thought out."

Kelly was in psychology, Lisa in political science, Zoe in marketing, and they rarely talked about their studies with one another, as it involved too much explaining, too many acronyms. There was just class and papers and exams, subject matter undifferentiated, the occasional lab partner or study group materializing in the living room.

THE CLASS INCHED together through *Ulysses,* page by page, all through the semester, as Victor and Isabel inched toward each other. Even the students most inclined to showing off, the ones with an aching, holdover need to be recognized as special, who forgot they were in supposedly free-form adult discussions and raised their arms with quivering hands like the tails of agitated dogs, even they eventually succumbed to the collaborative nature of the reading. Even they admitted they could not, on their own, make every connection, catch every reference, parse this web of near-infinite points. Victor, who treated the book like a puzzle or a game rather than a trove of philosophical meaning, fared as well as anyone.

Victor and Isabel came early to class, walked together afterward. They contrived to run into each other on their way there, running to catch up and slowing down to be caught, carving out small, noncommittal meetings. Victor had grown up on the opposite side of the Georgia Strait from Isabel, and she learned that he loved to surf. He dreamed of living in California. He seemed Californian already, or Isabel's idea of it: his drawn-out, easy way of speaking, the precise, rectangular teeth that suggested expensive orthodontics, his year-round tan, skin brimming with sunshine.

They went out for lunch after class. Once, and then after every class. He took her to a vegan restaurant and she was amazed by what could be done with raw mushrooms. She took him to a Portuguese chicken joint where customers were invited to draw on the walls. He took her to her first Ethiopian restaurant, showing her how to sop up curry with the spongy bread. She took him for what he declared were the best burgers of his life, accompanied by thick milkshakes in metal tumblers. They both gained weight as the weeks passed. Isabel didn't mind. Her new body felt soft and womanly.

They walked aimlessly along the quays and he told her about his honors thesis project, a slight modification to a computer program that plays Go, and about a project he was working on for fun with his roommates, something about the way data is managed on the stock exchange. She didn't try to follow the technical details. She caught herself just watching his mouth move. Their hands brushed as they walked, and he once closed his hand over hers but released it a block later, before she could figure out how to react.

She came home from one of these lunches and found her roommates together in the living room, sitting on the floor around the coffee table, which held a delivery pizza and a massive cookie they'd made by rolling out a tube of premade cookie dough onto a baking sheet. They too were losing their teenage sleekness. "What's with you?" Lisa said, as Isabel's head appeared over the landing of the internal stairs. "You're grinning like the Joker."

Isabel reached up and touched her face, surprised to find it locked in a giant smile. She had to work her jaw to release it. "Nothing."

"It's that guy from your *Ulysses* class, right?" Zoe said, plucking olives off her pizza slice.

Isabel sat down on the couch and broke off a corner of the cookie. The grin returned.

"Are you guys dating or what?" Kelly asked.

"I don't know. I think so? We've never talked about it." They hadn't even seen each other after dark.

"Has he made a move?" Zoe said.

"We've held hands, sort of."

"That's cute!" Kelly said.

"Sure, if you're ten years old," Zoe said. "Have *you* made a move?"

"He seems happy with the way things are."

Lisa brought Isabel a plate from the kitchen. "Are you happy?"

Isabel considered, taking a slice of pizza despite the two dozen dumplings she'd just shared with Victor. "I could . . . do with more."

Zoe pretended to be scandalized, gasping and fanning herself as she fell back onto the couch. She sat upright again. "Then go get more!"

THEIR FINAL PAPERS were due. Isabel's copy of *Ulysses* was now dog-eared, wavy with water spills, stained by coffee rings and smudged lead, covered in scrawled pencil notes that made little sense to her now. Victor invited her over for lunch this time. He lived in a basement apartment with two room-mates, one much like Isabel's, except down the stairs instead of up.

In their living room, in lieu of any other furniture, four unrelated tables had been pushed together to form one larger one, covered in computers and equipment. The two walls without doors were painted over with chalkboard paint and used for equations and doodles. Chalk dust hung in the air and coated every surface. His roommates sat at two terminals on the big table, a third computer off and expectant. The curtains were drawn over the high, street-level windows, the dim room glowing blue.

Victor's roommates didn't introduce themselves as he and Isabel passed through to the kitchen. They didn't even look up. Victor puttered around the filthy kitchen, making tacos, while Isabel sat at a Formica card table. She drank the beer he'd given her, a Corona with a lime wedge in the neck. She didn't offer to help. The beer tasted of nothing but lime. She could have sat back and watched him cook forever.

"I liked the last chapter best," Victor said.

"Really?"

"Oh, yeah. That would have been a better book. 'The Adventures of Molly Bloom.'"

Isabel laughed. "Is that what you're writing your paper about?"

"No . . ." He held the spatula aloft, thoughtfully. "We didn't have as much time to discuss it, and I'd just sound like an idiot going it alone."

After they ate, Isabel left by the back fire escape instead of passing through the living room dungeon again. Victor brought her shoes. As he held the door open, she leaned across the threshold to kiss him.

"I was waiting for you to do that," he said.

"I was waiting for *you* to do that," she replied.

"We could've been waiting forever." He opened the door wider. "Why don't you come back in?"

VICTOR'S BEDROOM, like the rest of the apartment, was spare but messy. A bike hung on the wall, another computer on an overturned milk crate, a mattress on the floor, piles of clothes and textbooks. "I didn't think you'd be coming in here," he said sheepishly.

Isabel was excited. She was excited that she was excited. She had known sex as a grand existential opera, she had known sex as a blank trauma, and this was yet something else, this was Isabel as a dumb, simple, happy animal; stroke the head and the tail wags. This pleasure frothed along the surface of her skin, weightless and lacy as ocean foam, bubbling upward until it reached her mouth and dissolved into laughter.

They stayed in Victor's room all afternoon and evening, all night. When they emerged in the morning, ravenous, ragged,

Mr. Davies patted her arm and looked out at the table with an indulgent smile, as if to say, *Doesn't she say the darndest things?*

The dishes started to arrive. Isabel's father started loading his plate with barbecued pork and her mother playfully slapped his hand. "*Aiyee!* You're the one who said we should eat less meat." Dina looked up with restrained interest. "Part of getting old, you know." Dina took one piece of bok choy, held it aloft in her chopsticks, nibbled lightly on the leafy end, and put it down again. She drank a lot of tea.

Isabel sometimes felt her parents affected being older than they were. She knew they would go back to the hotel room and change into matching tracksuits, then walk briskly in circles around the city, complaining about their backs and knees. They'd requested an accessible hotel room, with handrails that they didn't need in the shower and around the toilet. Or maybe Isabel was in denial, and her parents, who'd had her in their early forties, were in fact entering the last phase of their lives.

Below the table, Victor took Isabel's hand. He rubbed his thumb against the center of her palm.

"So," Mrs. Chang said. She ate noodles more tidily than anyone Isabel had ever seen. "What are *you* going to do in San Francisco, Isabel?"

"Well, I won't be able to work for the first few years, because I'll have a non-working visa. I thought I'd just . . . hang out."

"Hang out," Mrs. Chang repeated. She and Isabel stared at each other in mutual disbelief at what Isabel had just said.

Isabel tried again: "See the city. Make some connections. Figure out what I want to do next." These did not seem like better answers.

"And you support this," Mrs. Chang said to Victor.

"Absolutely."

Mrs. Chang addressed the Wens. "You too?"

Isabel's father kept on grinning. Her mother said uncertainly, "She's a lucky girl."

"Well, then." She folded her hands onto her napkin, in her lap. "I hope you have fun."

TWO MONTHS EARLIER, Victor and his roommates had been flown out to California by a company they'd never heard of called Jacquard. Jim had to get a passport in a hurry. On the plane, Shen and Jim drank complimentary business-class beers until they fell asleep, while Victor stared out the window. Their plane floated west over the clouds, the sun hanging, fixed in place, as they traveled against time.

They'd been too busy with finals to give this trip a ton of thought. They hadn't incorporated or consulted a lawyer. They didn't really think of the code they'd written as a product, worth anything to anyone. It was a mathematical curiosity they'd shared with the internet at large, an invisible populace of people like themselves, and now they were tired of it and one another. They were ready to move on.

They touched down at the San Jose airport in the late afternoon. Jacquard's offices were in the patchwork of tech-dominated municipalities around the bay, halfway between San Jose and San Francisco. The boys whimsically rented a red-striped convertible, using the email voucher Jacquard had provided. Victor drove them onto the gridlocked highway that led to their hotel. They put the top up to keep out the dense cloud of car exhaust.

Their hotel was a motor inn bought and renovated by an upscale chain, across the street from a strip mall of Chinese restaurants and stores. The renovation involved slapping walls up around what had been the parking lot and turning it into an indoor courtyard with a shiny new lobby, while otherwise retaining the motor inn's original layout. The net effect was preservation, imitation, a Disneyland version of the seedy motel it had been.

Not knowing what to do with themselves, they ate at a fried-noodle place in the strip mall. It took them twenty minutes to walk to the corner and cross the street, the block stretching uninterrupted for a mile in either direction from the hotel. Everything seemed larger than it should be, the roads wider, the parking lots deeper, their sense of distance thrown. They had more beers in the hotel bar, not talking much, an eerie orange light coming in through the windows. "What are you going to wear tomorrow?" Jim asked.

"This?" Shen said, in his hoodie and jeans. "With a different T-shirt."

"I brought a suit jacket," Jim said hesitantly.

"I don't think it matters," Victor said.

"We should go for a drive," Shen said, perking up. "Cruise around in the convertible. Or drive into the city? Where the hell is the city?"

"I've had too much," Jim said, gesturing with his empty glass. "You?"

"I don't want to risk getting a DUI in the States," Victor said.

"So what are we supposed to do? Just go to bed?"

Jim and Victor glanced at each other. "We should find internet somewhere and figure out where Jacquard *is*."

Shen slumped into his chair. "Well, this trip blows."

After visiting a Starbucks, another endless walk on the deceptive, baking concrete, there was some debate over the room's two beds. Victor offered to sleep in the bathtub, but Jim and Shen said they were fine sharing. The two were still glumly watching television when Victor fell asleep.

In the morning, they returned to the same Starbucks for breakfast. They budgeted an hour to drive eight miles, but they somehow kept getting on the wrong freeway, and made it just in time. They pulled into an anonymous concrete-and-glass low-rise in a business park, spaced far apart from several other, identical buildings. Low-lying fog obscured the horizon, making each building seem like it stood alone in the middle of nowhere. "I don't know what I expected," Shen said.

A receptionist led them through an open floorplan of desks pushed together that looked oddly similar to the setup in their apartment, multiplied fifty times over. The office seemed underpopulated, about half of the desks empty. Someone tossed a Nerf football to himself in his chair, someone else was asleep. The staff was almost entirely men. All of whom, in some implacable way, resembled Victor, Shen, and Jim, a thought that depressed Jim; he'd never thought of himself as a "type." Victor and Shen were less surprised.

The receptionist left them alone in a dark boardroom. A small amount of daylight came in through a high, rectangular window, but they couldn't even see one another's faces clearly. "Should we turn on the lights?" Jim asked.

"I don't know," Shen said. "I kind of don't want to touch anything."

Rolling chairs were clustered into a corner rather than around the table. It seemed safe to pull out a few of these to sit on. They left the light switches alone. When someone finally came to meet them, the lights flicked on and the three of them felt small and startled, blinking, vulnerable as nocturnal animals.

Two men and a woman sat down across from them, after the woman pulled out three chairs, introducing themselves as VP-Acquisitions, Legal Counsel, and Brenda from HR. Pulling papers from a thick, inexhaustible folder, the two men spoke briskly and severely, while Brenda stared probingly at the boys, like she was trying to see into their souls.

After ten minutes of this, Shen said, slowly, "So . . . you're asking if we want money or jobs?"

"Essentially," the lawyer said.

"You don't all have to make the same decision," Brenda said.

"But we would like a decision by tomorrow," said the VP.

SHEN, VICTOR, and Jim found their way to downtown San Jose and a steakhouse on a tourist strip, set among museums and luxury stores. The sense of emptiness and oversize buildings and streets persisted. The businesses seemed quiet, the sidewalks lonely. It had begun to rain.

Shen ordered a bottle of sparkling wine. The waiter asked, "Celebrating something?"

"Fuck yeah!" Shen said. "We're about to be rich!"

The waiter smiled politely. "May I see your IDs, gentlemen?" After they passed their licenses over, the waiter asked, "Where is this, exactly?"

"Canada."

"Ah. Pardon my ignorance. Three glasses?"

Jim waited for the waiter to leave before saying, "Not *rich*. But certainly not a bad graduation present."

Shen looked over the menu. "Rich enough for a good steak."

Victor stared out at the rain. California! Land of optimists and dreamers and perpetual sunshine. He'd wanted to live here his entire life. Had that changed in the last twenty-four hours? Victor had also thought — perhaps foolishly, perhaps as every entitled young person did — that he could escape working somewhere like Jacquard, a nine-to-five job in a claustrophobically grim, fluorescent-lit office, a computer on a little desk. His parents had. His mother had been a real estate agent and his father a contractor, tag-teaming properties in the real estate holy land of British Columbia's southern coast; his stepfather was a retired classics professor. He knew Shen and Jim thought the money was their way out, that this would happen again, they'd turn ideas into gold and forever be the masters of their own destiny, smoking pot in their boxers in a basement apartment.

But it was less than what he'd make in a year if he took the job. And what was a year? Victor was twenty-two. He had, it seemed, a million years in front of him.

· · ·

ISABEL AND VICTOR moved with just one backpack and one suitcase each. They arrived on a perfect day in June, emerging through the doors of the San Francisco airport to a blue sky and a breeze, like a habitat engineered for mankind.

That first weekend, they stayed in corporate housing in the financial district, a large but sterile set of rooms with a view of the bridge into Oakland. They walked to Fisherman's Wharf, and the teeming crowd of Saturday tourists and the smell of the bay and frying oil told Victor he'd made the right decision. They smashed crabs in a restaurant where the shared bench-tables were lined with newspaper, under a river of butter and lemon wedges. They rented bikes and rode along the water to the Golden Gate Bridge, across, through the winding residential streets of Sausalito, and back. Victor started work on Tuesday. On Monday, Jacquard arranged for the couple to tour apartments with a broker. They settled on a tiny, obscenely expensive studio in the Mission, a Spanish-style building with a persistent smell of mold from the damp air and galvanized rubber from the tire store next door. They bought painted terra-cotta dishes off a guy in the park who had them spread out on a blanket. The paint came off on the third washing and made their food taste faintly of turpentine. They decorated their windowsills with seashells and animal bones, both bought and found.

On the weekends, they rented a car and drove for hours

up and down the coast to beaches where Victor could surf. At work, he usually kept the tide report open in a window in one corner of his screen, noting where the waves would be good, what the weather was like, where it would most likely be crowded. When he rode, he felt like his blood was on fire, a high like nothing else. Afterward, out of the full-body exhaustion, he knew a kind of peace and clarity that lasted all week. Sometimes other surfers struck up a conversation as they paddled inland, or as Victor and Isabel sat at a beachside bar shack in the late afternoon, but they were mostly adrenaline junkies, who invited him to snowboard, raft, climb, cliff-jump, BASE-jump, skydive. As with programming and with Isabel, when Victor found something he loved, he stuck with it, unwavering as a blinkered horse.

Later, Isabel would remember these as their happiest years.

ISABEL'S ROOMMATE ZOE found an internship for a company in Germany, Lisa went to grad school, Kelly moved back into her parents' house in Ottawa while she looked for work. Graduation had brought on the kind of panic that accompanies a governmental regime change. On the patio of every pub, on the fields, students sat around and asked one another: In the new world order, who will you be? Will we be friends or enemies? The dependable progression of one year to the next, the way time had worked since kindergarten, became now versus the rest of your life. Keeners with five-year plans held smugly fast. Everyone else grabbed what they could or began the journey home.

Isabel had an excuse. She *couldn't* work. A piece of white card stock stapled into her passport said so: H-4 SPOUSAL VISA. Theoretically, a company could sponsor her the way Jacquard had Victor, but she told herself the odds were too low to bother.

One afternoon, as Isabel ate lunch at a café, she got a text message from Victor saying he'd be working late. How late? Before midnight, he hoped. As he hoped on many nights. Seated at a neighboring table was a group of women about Isabel's age, who stood out among the tech workers, tourists, young mothers, and aging hippies who frequented this café, a place Isabel had mentally marked as welcoming to those who eat alone in sweatpants. All four wore high heels, pencil skirts, and tucked-in silk blouses, with blazers and light sweaters over the backs of their chairs, a high-fashion gloss to their hair and nails. One arrived later than the others and announced, "I've been looking forward to this all week," and the others exclaimed their assent. They looked like a piece of art, a carefully constructed tableau. Rather than conversing back and forth, they seemed to take turns telling long stories. Only one person would speak at a time, with urgency and drama, the suggestion of great triumphs and cosmically unfair losses, while the others gasped, laughed, and cooed sympathetically.

Isabel recalled a morning when she was seven years old. Her parents left for work. They trusted her to make her own breakfast and walk to school alone, her house key tied to the mitten string on her coat. A routine morning. It never occurred to her to be afraid or to rebel, to eat ice cream for breakfast or skip school, to worry about burglars and monsters. Before Forevermore, she'd had a happy child's narcissism, a solid belief her parents would return in the evening.

She listened to their car pulling out of the driveway and suddenly thought: What was it that grown-ups did all day? As she had trouble imagining her teachers outside of school, she couldn't picture her parents outside of the house, or indeed the totality of any adult's life. Once, she'd been out with her father and run into one of his co-workers; another time, she'd seen her first grade teacher eating alone in a McDonald's. Both incidents had disquieted her, a break in the laws of the universe as she understood them.

Eating beside these women, Isabel felt like she'd never found an answer to that question. What did grown-ups do all day? What did these women do for a living?

Victor told her he was convinced some of his co-workers lived in the office. Even if he came in at seven and left at midnight, he'd see the same people at their desks. Others were digital ghosts: he got their emails, internal IMs, and code reviews, but he never met them, could never find them or get them to show up to a meeting. People either ate at their desks, still working, or quietly slunk away alone in their cars, as there was nowhere to eat within three miles of the business park. One of the senior engineers didn't eat at all — he subsisted entirely on nutritional shakes he made by blending oil, oats, vegetables, protein powder, and bulk synthetic vitamins.

When Victor returned to their studio apartment each night, Isabel was invariably there, dinner on the table or a plate put away for him, which he wolfed down cold right out of the fridge, standing there with the door open, in its light. Then he took off his jeans and slid into bed. She turned and pressed her face into his back until his warmth and smell blotted out all thought, until she stopped wondering how long love could be enough, how long it could count as meaning, how long it could structure her days.

THE YEAR VICTOR and Isabel turned twenty-five, Isabel's parents went on a trip to Mexico with a seniors' group. Between Chichén Itzá and their compound hotel in Cancún, their charter bus was stuck in traffic at the bottom of a hill, behind another tourist bus. Behind them, the brakes of a fruit truck failed. The truck collided with the back of the bus, forcing it against the bus in front, compressing the accordion folds of the frame. The Wens, asleep in their travel tracksuits in the back row, were the only casualties.

Victor and Isabel spent a month living in Isabel's childhood home, crying with the aunties, uncles, and cousins who came. A surprising number didn't come, Isabel thought, too busy or too old to travel. One of her father's sisters took care of everything. She had the bodies transported, arranged their cremation, and had been named executrix of the will. She sorted the flowers and made pot after pot of tea for the stream of relatives passing through. She didn't consult Isabel about anything, nor did she ask for her help, letting Isabel clutch Victor in her childhood bed and muffle her wails with his chest, or hang uselessly in the kitchen doorway, pale and emptied out. Auntie hadn't seen Isabel since she was a child and perceived little difference.

After only four weeks, Auntie told Isabel to mark things of her parents' that she wanted to keep, because she was going to donate or throw away the rest. Isabel didn't have the wherewithal to take anything beyond a couple of photo albums, her father's toque, and her mother's gloves. Auntie sold the house within six months. She mailed Isabel several checks with no explanation. Holding the first one in her hands, Isabel wished she had kept everything. It was more money than she'd ever seen in her life, but it seemed like a paltry amount to have traded for her parents' lives.

That same year, their green card process began. In another year, Isabel would be able to work. But Victor couldn't bring himself to mention it, not while Isabel was fighting the chill of the San Francisco summer in her parents' hat and gloves.

She dreamed one night of the fruit truck. In her vision, the radio played a jaunty mariachi tune as the truck rolled down the hill, unoccupied, driverless. The back doors burst open upon impact. Mangos and papayas tumbled into the wreckage, their skins shredded, their brightly colored flesh smeared across the asphalt, sweet juices running in rivulets.

In the morning, after Victor left, Isabel called Auntie.

Auntie was the tallest woman in their family of stubby-boned southern Chinese, with a steely countenance that Isabel envied. "Isabel," she said, "I know the way they died was sudden and violent. But for them, it was quick. And they were not young. They were happily married for forty years. They loved each other, and you. You gave them no trouble. They left this world together. They were very lucky. Most people are not that lucky. Do you understand? You are very, very lucky."

"I don't feel lucky," Isabel said.

"You are. You're young. This is not the worst thing that will happen to you."

Later, Isabel will remember this sentence as a curse.

FOR ISABEL DID BELIEVE nothing worse would ever happen to her. She emerged from her grief feeling immunized against further tragedy. The ordinariness she had seen in herself since she was a teenager meant there could be only petty sorrows from now on.

Isabel wanted something she couldn't describe. She wanted to be bound more permanently to the earth.

A house.

They wanted to buy a car and have a place to store Victor's boards, which made staying in the city out of the question. They found a three-bedroom California ranch in the suburbs, closer to Jacquard. When they emailed the listing to Victor's mother, the real estate magnate, rather than answering any of their questions, she responded with only: HOW CAN YOU AFFORD THIS YOU ARE SO YOUNG?????

They sold all of Victor's Jacquard stock, and, combined with Isabel's inheritance, it was just enough for the down payment as prices started to soar across the Valley and the Bay. They were young and rich, believing they would only, somehow, get younger and richer still.

5

ISABEL'S PHONE is ringing.

The doorbell is ringing.

They're always ringing, producing a soft, melodious, distant series of chimes that say, "It's not important. It can wait. It will go away."

The mail slot in their front door feeds onto a heap in the entryway. The heap grows until Isabel opens the door, which swings inward. The bottom of the door sweeps the mail into a corner and creates a secondary pile.

Her voice mail is full. The little icon at the top of the screen tells her so. It begins as a number that counts upward, one through nineteen, and then becomes an exclamation point. She can delete them all at once with a couple of sweeps of her index finger. The icon disappears, reappears later as the number one. The swipes feel soothing. A monastic exercise, like filling a water bucket with an eyedropper, emptying it out, and starting again.

When she was still charging Victor's phone, it rang and rang. She finally let the battery drain completely. His phone rests on the table in the entryway, where he'd see it if he were leaving the house.

HER BRAIN is made of mesh. Occasionally a question gets caught: What day is it? It doesn't bother her that she doesn't know. She could find out easily, but it doesn't matter. The difference between Wednesday or Saturday, April or May.

Automatic withdrawals keep the lights on, her phone on the network. She imagines their checking account ticking down in the same manner that her voice mail ticks up, equally abstract. She lives in the slippery now, with no future. It will bottom out in its own time.

She spoke to Victor's mother at some point, now living full-time in a condo in Hong Kong with Mr. Davies and a nurse/ maid, unable or unwilling to travel. There would be some kind of ceremony there. Victor's name written on a banner and burned. For family.

But Isabel is not family. She's not blood. She's more than that. She is flesh. One body and soul.

She said yes to a lot of people at the beginning. People in and out of uniforms, people in beige-and-gray rooms, people who wanted information or money or to know if someone was coming to pick her up. They kept asking yes-or-no questions and she just said yes until they let her go.

ISABEL IS in their SUV, in the parking lot of the twenty-four-hour minimart. The digital clock on her dashboard says it's just after three in the morning. She doesn't remember driving here. She's gone too long without eating. She's been led by her body, a survival instinct honed for the suburbs.

She goes inside. The mechanical bell dings. She takes a red plastic basket. The shelves are bright and abundant, a bottomless cornucopia. Glass doors reveal row upon row of bottles. She feels a gut-rumbling anticipation, a sense of wonder. She stuffs the basket with instant noodles and cookies and chips, glossy packages with enticing pictures. She pays. She tenses —does her card still work? Has the world changed, does it use a whole new method of currency?

As she's putting the bags in her trunk, she's suddenly, sharply aware of being *outside*. From here, the store glows gleaming-white, like a giant refrigerator. She gulps the cold air. An engine revs aggressively in the distance. She's outside. The dam holding her thoughts at bay begins to buckle. She can hear her inner voice gathering strength, the enormity of her grief and despair. She's outside. She leaps in the car and drives frantically home, running a red light along the way.

Inside the garage, out of her car, she hurls herself at the

inner door as though being chased, fumbles with her keys. Her breathing is fast and irregular. Staccato panic.

She falls inside and slams the door shut. Immediately the feeling subsides. She's safe now. In her house. Behind its walls. She tears open a package at random and pours the contents directly into her mouth. Salt shreds her palate and tongue.

• • •

TV HAS CHANGED. Isabel discovers a new genre: game shows without prizes. Aspects of people's regular lives—job-hunting, moving, clothes-shopping, finding out if they're pregnant—presented as game-show-style challenges, with no reward beyond the job, the home, the shirt, the baby. She keeps expecting the host to surprise them with a free renovation, a novelty-size check, a crate of diapers and formula, but it never comes. The contestants get nothing out of having the camera pressed in their stricken faces other than being on TV.

TV has changed. She remembers when the programming ended for the night, the test pattern rainbow and its continuous tone. The first time she saw it, as a young teenager, she imagined someone on the other end, like a lighthouse keeper: the man who lives in the broadcast tower and flicks the switch. Now TV is infinite. It streams from the internet, and she can have anything she wants, as much as she wants, anytime. Time speeds and ceases at will. Reverses.

SHE'S BACK THERE. She remembers sitting cross-legged on the ground, on a beach, the fire before her, her back to the open tent, mumbling to herself as though talking to Jan. Tending the fire carefully, as Jan had taught. The wind blew the popping embers away from her as she prodded it into shape, feeding it new wood from Jan's pile until there was nothing left.

She ate half of the sandwich and left the other half for Jan, just in case. She wrote HELP on the sand in letters made of rocks and pinecones, the way they did in cartoons, in case a plane flew overhead. It took hours to gather enough and arrange them just so.

She reentered the tent only when it was fully dark and too cold to stay outside. She kept her flashlight on all night, and found a corner of the tent where she could lie balled up and see the yellow of Jan's sleeping bag only out of the corner of her eye. She feared bugs would be drawn to Jan and she'd have to brush them away, she feared Jan's smell would worsen, she feared the yellow sleeping bag would swell and burst like an overfilled balloon, that Jan would change in some monstrous, undreamed-of way.

But none of these things happened. Jan remained immobile and inert, the same cloying, overripe sweetness. Morning came, and the battery in her flashlight had died.

Around dusk on the second night, a new sound tore through the lapping of the water and rustling of the trees, a mechanical roar. A motorboat rounded the bend, a few hundred meters out. Isabel stood at the water's edge and screamed. Her voice was no match for the blare of the motor. She jumped up and down and waved her arms. She cursed her dead flashlight, hoped they could see her tiny figure in the twilight.

The motor cut out. The boat continued to drift, parallel to the shore, and Isabel could see two figures on the deck. She redoubled her shouting. She can't remember what she was yelling, if it was even words.

The boat slowed and almost stopped, still a fair distance away. The figures appeared to be conferring with each other. Finally, one of them dropped an anchor, and the other jumped from the boat and swam toward Isabel.

Isabel ran out into the ocean. She saw that it was a man. Tall and broad-shouldered with a beard and a large, solid belly, dressed in a fishing bib. He strode powerfully through the shallow water. She threw herself at him, clutching the slippery, waterproof fabric over his legs. He scooped her into his arms, lifting her, cradling her against his massive chest like the baby he assumed she was.

What Isabel's body remembered, now, was the sight of her rescuer in the water, like an ocean god with the power to give and to take away. The strength of his arms, the warmth and smell and safety of his chest, how she trembled with relief in his embrace. She was eleven, and he was the true first, the one who woke her to the wonder and beauty and horror and violence that came from loving men.

WHERE'S VICTOR?

The sheets smell like him. Also like something else, something sour and oily. Like rancid peanut butter.

His slippers are in the front hall. Blue foam with raised massaging bubbles. Three dollars at the Asian supermarket. They had a distinct rhythm as he walked around the house, slapping his feet and then the floor, *thwap-thwap, thwap-thwap*, like a heartbeat.

His towel hangs in the bathroom. Black mold grows in streaks on the side of the toilet, fills the gap at the base of the drain in the sink, circular blooms on the windowsill above the tub. The house seems like an unnatural incursion on the land; the mold reclaims.

His swim trunks blown off the clothesline, a small mound in the center of the backyard.

His coffee mug on the counter, the dregs dried to the bottom, a solid block with cracks that weave like canyons.

A room of his half-unpacked computers and books. A book on the desk, with a bookmark thirty pages in. Where he'll come back to it.

WHERE'S VICTOR?

Right here, beside her. The edge of his shirt slips from her empty fist. The bed is warm on his side. Her skin is alert from a kiss.

At work. In another room. Around the corner.

ISABEL THINKS of her college roommates. There was a time before Victor. There was a time before Isabel, for Victor. There are friends and co-workers who probably deserve to come together and grieve, an event to give shape and closure to their loss. But why should they get that, when Isabel will never have it?

The entryway is filled with envelopes. Too many for anyone to sort through, a lifetime's worth. Twenty voice mails and none.

There are too many things that she should do. More than can be done.

THEY HAVE NO CLOCKS, only computers and phones that have to be prompted to display the time.

ORPHAN, WIDOW. As everyone must be, eventually. Orphan, widow, or dead. Orphan, widow, and then dead.

A HOUSE ONCE meant permanence. Now Isabel can see how flimsy it really is. How quickly a house goes up — studs, frame, drywall, roof, tossed together, quick pops of a nail gun, a thoughtless smear of mud. Slapped together in a couple of months, meant to last a hundred years. An eternity, with proper care. As though the water doesn't rise or recede, the weather doesn't turn. The splitting of a seam here, dripping there, a crack, a patch, new window, new shingles, new gutter, burst pipe, rewire, but see how it's unstoppable, entropy and time, how we have to be constantly building without rest, constantly redesigning the levees and draining the swamp, the illusion of city and settlement, the idiotic hubris, how plants can break through concrete then wither in your hand. How everything tends toward a smooth, featureless earth, uncomplicated by ambition, by life.

WHERE'S VICTOR?

Victor's body on the table in that room, where she relived the death of her parents, a long-repressed night in a tent. Every death the same death, each death every death.

Victor's body like the chickens her parents had boiled whole, beak to feet. Like the sheep's eyeball she'd dissected in a high school science class. Something base and biological, loosely held together, arranged to look like Victor. Except for his hair, dried stiff from the salt water. That hadn't changed.

Victor, get up. It's time to go.

WHERE'S VICTOR?

Ashes in a box, sent airmail to Hong Kong.

WHERE'S VICTOR?

Out on the ocean, where he was happiest. Open water in all directions, too far to see from land, too small to see by the satellites above. Catching a wave.

THE DOORBELL IS RINGING. It's always ringing. She goes to answer.

CAMP FOREVERMORE

AND THEN there were four. They trudged into the undefined woods, the only way to leave the beach without swimming. Bag straps crisscrossed their torsos, made them into lumpy, unwieldy creatures, lumbering forward. Nita at the back, carrying the heaviest load, a fact that had gone undiscussed. Siobhan at the front, compass in hand, checking it anxiously every few minutes to make sure they were still walking in a relatively straight line. Andee and Dina in the middle. Dina kept looking back, stumbling under the weight of the packs, her thoughts as clear as if they'd been projected in a bubble over her head: she wished she'd stayed back with Isabel.

Siobhan understood. Already the beach where they'd camped seemed safer, like a home, a place they had eaten and slept, a place they'd been happy.

They walked for an hour, then two. Siobhan had thought that they would walk into the trees and quickly find their end, emerge on the other side on a road full of rushing cars, enough that they could pick and choose: wait for a police car, or a mother with children, as Siobhan had been taught.

They were walking very slowly, careful of the vines and tree roots, looking for the best possible footing, the avenues presumably cut by animals. Siobhan was sweating buckets, but she couldn't take off her fleece or windbreaker without unstrapping the bags. They were climbing a hill, or a mountain, that hadn't been a visible part of the landscape from the beach. Siobhan searched her memories of this island, from visiting with her parents—ferry, motel, ice cream stand. It had seemed tiny, provincial, quaint. How could it go on and on like this? How could it be so large, contain so many discrete parts where people couldn't find one another?

When the ground started to level out, they stopped for water and each ate their camp-issued cookie ration, "chocolate chip" flecks that looked like rat droppings. Once Dina swallowed her cookie, her eyes filled, as though agonized that there wasn't more.

"I hope Isabel is okay," Siobhan said.

No one answered. They were too caught up in their own pain and fear, individually, to take on someone else's. They sat or lay on their backs on the ground, breathing heavily, until Nita said, "I guess we should keep going." No one argued. They helped one another re-knot the bag straps, swaying under the uneven weight distribution.

Now, from the elevation they'd gained, Siobhan expected to come to a lookout point, somewhere they could survey the whole island, see the road, the ferry terminal, know exactly which way to go. But that didn't happen either. They started to descend, digging in their heels to resist the pull of the slope.

"I can't," Dina gasped. She tilted in the direction of one of the packs and then fell completely over. "I can't keep going."

Andee flopped down dramatically, as if in protest. "Me neither."

Nita and Siobhan glanced at each other. Siobhan felt something had changed between them since Isabel had insisted on staying, since Andee had stabbed Jan in the foot. A necessary shift in allegiances. "I'm sure we're almost there," Siobhan said.

Andee held out her hand. "Sandwiches. Water. Now."

Nita snorted. She had the food bag. "Get up."

"And the marshmallows," Dina said. Sniveling, but mad.

"It's lunchtime anyway," Siobhan said. She wished they'd stopped in a more convenient spot. Sharp rocks jutted out of the dirt, and they were still on a downslope.

"Fine," Nita said. "I just want to remind you, these are our only sandwiches."

Siobhan tried to rub the dirt off her hands onto her pants, but they were no cleaner. Her PB&J seemed small, as all the camp-issued sandwiches did, white bread as thin and flavorless as card stock, a trickle of jam, barely enough peanut butter to stop up their dry mouths. The marshmallows, by contrast, tasted like salvation, and the girls shoved their hands into the mostly empty bag, racing one another, testing how many fit in their mouths, until they were gone.

"We'll be in town by dinner," Siobhan said.

"Maybe the police will buy us dinner," Andee said.

"There's a diner, I think." Siobhan tried to sound encouraging. "With burgers. And French fries. And chili and milkshakes . . ." Dina groaned.

They came upon a dribbling creek soon after lunch. Nita scooped an experimental sip into her mouth. "How does it taste?" Andee asked.

"Uh, metallic, I guess."

Siobhan asked, "Does it taste safe?"

"How should I know? What does safe water taste like?" Nita drank another handful.

"Well, you're still drinking it," Dina said.

"So we can just wait and see," Andee said darkly. Nita gulped a little more, took out the water bottle they'd emptied, and filled it with creek water.

They continued downhill, shaded by the thickening spruce trees, the light beginning to fall at an angle. The other Forevermore groups would be back by now, the neon-green army returning home, triumphant. When would their absence be noticed? By dinner? The electric lights of the cabins and communal buildings set aglow, the singing and fist-banging on the long tables under plastic tablecloths, the steamer trays of a hot meal. Would they send someone to Lumpen in the dark, or wait until daylight? Would they call the police? Their parents? An itch started inside Siobhan's T-shirt and fleece, under her ribs, creeping across her back and stomach, like leaves and hair were trapped inside. Or those minuscule bugs that lived in their Forevermore cabins, each the size of a pinhead, small enough to get through the window screens, distinct from dirt by their movement, small as dust in your eye.

A break in the trees ahead, a shimmer between them. Relief, and then. "No," Siobhan said, aloud.

"Is that . . ." Nita began.

Siobhan hurried ahead, through the gap, toward the steady thrum of sound that was not, not at all, the sound of passing cars. "No," she said again.

The ocean. The same type of gritty, inhospitable sand they'd left behind, now on the opposite side of the island.

Nita appeared beside her. "We walked all the way across," she said, astonished. "Without ever hitting a road."

Andee and Dina stayed a few steps back, radiating a dangerous emotion, like a smell.

Nita took off her packs. It was a slow process. The other

girls watched in silence. Nita picked up a solitary fallen branch from the brush. She started drawing in the sand. "Okay, so this is the island. We walked across it east to west, without hitting anything. So I guess tomorrow we should go north-south."

"Tomorrow?" Dina echoed, her voice tight and panicked. "*Tomorrow?*"

Siobhan looked out across the water. An anemic sunset, claw streaks of salmon. "Tomorrow," she said. She stripped off her bags and felt a deep release in her muscles. She scratched wildly at her skin.

"I DON'T THINK we have time to make a fire," Nita said. "We should just set up the tent as fast as possible."

"Do you know how?" Siobhan said. She'd been carrying the tent, the poles prodding her for hours.

"Um, I've never done it by myself, but we can probably figure it out. We watched Jan do it yesterday."

"That was only yesterday?" Siobhan said. "It feels like forever ago."

As they had at that morning's fire, Siobhan talked—"I think the first thing Jan did was the posts"—and Nita acted, Siobhan and Andee holding pieces in place while Nita experimented, saw which way each pole bent.

"Why is this so hard?" Siobhan groaned, after their arrangement of poles had collapsed for the tenth time.

"Maybe we're hungry," Dina said. "My mom says girls get stupid when they're hungry."

They laid down their poles and sat on the bare ground. They'd left the tarp with Isabel in an effort to reduce the load. They shared the two cold, slimy hot dogs, barely a bite each. After an unsatisfied pause, they took turns coating their mouths in instant hot-cocoa powder. Only Jan's stash remained. Nita said they would have to save it for the next day.

"That's probably a good idea," Siobhan said, an edge to her

voice. She was still ravenous, and she resented Nita for being so controlled, so reasonable.

"This is seriously all we're going to eat?" Andee said. The food bag was tucked between Nita's knees, the top unzipped, rounded and gaping like a mouth. Andee reached toward it. "What about Jan's candy and trail mix? Couldn't we just . . ."

Nita snatched up the bag, lifting it off the ground and holding it shut. "We don't know how long it'll take to get to town tomorrow."

"We'll need energy for walking, though," Andee said. She advanced suddenly on Nita, lunging forward, but Nita was quicker. She was on her feet and a few steps back, the food bag still in her grip, maintaining the distance between her and Andee. Dina's eyes flicked back and forth between them.

"No," Nita said. "You'll thank me tomorrow."

Andee, Siobhan, and Dina exchanged a look, and Siobhan recognized something feral in Dina's and Andee's expressions, something she felt too, in her gut. Their shoulders were up, their bodies alert. They were hungry, and Nita stood between them and food. Siobhan thought: *The three of us could overpower her.* Saliva pooled in her mouth. She could almost taste the gummy bears and the candy bar. She felt herself rising to her feet, not knowing what she planned to do.

A rustle in the nearby brush startled them. They turned toward the sound. "What was that?" Siobhan whispered.

Nita said, "It could be a person. Should we go investigate?"

"What if it's an animal?" Dina hissed.

Nita squinted into the woods. "Hello! Is anybody there?"

Siobhan caught a flash of movement. Not a person. A hunched-over shape, shorter and wider and longer and swifter, one dark hue that blended into the trees and the early-evening shadows as it barreled away from them.

"Wait!" Nita called. "Come back! We're just kids! Help us, please!"

Siobhan touched her arm. Nita jumped. "I don't think that was a person."

"What was it?" Dina asked. "Was it a cougar? A bear?"

The three girls looked expectantly at Siobhan. None of them had seen. Siobhan felt her front teeth catch her lower lip, the way they always did before she lied. "No, something smaller. Like a raccoon or something? Anyway, it's gone now."

They listened a little longer, leaning slightly toward the woods, their chins raised and ears pricked like pointer dogs. After a few minutes, their tired bodies relaxed, equally relieved and disappointed.

Nita sat down again, her arms still wrapped around the food bag. Andee picked up the empty hot-chocolate pouch and peered inside it. "You're right, Nita. We should save the food for tomorrow. I'm sorry."

"Me too," Siobhan said, though she hadn't done anything, not really. Not yet. The moment when she'd felt them turning on Nita, a shared, pack-animal instinct, had passed, retreating into the woods with the real animal. Dina was still staring fixedly in the direction that it had gone, but her eyes were strangely empty, the fear burned out.

She said, "What if no one ever finds us?"

Siobhan tried to conjure up the hope and affection she'd felt for Dina the day before, to once again see her physical beauty as moral goodness.

Andee stuck her index finger in her mouth. She ran her saliva-coated finger around the hot-chocolate pouch, trying to recover any dust caught in the seams. She looked sideways at Siobhan, and Siobhan knew that Andee hadn't quite believed her about the "raccoon." Andee said, "Then the cougars and bears can eat us."

Siobhan regretted leaving all of the fruit cocktail with Isabel. Then she felt guilty — Isabel was probably out of food too — and the guilt made her itchy all over again. "Do you think Isabel's okay?" she asked, scratching her stomach.

"Probably better than us," Nita said. "She didn't walk all day for nothing."

"What if we walk and walk tomorrow, and we still don't see anyone?" Dina continued. "What about when we run out of food?"

Andee finished sucking on her finger, drawing it from her mouth with a pop. "I vote we eat Dina."

"I'm cold," Dina said. Her voice had gone eerily flat. "I'm cold and I'm tired and I'm hungry and my stomach hurts and I hate this and I'm scared and I want to go home and no one's going to find us and we're going to die out here. Like Jan. We'll be nothing and empty, like Jan."

No one answered.

"I'm cold too," Nita said finally. "Let's give the tent another try."

THEY WERE FINALLY making progress, the tent resembling its intended shape. "It's getting hard to see," Nita said. "Can someone grab a flashlight?"

Both Siobhan and Andee had their hands full. "Dina," Andee said, "get a flashlight."

Siobhan looked around. "Where's Dina?"

Nita turned her head. "What? Did she leave? I thought she was right next to us."

Siobhan already knew. "Where's the food bag?"

They dropped their poles. "Dina," Nita called. Shrieked. *"Dina!"*

"She's over there," Andee called, pointing to some motion behind a rise close to the water.

They ran. Dina, seeing them approach, stuffed gummy bears into her cheeks at an accelerated rate.

"You stupid bitch!" Andee shot ahead. She tried to yank the package of gummy bears out of Dina's hands, and it tore between them. The remaining bears scattered on the ground.

Nita dove for the food bag at Dina's feet, but Dina grabbed it first. Nita caught the end of one strap. "I'm not going to die first!" Dina screamed. "You're not going to eat me!"

Nita wrestled and pulled, choking up on the strap to get a better grip. "It's been one day. One day! You couldn't go one day!"

Andee was kneeling in the sand, trying to gather up the gummies and dust them off, but it was impossible to tell them apart from the rocks and other detritus in the dark. The tide rushed toward them, washing over the edge of where the candy had landed. "You saw her," Dina said, struggling to get the bag back. "We all saw her! I woke up beside her. You saw what's going to happen to us."

Siobhan joined Nita, and the two of them wrested the bag away from Dina with such force that all three of them fell backward onto the ground. Siobhan sat up and peered into the food bag. She could just make out the shredded ribbons of the empty candy-bar wrapper. The trail mix was the only thing left. Siobhan's stomach growled awake, vicious once more. "How could you?" she snarled.

"Andee said you'd eat me!"

"She was joking! You're insane!"

Andee rose. She pitched the few dirty gummies she'd recovered into the ocean. Something twisted in her face. She's going to hit her, Siobhan thought, almost excited, her own body tensing to anticipate the blow. But instead Andee turned away. "Leave her," she said, over her shoulder. "We have to get the tent up."

Siobhan stared at Andee's back as Andee walked back toward the half-built tent. She looked at Dina, who was blubbering pathetically, pulling at the fabric of her thin jacket, clutching at herself around the armpits. Siobhan and Nita came to a silent agreement. They followed after Andee, Nita clutching the near-empty food bag to her chest.

They worked quickly and quietly now, without any more bickering. Nita held the flashlight between her teeth. Each pole slid into place, and the tent came together at last. They stood back to admire their work, before hurriedly tossing everything inside.

Nita hadn't let go of the food bag. "Should we try to hang it?" Siobhan asked. "So it doesn't attract the . . ." She caught herself. "So it doesn't attract any animals?"

"I don't know how. And it's too dark." Nita said.

They could hear Dina continuing to snuffle and weep.

"Can we just leave her out there?" Siobhan said. "It's getting kind of cold."

"Serves her right," Andee said.

"We can't trust her anymore," Nita said. "I don't want her in the tent with us and the last of the food."

But Nita was eyeing Andee and Siobhan too. Siobhan knew she didn't trust any of them anymore, and she wasn't wrong; as angry as Siobhan was at Dina, she was also jealous. That she'd gotten to the food first, that she'd been the one to seize a moment when Nita was distracted, that she no longer had to bear this emptiness in her rib cage, this singlemindedness of need.

"Let's tie her up," Andee said.

Andee had already dug the food-hanging rope out of one of the supply bags. She held it in one hand and rubbed it against the opposite palm.

Siobhan found herself nodding. "Yes," she murmured. She quickly added, to Nita, "Then you—then *we* won't have to worry about her anymore. We can let her into the tent, and she won't freeze, but she won't run off with the trail mix in the night either."

Slowly Nita replied, "I guess that makes sense." Her grip on the bag loosened. She placed it carefully inside the tent.

They marched toward the dune where they'd left Dina. She was sitting in the sand, her knees pulled up to her chest and her arms wrapped around them, rocking gently on her tailbone. She jumped to her feet when she saw them, poised to bolt.

Nita and Andee, quicker and stronger or just readier than Siobhan, leapt upon Dina. Andee dropped the rope. It took both of them to yank Dina's arms behind her back while Dina squirmed and bucked. Dina screeched in a way that made Siobhan's abdomen clench. She didn't want to be responsible for that sound.

"You have to do it, Siobhan," Nita shouted. "Tie her up."

The rope, Jan's rope, was industrial yellow. Coiled on the ground, it looked like a venomous snake, a bright color of warning.

"Siobhan!" Andee snapped.

Siobhan picked up the rope. She circled behind Dina. She looped the rope around the other girl's soft wrists, laying it gently at first, just resting against her skin. She felt faraway, disconnected from the moment. She knew they were crossing a line, going somewhere they couldn't come back from. But also — what? That this had to happen to someone, and she was glad it wasn't her. She pulled the loop taut. She looped it again, tightened it, again and again. She tied a knot, she doubled the knot, she tripled the knot. Like a shoelace. A package. Not a person, a girl, Dina, howling in her ear.

Several feet of rope still trailed from the ends. Nita and Andee released Dina, and Andee picked up the loose rope like a leash. "Walk," she commanded. "To the tent."

Tears and snot coated Dina's face. They left her kneeling at the entrance of the tent, bound, as they unrolled and arranged their sleeping bags. Siobhan took off Dina's shoes. Dina cried and cried as they ordered her into her sleeping bag, as they zipped her inside with her shoulders still forced backward. She cried as they took turns guarding her and walking a discreet distance away to go to the bathroom, as they climbed into their own sleeping bags, as they turned off their flashlights. Dina cried as they lay breathing in the dark. She was still crying when Siobhan slipped easily into a black, emotionless sleep.

DINA

1

DINA WAS DROPPED off by a friend's mother after ballet class. Her father was shoveling the mashed-potato mush of salt and snow from their driveway; she blew by him without saying hello. She ran inside the house and straight into her mother's study without knocking, barely pausing to kick off her mud-and-ice-encrusted boots.

She held out a costume pattern to her mother, gripped in her six-year-old fists. "Mom! You're supposed to sew this for me!"

Mrs. Chang peered at her daughter over her reading glasses. She turned back to the contracts on her desk. "I don't have time for that," she said.

Dina stood there, blinking dumbly, arms extended.

Her mother looked up a second time. "What are you still doing here? Out, out."

The following week, Dina went to the fabric store after

ballet class with her friend and her friend's mother. The week after that, she burst into her mother's study again to show her: shoulder-strap wings and a red tulle skirt with suspended black dots. She held the skirt against her body and spun around. "Isn't it pretty? Don't I look like a ladybug?"

Dina twirled until she started to feel dizzy. She realized her mother's silence had gone on for an ominously long time.

"Where did you get that?"

"Jenny's mom sewed it."

Mrs. Chang rose slowly from her chair. "Why do you insist on embarrassing me this way?"

"What?" Dina stopped spinning. She wavered slightly on her feet.

"If it was that important, you should have said so. I would have given you the money to buy your costume. Instead you run around town begging for charity."

"You can't buy the costume. The moms have to make them."

Her mother smacked the wall. Dina jumped. "You can buy anything! Stupid girl."

Dina flung the skirt into the corner.

"Ungrateful!" Mrs. Chang shouted. "Pick it up! Pick it up right now."

Dina snatched it up again. "I hate you! You don't understand *anything!*"

"Who do you think pays for ballet, eh? You think they teach you out of the goodness of their hearts? Apologize to me for talking back." Dina raised her chin defiantly. "Apologize to me on your knees, since you insist on acting like a beggar." Still Dina didn't move. "Apologize to me or no more ballet classes."

"Fine! I won't dance!" Dina fled. She felt exhilarated, like she'd just poked a tiger in the face with a stick, convinced her mother would chase after her and something new and terrifying was about to take place. Instead, her mother just shut the study door with a controlled, final-sounding click, and that was that. No more ballet classes.

For the rest of her life, Dina was secretly convinced she could have been a prima ballerina, if not for her mother. She saw *Swan Lake* on a field trip to the mainland, and though she fell asleep for part of it, the finale worked itself into her fantasy life. She saw herself as the white swan, lithe arms undulating to the rippling of the harp and the imagined lake as though she had no elbows or shoulder joints, her calves as fine as an insect's legs. The swelling, bombastic sadness of the music. Even more vividly, she pictured the curtain call. Curtsying to her adoring audience as they flung roses and cheered with frenzied admiration.

She practiced her useless curtsy around the house, right leg far behind the left, arms spread. She spaced out while she was supposed to be doing her homework, hearing the clapping and the whooping, until her mother struck Dina on the back of her head.

Sometimes a tap with an open hand. Sometimes a thrown object, a slipper, a hairbrush, a melamine bowl. Mrs. Chang had impeccable aim.

In the waiting room for an audition, many years later, Dina fell into a conversation with a group of other Asian actresses (the call: "Asian woman, early to mid-twenties, VERY sexy, non-speaking, non-union") about how their parents had beat them as children. Dina said, "Oh, my parents never hit me," and as she said the words she realized that of course her mother had. It just didn't fit her idea of "parents who hit." She was never spanked as punishment, never taken over her mother's knee as the direct result of something she'd done. It was constant, casual, meaningless. Mrs. Chang didn't even stop walking as she slapped Dina's skull, her palm like a swinging cat door. Dina didn't fear it. She was almost fond of it, the dull sting through her childhood and early teens, something like affection.

DINA WOULD ALWAYS remember her mother as a withholding tyrant, a wall of no, but if she thought about it, Mrs. Chang wasted unfathomable sums of money on her: ballet lessons, piano lessons, swimming lessons, soccer camp, horseback riding camp, French classes, Mandarin classes, all before the age of ten, all rapidly quit and immediately forgotten.

An all-girls' sleepaway adventure camp on the coast.

Mrs. Chang blustered about a lawsuit that never materialized. She seemed unconcerned that Dina, after Forevermore, lost interest in eating. Putting food in her mouth made her stomach seize up; she could feel it closing like a fist in refusal. She felt stalked by a predator, like she couldn't let her guard down long enough to eat. For years, she preferred soft, bland, quickly swallowed food, bananas and vanilla pudding, tofu and rice porridge, and being left alone at the table. Her parents talked about it when Dina was lying on the couch in the same room, as though she couldn't hear them. "Oh, it's fine," her mother said. "My sister was like that at her age, picky picky. She'll get over it. The women in our family all get fat eventually."

UNTIL HE GOT SICK, Dina saw her father as a quiet man who did or said little of note. His only hobby or vice was watching hockey in his recliner after dinner with a single can of Kokanee. When Dina kissed him goodnight, he patted her on the arm as though embarrassed, urging her to hurry up.

Dina thought he and her mother were mismatched, especially when they left for work in the morning. Her father, a contractor, had gnarled hands and a dark complexion. When he put on his denim overalls, he looked physically tough but spiritually diminished, hunched into his sunken chest and small potbelly. Her mother, a real estate agent, strode out the door resplendent in silk blouses and trousers, a sleek bun, the many rings on her fingers clicking against one another: real gold and fake, diamonds and cubic zirconia, creamy mutton-fat jade tapping bits of painted glass.

Mrs. Chang liked to talk about Mr. Chang after he died, even in front of her eventual second husband, Mr. Davies, who only smiled his perpetual, inscrutable smile behind his bushy gray mustache. In retrospect, she said, Mr. Chang was sick much longer than they realized, but he didn't like doctors, didn't want to cause a fuss. His bones had always ached, his stomach had always troubled him, and so what if it was getting worse, wasn't that just getting older? And wasn't he lucky to have a team of young men who worked under him so he could scale back his hours, to have an industrious wife who brought in more than enough money on her own?

Mrs. Chang claimed Mr. Chang had been demonstrative and affectionate in private. What a wonderful, clever, beautiful wife I have, he'd say.

Dina could not recall ever seeing her parents touch.

MR. CHANG STARTED coming home from work in the afternoon. He took off his overalls and hung them on a hook by the door, and cooked dinner in just his white boxers and long-sleeved white shirts, both bought in bulk at the Real Canadian Superstore, a fact that embarrassed Dina so much she stopped bringing friends home. With a cleaver, he hacked up large joists of meat and overgrown vegetables from the Chinese market—carrots thicker than Dina's arms, bundles of bok choy and Napa cabbage the size of babies—and either fried them in soy sauce and garlic or boiled them for soup. He ate a little less, went to bed a little earlier, slept in a little later, slipping away from them unnoticed.

Dina announced at the dinner table that she was going to be a movie star.

Mrs. Chang set down her bowl of rice. "You want to act?"

"Or sing," Dina said. Movie star, rock star, the generalized famous. She'd seen how, once you broke into one, you were allowed to switch at will. "Or model."

Mrs. Chang looked at her daughter appraisingly, tilting her head from side to side. "Yes, you have a very pretty face." She addressed her husband and son. "Doesn't she have a pretty face?"

"Very pretty," Mr. Chang mumbled agreeably.

"I don't see it," Victor said. He speared a piece of meat with his chopsticks for emphasis.

Mrs. Chang made a scolding sound with her tongue. "Eat properly, Victor." She turned back to Dina. "Little bit chubby," she added. "But maybe you'll grow taller and it will balance out. Are you the prettiest girl in your school?"

"No way," Victor said.

"One of them," Dina said. She kicked Victor under the table and the dishes jumped.

"Hmm," Mrs. Chang continued, ignoring their bickering. "How many girls in your school? Let's say two hundred. You are pretty, but not the prettiest of two hundred." She spoke methodically, solving a math problem aloud. "How many schools do you think there are in Canada? And the U.S.? And China? All of Asia? Those are the girls you'd be competing with eventually — girls with your kind of face. Not very likely, you see. Who do you like? Who is your favorite actress?"

Dina slumped in her chair and scowled, refusing to answer.

Victor piped up. "She likes Jennifer Aniston."

"I don't know her," Mrs. Chang said. "Is she rich?"

"Super rich," Dina said, brightening.

Mrs. Chang nodded. "How many Jennifer Anistons do we need? The world, I mean. How many do we need?"

"One," Victor answered.

"Yes. And there is one already. What do you want to be, Victor?"

"I want to work with computers."

"Suck-up," Dina muttered. "Mama's boy."

"Shut up!"

"You shut up!"

"And how many computer people do we need?" Mrs. Chang asked.

"Thousands? Millions?" Victor guessed.

"Right. And they make good money."

Dina interrupted, "Actresses make lots of money."

"No. A few of them, the Jennifer Anistons, make *all* the money. The other actresses make nothing, or almost nothing." Mrs. Chang picked up her bowl and resumed eating, the matter resolved. "You could teach, maybe. Teach acting or singing. Or you could design clothes, write songs. These are hard, but not so hard."

Dina knew her mother's argument was flawed, but she was too angry to articulate why. She was telling Dina to capitulate to failure without even trying. Like she was a born failure. At school, they always said the opposite. You can be anything you want to be, as long as you work hard and stick with it! They said it in slogans. They said it in songs. They said it on stickers.

And Dina knew she *was* pretty, perhaps the prettiest. She was sometimes transfixed by her own reflection when it caught her unawares, when she passed a reflective surface unexpectedly, polished metal or still water. As they fussed with their hair in the girls' room during first recess, one of her white girlfriends remarked, "You're lucky. Asian girls can be so weird-looking, but you look totally normal." Yes, Dina had thought, now seeing herself through that prism: she had relatively round eyes, a relatively high, neat bridge in her nose, paintable folds in her eyelids. She had her mother's height and her father's delicate bone structure, a combination that surpassed them both.

Dina liked lying in bed on weekend mornings, lifting one leg and turning it this way and that, seeing from which angle it looked the thinnest and most elegant. She liked the long bones of her dainty feet, the sunken canyon of her stomach, from which her hip bones jutted like mountain peaks. She ignored her mother, who banged on the door and said, "Ai!" in a short, authoritative bark, a sound that was neither Chinese nor English. When Dina wandered out into the kitchen in her pajamas, after the rest of the family had already had half a day of living and were sitting down to lunch, her mother said, "You act like an invalid. Idle, useless, garbage girl!"

THEIR FATHER HAD a quick death: a whirlwind ER visit, diagnosis, one week of Mr. Chang sitting in a hospital bed and apologizing for being a burden, asking tentatively for water and who won the Stanley Cup and how the business was doing; two weeks of ashen silence and stillness, brief, mewling hallucinations, a barely heard and denied request to go home; three days of morphine instead of food and water. To the palliative care doctors, Mrs. Chang said, over and over again, "Are we there already?" as though she'd fallen asleep on a road trip.

Dina and Mrs. Chang reacted similarly, with numb disbelief. It had been so fast, he was there and then gone, a sudden hush in place of the background noise of his presence — the TV on in the evenings, his small form shuffling through the house, his puffing blue truck coming and going. Yet everything went on. Mrs. Chang went back to work almost immediately. Dina went to school.

Victor, on the other hand, stayed home to cry in his room. Their father had passed at the end of his last year of high school, and he'd already been accepted to university, so what did it matter? His teachers were understanding, shuffled him quietly out. He backed out of his summer job lifeguarding and spent the three months before college moping around the house. He had been like Dina, or so Dina had thought, effortlessly popular and attractive. Dina's girlfriends had hung around the house gawking and made Dina accompany them as they followed Victor to the beach, sighing as he emerged from the water and peeled off his wetsuit, dropping hints about the prom he ultimately wouldn't attend. Now he was a soggy-eyed sap who insisted on hugging Dina hello or goodbye whenever they'd been or were about to be apart, no matter how brief the interval, until she asked him to stop. "We never hugged before," she said.

Even Mrs. Chang thought he was being melodramatic. "It's not like him," she insisted. Dina recognized this was a nonsensical statement—Victor had never lost a father before, so how would they know what he'd be like? But the extravagance of Victor's grief made Dina wonder what she'd missed. He must have had a relationship with their father that she didn't know about. They must have talked when no one else was around. Secret man things, father-son things.

When Victor came home for Christmas after his first semester at university, he'd gained weight, his wiry muscles reformed into stocky, bricklike blocks. His sparing adolescent acne had been aggravated into red craters. Dina stared at his changed face all through their first dinner together. She felt betrayed. Alarmed. Someone beautiful could become ugly. Beauty, before, had seemed intrinsic, something she possessed as certainly and irrevocably as her brown eyes. And what was the cause? Had he lost it through neglect, or had he willfully destroyed it? Could it happen to her?

ALONE, DINA and her mother lived like roommates. Without Mr. Chang's cooking, Mrs. Chang went out every evening. Dina more or less stopped eating altogether. The panic had lessened as the years passed, but meals continued to be tedious, all that chewing and gnashing and sitting around, made worse by other people's seeming rapture: *This is soooo good!* When she'd been required to attend family dinners, Dina had managed a small bowl of rice and bits of meat and vegetables from her father's soups and stir-fries. Left to her own devices, she forgot to eat dinner, woke up late and hurried to school without breakfast, bought a can of ginger ale and a packet of crackers from the vending machine at lunch.

In class, her daydreams wove a soft, protective barrier around her mind, blocking out whatever the teacher was saying, cushioning the feeling in her brittle bones as she carefully sat them down on the hard wooden and plastic seats. Prima ballerina, pop star, rock star, movie star, runway model. In her mind's eye, red carpet unrolled beneath her feet down the school hallways. The flickering at the edge of her vision was from camera flashes, the roar in her head from applause. Sleep and waking life flowed into each other easily, were almost one and the same.

Over the girls' room sinks, her girlfriends complained, "God, you're so thin, and I'm such a cow." Dina couldn't summon the energy to respond. It felt like they were speaking to her from the other end of a tunnel, echoing, at a remove. "You're so lucky. You have that Asian metabolism."

VICTOR CAME HOME for the summer. Mrs. Chang had booked his flight for him. They picked him up from the airport on the mainland in Mrs. Chang's new car. She had to honk and wave from the silver Lexus before he recognized them.

"You guys didn't need to drive all the way out here," Victor said. "I could've easily taken the bus and the ferry across myself. And I still don't understand why you had me fly to Vancouver instead of Victoria. Was it that much cheaper?"

"Oh, I wanted to show you something," Mrs. Chang said.

Victor craned his head around in his seat, trying to talk to Dina with the forced interest he'd had in her since their father died. Dina strained to answer his questions. School was fine. She was fine. Her friends were fine.

They pulled into a private parking lot underground, beneath a skyscraper of turquoise glass. Mrs. Chang waved a bar-coded plastic card and the gate opened. She parked in a numbered spot. "What are we doing here?" Victor asked. Mrs. Chang got out of the car and headed toward the elevator, her children rushing to follow.

Once they caught up to her, Victor asked, "Is this a property you're showing?"

Mrs. Chang watched the numbers increasing on the digital dial.

"Mom? Hello?" Victor said.

She used the key card to open the door to one of the condominiums on the twenty-eighth floor. The door swung open to a startling vista, through a wall of glass: the harbor and the waterways, the snow-laced mountain range beyond.

The condo was empty of furniture, so the two Chang siblings gravitated to the windows. It was a corner unit, with one bank of windows facing the water and the forested coast to the north, while the other showed the glittering towers of the city.

"We're going to move here," Mrs. Chang said.

Victor turned, distraught. "What? Why?"

"I'm getting remarried. His name is Mr. Davies."

"You never mentioned him before," Dina said, still gazing out the window.

"Well," Mrs. Chang said, "I didn't think it was any of your business. It didn't affect you, until now."

Victor asked, "Is this his place?"

Mrs. Chang chuckled, a private joke. "No, I own this place." She considered for a moment and then added, "I own lots of places."

Victor said, "What do you mean?"

"What do you mean, what do I mean? What I said. I own lots of places. Here, and in Toronto, and in Hong Kong, New Jersey, San Diego, Los Angeles . . ."

The house they'd grown up in had been a quaint, ramshackle three-bedroom bungalow, twenty minutes from the beach. The small kitchen centered on an olive-green dishwasher that didn't work; their father had washed everything by hand. The detached garage had leaned during the winters, under the weight of snow. Victor gaped. "Why didn't we know about this?"

"It wasn't any of your business either. You were children. They're just investments."

"I can't believe this," he said.

Dina smiled quietly to herself, the million-dollar views spread out beneath her like a feast. Like the girl who found out she was a princess, the boy who found out he was a wizard, she'd always known. Of course they were secretly rich.

2

THEY KEPT ALMOST nothing from the old house. Mrs. Chang supervised as all-new furniture filled the rooms of the condo. Dina's favorite piece in her new room was a heavy standing mirror in the corner, the border made of real mahogany. It was no child's toy, not something you'd cover with puff paint and stickers.

Mr. Davies arrived as stunning, early-evening light poured in through the floor-to-ceiling windows, where Victor stood. Dumbfounded, still or again. Cheerful and blathering, Mr. Davies and his mustache rolled in a suitcase full of cookware, his free arm loaded with groceries. He put the food away and cooked while the Changs watched and didn't offer to help. Mrs. Chang sat in a new, relaxed pose on her new sofa, drinking a glass of wine, her feet bare — no slippers. Dina had never seen their mother drink alcohol. Her feet were swollen and square in a way that looked unhealthy, her toes hard little nubbins of yellowing flesh and nail. Dina had never seen her feet before either.

Mr. Davies served them scallops in cream sauce. Fat, buttery white orbs in a slick white puddle. Dina's only previous experience with scallops were the stringy yellow bits her father had rehydrated to flavor soup. Mrs. Chang ate with relish, her knife scraping the plate. Dina and Victor picked at their dinners.

"Oh, dear me, I didn't think to ask if either of you is a vegetarian," Mr. Davies said.

"They're not," Mrs. Chang said.

"Vegan," Dina said, inspired. She pushed her plate away. "I'm vegan now."

Mrs. Chang wiped the last of her cream sauce with a hunk of bread. She took a bite, swallowed, and said, "The nonsense with you is endless, isn't it?"

"That's no trouble," Mr. Davies said. "No trouble at all. I bought a nice piece of liver for tomorrow night, with cabbage and oranges, but I'll make extra cabbage."

As he cleared their dishes, Mr. Davies said, "No need to help clean up. I've got it," though no one else had moved to stand.

Victor led Dina out onto the balcony. They were buffeted by strong winds up that high, and they pressed back against the glass door. Victor had to speak loudly and close to Dina's ear to be heard. "What do you think of Mr. Davies?"

"He's ridiculous."

"Do you think he's after Mom for her money?"

"Maybe. Better someone her own age than some young boy toy, I guess."

Victor shook his head. "I can't tell if it's weird seeing her with a white guy, or if it's just weird seeing her with anyone who isn't Dad." Quieter, almost to himself, he added, "It's like she just threw away our whole lives before now, like none of it ever happened. Like I dreamed it."

But that's how you become someone new, someone better, Dina thought. Someone rich and famous. She rubbed her wrists to clear away a sudden sense memory, the sensation of ropes wrapping around her skin. Victor said something more, but the wind swallowed up his voice, and Dina let it go.

ONE OF MANY things Dina loved about living on the mainland: the malls. To counteract the elaborate breakfasts and dinners Mr. Davies managed to foist upon her—the bites she took to get him off her back—she walked through the connected downtown malls after school. She liked looking at the window displays, the faceless mannequins arranged in dispassionate groupings, elbows cocked for shining handbags. Sometimes alone, sometimes with the group of girls who had claimed Dina on her first day at her new school, identifying her as one of their own. They were, in a way, indistinguishable from her girlfriends at her old school. Richer, more ethnically diverse, quicker to whip out their parents' credit cards for a tube of lip gloss or a Frappuccino, but the same overexcited voices, the same walking with linked arms, the same topics of conversation, tolerant of Dina's drifting inattention and mindless mimicking.

They squealed about some boy, so Dina squealed along with them. Dina hadn't developed a sexual interest in men or women. Men's bodies all looked the same, a doll-like contiguousness, one undifferentiated lump and a sad little offshoot, an accidental skein of flesh. Taller, shorter, fatter, thinner, yes, but somehow all the same, the same basic figure underneath. Women, on the other hand, were too varied, a universe of alien life. It was hard to believe they all belonged to the same species. To Dina, most of them seemed ill made, factory defective, to be tossed aside at the end of the line. It was clear to her how they should look and how they fell short. Men's bodies bored her; women's bodies made her uneasy, like a painting on a wall hung askew, a hair in the icing of a cake.

Dina was with her new friends when she saw the poster. Hot-pink text on a black background. It was an open call for a modeling agency, that Saturday at the mall at 9 a.m. "Oh my God," one of her friends said. "You have to be there."

They followed Dina back to the condo, rooted through her closet for the right outfit. Mrs. Chang appeared at the open door to Dina's bedroom. Dina was the only one who noticed her. Her mother leaned on the door frame as she listened to the chatter, the heap of rejected clothes building up on Dina's bed.

"Maybe your yellow dress," Mrs. Chang said.

The other girls stopped. "Hello, Mrs. Chang," one of them said in a deferential voice that made Dina want to roll her eyes.

"Yellow washes me out," Dina said.

"No, no." Mrs. Chang stepped into the room and the girls stepped aside. Mrs. Chang had recently developed a problem in her left knee. She had surgery scheduled for later that year. Sometimes she used a cane, but on this occasion, she limped forward under her own power. She took the yellow dress from Dina's closet and laid it out on an empty spot on the bed. "It makes you look young. Fresh."

"Ooh," her friends cooed. "Yeah, that. Definitely."

"You should go early," Mrs. Chang said. "I can drive you."

"It's only at the mall," Dina said. "I can walk."

"You're not worried about getting sweaty? Your hair getting" — Mrs. Chang made a fussing gesture with her hand — "by the wind?"

"Good point," said the chorus.

"Okay, I guess I could use a ride," Dina said slowly. "Thanks."

On Saturday, to a rapping on her bedroom door, Dina lifted her head partway from the morass of dreams and pillows, then rolled over and fell back asleep. When she woke again, the clock face read 8:50. She jumped up and ran to the bathroom, swearing. It would take at least fifteen minutes to do her face — thirty minutes to do the look she had originally planned, which was out of the question now. In her yellow dress, powder choking the sweat her skin strained to produce, she hurried into the main room. Her mother and Mr. Davies sat at the glass dining table, another grossly rich meal between them, a tray laid with brie, custard buns, and tea. "Why didn't you wake me?" Dina demanded.

"I tried," her mother said.

"Well, let's go already!"

Mrs. Chang took the cane off the back of her chair and pulled herself to her feet. Spitefully slow, Dina thought.

They were quickly stalled in a construction-heavy web of one-way streets. The leather interior of her mother's Lexus still had a new, outgassing smell that turned Dina's empty stomach. "It might be faster for you to walk," Mrs. Chang said.

Dina touched her flat-ironed hair. Showing up a mess was worse than showing up late, she decided.

When they pulled up alongside the mall, they could see a line of girls that stretched around the block and out of sight. Dozens, maybe hundreds, many with their mothers. "I told you that you should have come early," Mrs. Chang said, her tone flat and unscolding.

Dina hopped out of the car and navigated her way to the back of the line.

The day was gray, a damp chill in the air. Dina stood for almost three hours as the line crept forward. Some of the girls took off their heels and stood on the filthy sidewalk in their bare feet or stockings. Some sat down, tugging at their tight skirts. Without thinking, Dina rubbed her eyes, which were starting to strain against the diffuse brightness of the overcast sky, wishing she'd brought sunglasses. She saw the smudge of black and shiny flesh-tone against her hand and cursed aloud.

She didn't have a headshot/résumé or a portfolio binder, like most of the girls. It hadn't even occurred to her. What had she expected? To walk into a room and have someone behind a table leap up in delight and recognition. *Yes,* he'd cry. *You. You're the one I've been waiting for. You have* it!

Finally, someone came outside and told them that was it, they were done for the day. Dina trudged home. Her mother and stepfather had gone out, and when they returned, they left her alone to mope in her bedroom without the I-told-you-so she'd expected.

Six months later, she saw a similar poster for a nationwide talent search at the same mall. This time, she had four weeks to prepare, and she wasn't going to screw it up again. She asked her mother if she could take singing lessons.

Mrs. Chang was lying on the couch. The silky fabric of her trousers revealed the shape of her legs. Her left leg had shrunken and atrophied, while her right had solidified, grown visibly muscular, the calf bulging like a melon. "Singing lessons?" she repeated.

"Yes. I picked out a school and a teacher and everything."

"How much?"

"A hundred and twenty dollars a session."

"How many?"

"I called and they said they have room for me to do one a week, for three weeks, before the talent search."

Dina had come armed with the teacher's credentials, the history of the school, its location — near their home and her school, she wouldn't need a ride — but Mrs. Chang just closed her eyes. "Bring me my checkbook. It's in the top drawer of my desk, in the study."

In the hallway outside her teacher's room at the music school, children and their parents passed where Dina sat on a wooden bench. Young children. Dina was the oldest student there. The door to her teacher's room opened and a boy of perhaps nine or ten walked out. Dina was called next.

The room was small, with a high, angled ceiling that ended in a line of windows, and just enough floor space for a grand piano, a stool, and a bookshelf. Her teacher was an older woman named Linda, a once-famous jazz singer, her silver bangs flattened by a barrette, in a sweater and wool jumper. When Dina came in, Linda was sitting at the piano. They shook hands awkwardly. Linda told Dina to sing anything she liked.

Dina thought she had a great voice, the kittenish vibrato of a pop star. When she finished, Linda was squinting at her from the piano bench, like she couldn't quite bring her into focus.

"Well?" Dina said.

"Next," Linda said, "why don't you tell me why you want to take singing lessons?"

Dina explained about the talent search. "I want to prepare for it. Refine my voice."

"How soon is this competition?"

"About three weeks. I have three lessons with you booked."

Another long silence. Linda looked down at the piano keyboard, ran a finger over the keys without depressing them. "There are some exercises we can do," she said at last.

So it went. Two hours of breathing and scales, Linda holding Dina by the hip bones and turning her pelvis one way or another, prodding a tight, almost painful muscle just above the waistline of Dina's jeans. One hour of practicing the song Dina was going to sing at the talent search, while Linda struck the same high piano key and clapped and hummed aggressively, sending a signal Dina couldn't understand. "Should I pick a different song?" Dina asked, frustrated. Perhaps her voice was better suited for something higher or lower, something simpler or grander.

"The song is fine," Linda said.

At the start of their lessons, Dina had expected to be told she was a natural, for Linda to be ecstatic and awed at having Dina as a pupil, to have finally found true talent. By the end, Dina would have settled for a pat on the back and a simple "You'll do great."

DINA ARRIVED at the mall an hour before sign-up began. She'd meant to come two hours early but getting dressed and primped had taken longer than she expected. She was given a slot about midway through the competition. She paced and breathed, she double-checked the instructions to the technician and the CD with her backing track, she sipped at the tea with honey she'd brought in a metal thermos.

Finally, it was her turn. As she climbed onto the small stage to face the table of judges and the smattering of people in fold-out plastic chairs, she didn't feel nervous. She felt the stage lights hit her, along with rays from the mall skylight, making the sequins in her white halter top and the jeweled pin in her hair sparkle. Waiting for the music to begin, she wrapped her hand suggestively around the microphone stand. She bent one knee and did a quarter-turn to the side. She smiled at the judges, who, in spite of their boredom and the long, torturous morning, smiled back. For Dina, they perked up and leaned forward in their seats.

A camera was trained on her, her image projected larger immediately behind her head, with two large speakers on either side. Shoppers stopped and stared, arrested by her image.

The backing track began. She swayed side to side. The judges' smiles grew.

From the first note, she was startled by how loud her voice was, booming from the monitors behind her. Loud and unfamiliar. A wholly different voice. Not the voice she heard in the shower, or layered atop the radio, or with Linda in the music school. Not at all the voice she heard reverberating in her skull.

This voice had almost no melody at all. Almost talking instead of singing, with a horrible falseness, like a bad affected accent. It went shrill and broke on high notes. It rounded eerily on low notes, like whale vocalizations in a nature documentary.

It was the worst thing she'd ever heard.

She sang the whole song. She even held the last note as she'd practiced, hearing now how off-key she was. The bland, blaring unpleasantness of the held note like an air-raid siren. Her eyes filled, beading on her waterproof mascara.

She stumbled a little on her white pumps as she hurried off the stage. She pushed blindly past the stage techs and their clipboards, past the rows of fold-out chairs and gawking faces. In the last row, the seat closest to the aisle, something caught her eye, caused her to falter momentarily. Her mother. She'd seen. She'd *heard.*

Mrs. Chang pushed swiftly up on her cane and her good leg. She loped after Dina, who let her mother catch up, allowed herself to be guided into the parking garage through a blur of tears, climbed into the Lexus on autopilot.

In the artificial night of the garage, orange safety lights and enclosed dark, Mrs. Chang let Dina cry for a few minutes before she said, "I'm going to tell you a story now."

"Once, there was a baby chicken who got lost," she began. "His mother got chopped up for stew. The baby chick wandered around the yard, confused and alone. He found his way down to the pond at the edge of the farm. There, on the shore, he found a nest of ducklings. The mother duck took him in. She fed him. She cared for him like the rest of her babies. The chick didn't know what he looked like, and for a while, he was happy. Then, when the ducklings were big enough, the mother duck led her family into the pond for their first swim. The baby chick drowned."

Mrs. Chang turned the key in the ignition and the engine shuddered to life. "Do you understand?"

Dina didn't speak for the rest of the drive home. As soon as they got back to the condo, she went straight to her room and shut the door. She took off her clothes and stood before the mirror. She examined her face and body, every inch of it, where there were straight, unfettered lines of bone and where it curved gracefully, the swoop of a swan's neck. Where she had stripped it of distracting hair, where she had evened out the color, where she had smoothed out the roughness. What she had perfected. Which was a talent. Which was a gift. She had a dim sense of what her mother was trying to say, but she blocked it out. She was no fucking chicken.

3

DINA FINISHED HIGH SCHOOL, somehow, more than one 59 bumped up to 60 just to get her out the door. Her mother had a third knee surgery to correct the damage done by the first two surgeries. Her back and hips were shot from overcompensating on the right side. Mr. Davies pushed her around town in a wheelchair. They bought a second car, a luxury SUV with a chair lift. Dina thought of her mother as only temporarily weakened, a wounded dragon.

That summer, Dina won fourth "princess"—fourth runner-up—in a Miss Chinatown pageant. Dina posed for press pictures in a group of two dozen women, styled to look identical, their faces lightened to the same shade, moles and marks painted over, their eyes rounded by makeup, their chins contoured and their hair parted to give the impression of heart-shaped faces. They wore the same leopard-print leotard with a peplum skirt of feathers, a confusing hybrid-animal costume.

Then there were fashion blogs and local stores, who didn't pay or paid in store credit, the clothes always a little too long, a little sloppier-looking than they should be, the camera always catching her in the middle of a fake laugh with too much teeth, or squinting into the sun, or her body in an awkward pose, her thin arms squashed outward in two dimensions. Or just revealing her bleary disappointment, the expression of someone on a bad first date. The images appeared on the stores' websites and hung in their windows, images she'd always assumed were of professional, high-paid models, not a beauty-queen runner-up with a gift card worth one scarf or half a pair of shoes. Her highest-paying—her only *paying*—job was a commercial for the provincial government, where she played a college student, nodding earnestly at the actor playing her professor. American movie and TV productions rolled into town with their casts already complete, fake police cars marked CHICAGO PD or BOSTON PD or NYPD flanking the downtown streets, and the trades were filled with dinner-theater roles.

This city was the problem, Dina decided. This whole underachieving nation, filming ugly people on low-definition cameras and putting them on TV, failing to recognize greatness.

TIME PASSED with unnerving rapidity, without school to demarcate the years, highlight and rarefy the summers. Mrs. Chang was running out of ways to call Dina useless, shiftless, hopeless. Eighteen blurred into nineteen. Twenty blurred into the rest of her life — the girls in the magazines seemed to be getting even slimmer and younger, emaciated heroin chic or a dewy, just-sprung preteen look. Dina couldn't shake the feeling that she had finished high school only days ago, that she was still growing, still almost a child, green on the vine. She was a diamond in an untapped mine, in the deep, dark unknown, ready to be unearthed and glitter in her first light.

Victor got married and moved to San Francisco. Dina was shocked when she saw Isabel for the first time in more than a decade. "You're so short," she said.

"I didn't shrink," Isabel joked.

Victor was goopy with love, and Dina struggled to see what he saw in her new sister-in-law. She did like Isabel, a bit irrationally, because Isabel had — through circumstance — opted out of what Dina now remembered as pointless, purely sadistic torture, a punishment for nothing she could recall. The other girls attacking her out of nowhere and Isabel absent, innocent. But even in Victor's diminished, adult form, his glowing adolescent beauty all but erased, Isabel looked strange beside her husband. In her old-lady glasses and old-lady clothes, underdressed for her own wedding, she deflected attention almost to invisibility. Dina tried to be happy for Victor even as she wanted to whisper, *You could do better.* She noticed their mother's lips thinning in disapproval as the meal went on, and knew that she saw it too. Maybe Mrs. Chang thought Dina was delusional and arrogant, but what Victor was doing was worse: selling himself short.

WHILE MRS. CHANG was at physical therapy, Dina went into her study and found the series of marked envelopes containing keys and key cards. Dina almost couldn't believe objects in one place could open doors thousands of miles away, magic that seemed like it should fade with distance. She took the envelope marked with an address in Santa Monica, California. She also pinched a wad of cash from the cookie tin at the back of one of the kitchen cabinets that her mother thought she didn't know about.

After Mrs. Chang came home with Mr. Davies, who had driven her and stayed through the appointment, Dina said, "I'd like to go visit Victor. See his new house."

Mr. Davies left his wife in a chair in the living room and went to start dinner. "Did he invite you?" Mrs. Chang asked.

"Well, no. I kind of invited myself. But he said he's fine with it."

"Is he paying for your ticket?"

"Uh, no."

Mrs. Chang muttered something in Chinese. "Fine, whatever. Get out of my hair for once. Take my credit card and book it."

On the day Dina left, after Mr. Davies dropped her off at the airport, she went to the ticketing counter and had her return flight changed to a flight to LAX, paying the difference and fee in cash. All she had to do was get to Hollywood, she thought.

VICTOR AND ISABEL'S house was on a street of nearly identical houses, in a neighborhood of almost identical streets. Wide, street-facing, single-story homes that spoke of an optimistic past, a country that had more land than it could ever need.

They were almost finished unpacking. Only a few boxes remained stacked against the wall in the living room. The house still seemed empty, the furniture from their studio apartment dinky and far apart in the larger space. But Dina found the house strangely claustrophobic, the low ceilings and long, low windows, the suburban silence of unshared walls.

On Dina's first evening in California, they ate an early dinner at home, cleaned up, and watched a DVD together before Isabel rose and said she was going to bed.

"It's not even nine o'clock," Dina said.

Isabel yawned and gave Victor a peck on the cheek. "I might read for a bit. I'll let you two catch up."

After the bedroom door closed, Dina turned to Victor and said, "Really living it up out here, huh?"

"Hey, come on. That's not fair."

Dina stood and shook out her limbs. She'd been sitting with one leg tucked underneath her on the overstuffed couch, and her foot had fallen asleep. She felt pent-up and restless, the way she had in their childhood home, conscious that there was nowhere to go and nothing to do for miles. "Why don't we go get drunk somewhere?"

"We can go to a bar, but one of us will have to drive. I can make us drinks here, if you want."

Dina paced a circuit of the room. The curtains had been left behind by the previous owner, a heavy brocade in mustard yellow. She tugged one back and peered into the backyard, visibly shaggy and overgrown even in the dark. "Mom said your house was like a zillion dollars. It's not what I expected. It reminds me of our old house."

"Yeah, me too," Victor said, smiling.

She put her hands on her hips. "So you're happy? Living

like an old person?" She meant it as a joke, but it came out straight.

"Sure. I mean, I don't love my job. But it's just a job, and it pays really well. And I get to surf almost every weekend."

"But you're at work, like, forty hours a week."

"More like fifty or sixty. More with the commute."

"Right. Basically your whole life. Why don't you become a—what's it called? A sponsored surfer. Some guy from high school did that. One of those dudes you used to hang out with."

"I don't think he pays his bills with that. He just gets free boards and gear sometimes."

Dina looked down at Victor, who sat dead center on the kind of plush, rounded, too-soft sofa that their father had liked. "It just seems sad," she said, "that you spend all your time doing something you hate, so you can spend a couple hours doing something you actually like."

"Everybody does that. And I don't *hate* my job."

"But what do you want? What do you really want?"

"What do you mean? I have what I want." Annoyance had finally entered Victor's voice, which seemed like an improvement to Dina, better than complacence. "I wanted this house. I wanted Isabel. I wanted to be a programmer. I wanted to live in California. Why are you trying to shit all over my life?"

"That's not what I'm trying to do!" She took a breath. "I'm sorry. If you're happy, I'm happy for you."

The movie they'd watched had been a mediocre romantic comedy, two big stars and a forgettable summer script, beautifully shot but so poorly written that Dina and Victor had spent most of it mocking the lines and chatting about other things. The story made no real argument for why the two leads should be together, other than their initial dislike and that they were, of course, the two loveliest people in this universe, too gorgeous to belong to anyone else, their less-attractive friends, family, and red-herring romantic interests mugging on the sidelines.

At the climax of the film, after ninety minutes of unlikely obstacles and misunderstandings, after the female protagonist fled weeping from a wedding and was chased to a cliff above the Hollywood Bowl at sunset, after a metaphor-dense declaration of love that had made Dina and Victor howl, Dina had seen, out of the corner of her eye, that Isabel was tearing up.

Dina then turned her full attention to the screen, to the image there divorced from its context. The camera closed in slowly on a man and woman, from his impeccable suit to his blond stubble and perfect chin, from her plunging emerald bridesmaid gown to her wetly shining green eyes and mile-long eyelashes. A cathartic swell in the score, the sky an unlikely combination of pale violet and orange cream, the valley filled with earthbound stars. The kiss! A kiss that could only exist between those two people—the actors, not the characters. What made it romantic wasn't the thinly drawn story, but the sheer aesthetic, charismatic sublime of movie stars.

Their kiss had moved Isabel. And Dina, out of genuine affection for her brother and his wife, wanted, but did not have the words, to say: Then don't settle for this! For beauty only on the other side of the screen, for your ugly house in the middle of nowhere where you're already letting your bodies soften and turn, for a settled and dreamless existence so early in life. You can *be* those people on the TV. You can look like that, exist in a scene like that, have a moment like that one. If you didn't believe that, what was the point?

Victor said, now, "You're not going back."

"What?"

"You left your passport and stuff on the counter. Your ticket. You're going to L.A."

Dina crossed her arms. "You're going to tell me it's a stupid idea. That I'm being stupid."

"No, no. I think it's great. I think . . ." He paused. "I don't know anything about modeling or acting or whatever, but you've always had something. Something everyone can see, something that they want to be around. More than just being pretty. Some kind of magic." He gestured at the TV, where the menu screen for the DVD persisted, an image of the central paramours standing nose to nose. "Like them."

Sometimes, in the middle of the night, Dina wondered if her gifts were more useless and common than she could bear. For now, the thought always dissolved by morning. And even if it was just her sentimental, weak-hearted brother, at least someone, at least once, had said what she'd always wanted to hear.

DINA TOOK A SHUTTLE from LAX to the Santa Monica Pier and walked to the address on the envelope she'd stolen from her mother. The building faced six lanes of Ocean Avenue, a line of palm trees, and the ocean itself beyond. Her mother knew the value of waterfront property. The lobby was so cold that opening the door felt like opening a freezer, the air-conditioning prickling her skin immediately. String lights dripped from a modern silver chandelier, reminiscent of icicles. Potted ferns and bamboo smothered the windows.

The woman behind the concierge desk looked like a model. Blond, vertiginously tall, in a lacy white dress and a navy blazer, face and body defined by straight slices of an artist's knife. "May I help you?" she asked. She had a faint, implacable accent. Dina was in the right place, she thought, the place where all the world's most beautiful people gathered.

"No, I'm fine," Dina said, trying to stride purposefully for the elevators. She was grimy from the plane, her hair pulled back. One of the wheels on her suitcase had been busted in transit. The suitcase skittered and bounced loudly along the marble floor.

The woman stepped out from behind the desk and cut off

Dina's path. She was wearing knee-high brown boots. "Are you expected by one of our residents? Would you like me to call someone for you?"

"I, uh." Dina produced the key card from her purse, thinking now that the envelope looked suspicious, obviously stolen. "My mom owns Unit Eight-oh-eight. I'm going to be staying here for a while."

"May I see that?" She plucked the card from Dina's hand before Dina could respond. "Thank you." She went back to the desk and Dina stayed standing in the middle of the lobby, tethered to her broken suitcase. The receptionist poked around at a computer and then said, "You're Mrs. Chang's daughter?"

"Yes."

"She hasn't informed us about any new renters or guests."

"It was kind of last-minute."

"If you'll just stay there, I'm going to give her a quick call to confirm."

Dina wondered if she should make a run for it. Would her mother call the cops on her? To teach her a lesson? The things Dina had seen on TV and in movies about the LAPD were not encouraging. Before Dina could decide, the receptionist brought her the cordless receiver. "Your mother would like to talk to you," she said.

Dina lifted the phone to her ear.

"Well, aren't you a clever little thief. Cleverer than I thought."

Dina didn't respond.

"I tried not to spoil you, but I've clearly failed," Mrs. Chang continued. "A wise mother would have you kicked out of the building, leave you to starve in the street until you came crawling back, humbled. But I'm too soft-hearted. I don't know what your plan is, what you think you're going to do out there with no money and no legal way to work, but go right ahead."

"You'll see," Dina said. And then, glancing at the receptionist, she added, "Thank you."

She gave the phone back. The receptionist smiled sweetly and said, "I'm sorry for the confusion. Security is very important to our residents. I'm sure you understand. Enjoy your stay, Ms. Chang."

THE AIR in the condo was stale, dust coating its elegant wood, quartz, and stainless-steel surfaces. There was no furniture or linens in any of the rooms, nothing in the cabinets or drawers. The building had been a new construction when Mrs. Chang had bought it, acquired when it was just an artist's rendering and a pit in the ground, so there were no remnants of staging or previous owners. Dina slept on a pile of her clothes that first night.

In the morning, she went to a nearby coffee shop and used her laptop to find under-the-table, non-union acting and modeling gigs. Nearly all of them alluded to nudity. The ones she called turned out to be student filmmakers and hobby photographers who couldn't pay, and out-and-out pornographers.

By the end of the week, she conceded to the student filmmakers if they provided lunch and a ride, the hobby photographers if they sent her copies, more to feel like she was doing something than for the bagels and sweaty slices of cheddar she stuffed into her purse. She built a portfolio website on a free hosting service, but no one ever emailed or called. Dina's mother stopped paying her phone bill—the roaming charges were astronomical—so she bought a prepaid burner from a guy who ran a stall near the beach. She sweet-talked a couple guys off the street into dragging the free futon she'd found on Craigslist inside; the real trick was getting rid of them afterward. The garbage bag she used as a trash can and the bare, plaid-patterned futon looked absurd in the middle of the large main room of the condo.

Eventually, she found a few paying gigs—handing out cans of energy drink at a gas station while wearing a crop top and short shorts in the drink's signature colors, handing out fliers for boat tours in a sailor suit—but generally even the party promoters and booth-girl organizers wanted a Social Security number.

She spotted celebrities all the time, in open-air restaurants and coming out of specialty bakeries, waiting for valets, walking their dogs. They were invariably shorter and more shopworn than she expected, without the aura of specialness they'd had in pictures and on-screen. To the point where she wasn't sure she'd seen them or just someone who looked an awful lot like them: an older sibling, a body double, a malformed twin.

Some days, discouraged, Dina just hung around the pier, waiting for someone to come up to her and remark on her beauty. Which plenty of men did, but they were never the right people, never people who could even plausibly pretend to have money or power, the ability to make her famous.

One afternoon, someone approached her who looked no different from the others, a youngish guy with glasses, in khaki shorts and a plaid shirt. His opening line was a common one. "Are you a model?"

"Yes," Dina said.

He took his business card out of his wallet. "My name is Steve Marsh. I run a modeling agency."

Dina took his card warily. He did not look like someone who ran a modeling agency. He looked like every other internet sleazebag she'd met and worked with. Maybe a little younger, which seemed only more suspect. She'd also never heard of the agency on his card.

"You're just stunning," Steve said. "I'd love to get to know you, with an eye to signing you on with us. Can I take you to lunch sometime?" Her doubt must have showed. He added,

"I'll bring one of our models. To show you everything's on the up and up."

Dina wasn't really in a position to say no.

THE RESTAURANT was a gaudy indoor-outdoor place in West Hollywood, red-and-steel heat lamps dotted between tables like alien spacecraft. The hostess showed Dina to the table, where a woman was waiting. "Steve is running late," she said, standing to greet Dina. "I'm Janice."

Janice was tall and willowy, with an older, sun-damaged face, her eyes ringed by black eyeliner, her knitted fuchsia dress casual for the surroundings. "I'm Dina. Are you a model?"

Janice laughed. "I'll pretend I'm not offended by that."

"I'm sorry, I didn't mean—"

"Yes, I'm a model. I was with a different agency for ten years and I just signed with Steve. And, you know, nobody sings praises like a new convert."

"What made you switch?"

"Let's get some drinks first," Janice said. "Steve is paying for lunch. We should make the most of it." She waved over their server. She ordered herself a martini, and after glancing at Dina to confirm, made it two. She checked her phone, in a pink case on the table. "Where the hell is he? Anyway. Basically—I'm sure you've had this problem too—I was tired of my agency taking such a huge cut. Forty percent since my first job and never negotiable. Steve only takes ten. It's revolutionary."

"That sounds . . ."

"Too good to be true, I know." The server put a basket of bread on the table and Dina resisted the urge to tip it into her bag. She thought often of all the food her father and stepfather had made over the years that she'd refused. Real hunger was very different from self-imposed. "There's no big secret to it.

Basically, there's less legwork for him than a traditional agent. All the bookings are managed by a computer system, between clients and us. All he has to do is vet the models and the clients on both sides, and then we deal directly with each other. It's cheaper for everyone." Janice's phone buzzed. She read the message on-screen and said, "Steve's meeting with investors. He's going to be a while. We can order."

"Investors?"

"Yeah. The thinking is that he's going to—what is it they say?—'disrupt' the modeling business, and make a fortune. Plus, rich guys like to be around models, so nobody turns down a meeting with Steve."

Dina waited until the food arrived before saying, "That all sounds great, but I should tell you right now, I'm not in the country legally."

Janice waved this away. "Oh, Steve's lawyer can deal with that. The agency can sponsor your visa. Steve has capital coming out of his eyeballs but he needs users—models, I mean, and clients—to really get this off the ground." Janice gave Dina a knowing look over their salads. "Imagine if the new fashion it-girl was discovered through Steve's system. That would change everything for him. And for her."

It was exactly as Dina had always hoped. Someone had seen her on the street, recognized her potential, offered her everything she needed. Representation, residency status. Steve rushed in at the end of the meal and she signed a contract right there and then. But her time in Tinseltown had ground something out of her. Too much time deciding whether or not to go down the stairs into a photographer's basement "studio," whether or not to undo one more button or let him pose her limbs, whether that would lead to more buttons or a hand on her ass, at what point a "student film" tipped into soft-core. Expected to provide her own products and do her own makeup and hair, "working" at a loss. Days where it was easier to just lie on the floor of the condo and try to crawl back inside the teenage fantasies — flashbulb, limo, applause! — that were becoming harder and harder to access. What was she even doing here?

When she signed with Steve Marsh, she didn't think, *All my dreams are coming true!* She thought, *I have nothing to lose.*

Steve and Janice arranged a shoot for Dina to fill in a gap they perceived in her portfolio. In these pictures, she wore a tight-fitting white T-shirt and jeans, her hair clean and brushed away from her face, her makeup natural and merely corrective, hiding the stress hives at her hairline and dark circles under her eyes. She stood before a plain black backdrop, her dark hair fading into it beneath the studio lights. It took several attempts before she could summon the right expression. "Chin up. Tilt your chin up. Not that far. Give me a little bit of a smile. Not that big. Don't smile so big. No teeth. But not like you're scared. Well, maybe a little bit scared. Uncertain. Uncertain but happy. Let's try this — can you open your eyes a little wider? Yes, good. Okay, look at me straight-on. Right at the camera. Right here." On and on, until finally the shot they needed: wide-eyed, credulous, full of hope.

DINA SCRAPED THROUGH six more months. She texted Steve periodically and his occasional reply assured her that her visa application was going forward, all was well, she'd start getting bookings any day now.

The call box phone in the condo rang. It took Dina a few minutes to identify the sound and its source — a sleek, discreet metal panel by the front door — as it had never rung before. She pressed the single button, encircled in blue LED light. "Um, hello?"

The concierge's voice responded. "Good morning, Ms.

Chang. This is Ariana at the front desk. You have a visitor, a Ms. Janice Morgan. Can you confirm that she's expected?"

Dina looked around the condo, down at herself. Well, shit. "Yeah, you can let her up. Thanks."

The elevator dinged. Janice swept in. She was wearing a swimsuit cover-up, a diaphanous blue-gray tunic, translucent enough to reveal the bikini underneath. She was clutching a newspaper in one hand, a wicker beach bag in the other. "I'm so sorry, Dina," she said. "I wanted to tell you in person, since I'm the one who convinced you to get mixed up with that idiot in the first place—"

She stopped talking as she came inside. Futon, garbage bag, suitcase, empty expanses of hardwood floor, luxuries built into the walls. "Are you squatting here?" She pushed past Dina. The room was blazingly hot. The large, sunny windows had no coverings, and the digital air-conditioning units had been remotely disabled. Faintly, almost impressed, Janice added, "How did you get the concierge in on it?"

"I'm not squatting. My mom owns this place."

"Does she know you're here?"

"Yes," Dina said, impatiently. "What happened to Steve? What's happening?"

Janice threw down the newspaper on the kitchen island. "The article's not even about him," she said. "It's about over-valuation in tech and new labor models. He's just one of the sad, sorry examples, a company in a list."

"What?"

"It was a good idea, wasn't it?" Janice said wistfully. "I mean, didn't it seem like a good idea?"

"What are you talking about? What are you saying?"

"Steve was desperate for clients and models and he stopped vetting. He wasn't even *signing* people, per se, just inputting data. The system filled up with garbage. The same garbage you'd find on any of the other online listing sites," Janice said. Dina knew these well. "So the legit clients and models, the few there were, got spooked and quit."

Dina could not find it in herself to be surprised. She slid quietly to the floor and sat with her back against the wall. "So that's it, then."

"I'm sorry." Janice looked ridiculous, somehow, in her beachwear and clunky sandals, her heavily made-up eyes. "I want you to know, I'm really sorry. And if I can . . . if I can help you, somehow . . ."

Dina glanced up, not knowing what to ask for. *Tell me I'm pretty*, she thought. Quietly, she said, "I think I'm done here. I think it's time for me to go home."

"That's your choice. But you have my number, if you think of something."

"Actually," Dina's eyes flashed, "I don't. You never gave it to me. I had Steve's number. He kept saying everything was fine."

Janice stood up straighter. She opened her mouth and closed it again before another "I'm sorry" flew pointlessly out. She took out a business card and put it on the counter beside the paper. "You have it now."

DINA CALLED HER MOTHER collect that afternoon, listening to the hiss of the overseas connection. Her mother had been living in Hong Kong full-time for just under a year. Dina had been dodging her calls for most of that time — her burner didn't have voice mail — because despite Steve's assurances, she'd sensed that this moment was coming. She thought her mother would be able to hear the mounting failure in her voice and wanted to put it off until it was absolutely necessary.

"Dina." Mrs. Chang said her name like a sigh, like it pained her. "You finally called me back. You have to come home to Hong Kong."

Dina had called to say the same thing, but somehow she couldn't face it, that her mother had been right all along. The scale of this I-told-you-so, among all the others.

"Your brother died."

Dina still had not spoken.

"Dina? Are you there?"

"How?"

"A surfing accident."

"When?"

"Three weeks ago."

Dina unleashed a flood of questions, informed by memories of when Victor had first learned to surf as a teenager. Was the water rough that morning, was there a weather warning, how long did it take to find him, what did they do when they found him, did they try to resuscitate him? Where the hell was Isabel in all of this, did she try to stop him, did she call the coast guard, why didn't she call them *sooner?* Dina realized, as her mother answered—inadequately, tersely, she seemed to know so little—that what she really wanted to know was how it could have been prevented, how Dina could still prevent it.

Then Dina had a flash of understanding. Something that made so much more sense than her young, healthy brother being dead. "You're lying."

Her mother sighed her name again. "Dina."

"You're lying! You're trying to trick me into coming home. I'm not buying it."

"You think I'd lie about this? About my own son? Do you want to talk to Mr. Davies? He'll tell you the same thing."

Dina felt a pang of fear. She had the sensation of being chased, footsteps on her shadow. "Of course he will," she said. "He's your little lapdog. He'll do anything you want."

"Why . . ." Mrs. Chang's voice cracked. On the verge of tears—no, of course not. Dina had never seen or heard her mother cry, not even during her father's illness and death. "Why are you like this?"

Dina knew her mother had gone to Hong Kong in case the doctors there could do something about her ruined musculoskeletal system, to see if money could buy something there that it couldn't in Canada. She knew that her mother was disabled, aging, that Mr. Davies and a nurse/maid took turns lifting her into the bathtub, that she had been once widowed and had possibly—no, it was a demented lie, it wasn't true—lost her first-born child, a loss so tremendous there was no word for it in English or Chinese, as if not naming it made it impossible. But Dina couldn't stop picturing her mother as young and strong, solid and unchanging, a force of nature to be resisted.

Dina pressed the end-call button. A small gesture that made such a small noise, *beep*, to make her mother vanish, put her out of mind.

JANICE TOLD DINA about her career as they drove. The sky was open and featureless above them, mountains hidden by smog at the horizon line. Under sunlight so glaring that filthy, dust-smothered cars were as blinding as polished chrome.

Janice had done all the things that Dina had wanted to do: walked for labels in Paris and Milan, swimsuit shoots in Bermuda and Thailand, a mysteriously short stint as a Victoria's Secret Angel—"It didn't work out," Janice said curtly. Background parts in major films, mostly the woman who glides through an early scene to make the lead "relatable" by comparison. Enough that she was called "model/actress" in the trade papers.

"Your life sounds so glamorous," Dina said.

"Sure, with all the highlights lined up back to back like that," Janice said. "That's it. That's everything. In twelve years. Sometimes absolute chaos and snowballing runs of work, where people knew who I was and were excited about me. Sometimes desperate, hungry months, where I thought I'd never work again. Friends getting strung out and fucked up, or just disappearing. Maybe they gave up and went home to Ohio to get married or whatever, or maybe they OD'd or got murdered or are working a corner in La Jolla—who the hell knows? A lot of it was fun, don't get me wrong, but a lot of it took some seriously thick skin. Especially now that I'm getting older."

"It still sounds better than what I've been doing."

Janice drove with one hand, leaning back in the driver's seat, her knees apart in a masculine pose. "I'll be honest with you. There's a lot less demand for ethnic girls. Maybe that's changing—I don't know. But your best bet would be to go back to Asia, make a splash there, and use that to leverage a career here. That's the only way I've seen it happen."

"I can't go 'back' to Asia. I've never been there."

"I thought you said you were from Hong Kong."

"No, I said my mom's there now." Dina felt a squeeze in her a chest, a cold grip. No more talk of her mother.

"You have a lot working against you. You're short for high fashion, you don't have the boobs for lingerie or swimwear. Plus, your look is a little generic. Your face isn't—interesting. Memorable. I'd say you'd do best in teen/college commercial stuff, but they mostly want whites and maybe a handful of light-skinned blacks. Has to play nationally."

Dina crossed her arms over her chest, mortified. "Why didn't you tell me all this when we first met?"

"You know why."

"Because you were shilling for Steve."

"Because Steve's system was supposed to change every-thing. Even though I couldn't see where you'd fit, I thought maybe it would create opportunities I didn't know about.

Maybe everything was changing. You hear all these things. Plus-size working mainstream, minority breakouts in *Vogue*. You hear it, but I've never seen it."

They passed through another town marked by American flags, towering palm trees, and stubby, solitary oaks. Past another craft store, another dry cleaner, another fast-food restaurant styled like a hacienda, another pink-stucco motel. Empty strip-mall parking lots. Farther and farther from Los Angeles County. "How long have we been driving?" Dina said, unable to keep the dejection out of her voice. "Are you going to drive me all the way to San Francisco?"

"Not quite," Janice said. "I'll leave you at a bus station that'll take you the rest of the way, as promised. I want to show you something on the way."

They turned off the main highway onto a state road, uphill, the elevation climbing. They passed a school bus with missing wheels, propped on cinder blocks on a turnout, the windows covered from the inside by cardboard. Below the guardrail, red and brown canyons and crags began, every now and then a jut of white rock like some giant and ancient bone.

They turned again at a wooden sign, onto an unpaved road. The sign was written in white spray paint: SWIMMING HOLE. Dina asked, "Where are you taking me?"

Janice tried to look at Dina as they bounced over the deeply rutted gravel. "You've been thinking about your body one way for a long time. I know — I've been doing it a lot longer. This is something that helps me — maybe it'll help you too."

The road widened where it ended. Cars, camper vans, and a couple of RVs were parked at haphazard angles. Janice pulled up alongside the others. She and Dina stepped out of the car and into the brutal desert light. It was around two in the afternoon, the hottest part of the day. Janice grabbed a couple of towels from the trunk and slung them under her arm.

Dina followed Janice up and then downhill, over a rise, on

a path through dry scrub and a scattering of bare-branched trees. They were descending into a valley. At the bottom, sheltered by slopes on all sides, lay a mud hole the size of a small lake, with a wooden platform at one end. Dina could hear voices and laughter, smell meat on a grill. Closer, and the figures pinkening in the sun and splashing in the murky water resolved: Everyone was naked. Families with children, clusters of young people, elderly couples.

Janice put down the towels beside a group of middle-aged women who smacked a volleyball back and forth without a net. One of them had a sunburnt face and arms while the rest of her was startlingly pale, white as the forebody of a stork, as if her legs and torso had never felt the open air before. Dina stared openly. "Why did you bring me to a nude beach?" she asked.

Janice kicked off her sandals. She peeled off the sundress she was wearing and stepped out of her underwear. Dina thought Janice's tan, statuesque body — tall enough for high fashion with the boobs for lingerie and swimwear, Dina thought grimly — would attract more attention, but no one paid them any mind. "Just hang out for a bit," Janice said. "You don't have to take off your clothes if you don't want to."

Dina held her hand over her face. She could feel, almost hear her skin starting to cook.

Janice added, "I'm going to get in the water to cool off."

Dina peered down. "But that water looks disgusting."

"Again, your call. See you in a second."

Dina watched Janice run to the end of the platform, jump, and pierce the water feet-first like a blade. Her blond head resurfaced and she lazily paddled around the crowded mud hole.

Dina didn't want to go to her brother's house anymore. She didn't want to call again either. His unanswered phone could have meant anything. Even though Dina didn't believe her mother, she was afraid to find out for sure. She wanted to stay in this suspended moment for as long as possible, her logic as an unbroken circle: it wasn't true, because it couldn't be.

She took off her shorts and T-shirt, felt the light on more of her skin, the dry heat melting her brain and relaxing her joints. She looked out on the valley. The scaly, scarred, bloated, potato-shaped bodies littering the beach, flopping along the dirt paths, bulging out of the opaque water. Vulnerable, raw as a wound, plucked chickens or hairless cats. But also anonymous, nonspecific in their nakedness, a contiguous blur of humanity. Taken at a distance, taken in aggregate, Dina thought, surprised at herself, they were almost beautiful.

THE BUS LEAVES DINA at the Greyhound station in San Jose. She takes a cab to Victor and Isabel's house. Their front walkway is overgrown, the tall yellow grass concealing the flat stones that lead to the door. She rings the bell.

The door swings inward slowly, Isabel appearing sliver by sliver. Isabel grips the door handle, cowers mostly behind the door. She seems even smaller than before, broken in a way that Dina suddenly remembers. She hears Isabel screaming at Andee to stop, hears the loose-nail rattle of the knife flipping open. The years compress. They'd succeeded for so long at not talking about it. "We left you," Dina says. "We left you behind."

"I asked you to," Isabel says, as though they're continuing a conversation. "I didn't believe it. I couldn't believe it."

Dina confesses, "I stole food and they tied me up." Isabel looks confused, and Dina tries to shake her head clear, find her footing in reality, in this moment. "Is Victor home?"

Isabel's face crumples, holding herself upright by the door handle. Dina presses on as though she hasn't seen. "I'm sorry for just springing on you like this. Our mother told me the most hideous lie."

CAMP FOREVERMORE
(SIOBHAN)

SIOBHAN WOKE JUST before dawn, a bare gray light seeping in. As her eyes adjusted, she saw that Nita and Andee were both awake, sitting up in their sleeping bags. The murmur of voices came to Siobhan. They'd been engaged in a low conversation, but stopped when they noticed Siobhan pushing herself upright. Nita looked like she hadn't slept, her eyes red-rimmed and cradled in purple. She'd used the food bag as a pillow. "Let's get going," she said.

In a small voice, Dina said, "Can you untie me now? It really hurts."

The other girls looked to one another. Nita unzipped Dina's sleeping bag and Dina rolled onto her front with a moan. The ropes had loosened slightly in the night and rubbed the skin of Dina's wrists raw, leaving bands of pink and red.

"Please?" Dina said, her face muffled by the stuffing of the sleeping bag.

Nita picked up the free ends of the yellow rope. "Help her get up," she said.

Andee and Siobhan pulled at Dina's limbs until she was on all fours, then guided her in a crawl out of the tent. Andee put Dina's shoes back on, closing the Velcro tabs with a strange, hesitant tenderness, like putting a Band-Aid on a baby.

Nita sat beside Dina, one end of the rope wrapped around her fist, as Siobhan and Andee packed up and disassembled the tent. Then Nita passed the rope to Andee, and she transferred the water bottles and Jan's cloth drawstring bag—the trail mix, Jan's tin cup and pot—to the tent bag, leaving the food bag itself behind. It contained only garbage—balls of tinfoil, their dirty bowls and spoons. Siobhan thought of Jan's absent knife, which likely remained where it had rolled from Andee's grip, on the floor of the tent they had left behind, beside Jan.

Nita handed the tent-and-food bag to Siobhan, and she felt both touched and unnerved. Uniting against Dina had worked almost too well.

Dina said quietly, to no one in particular, "I hate you. I'll hate you forever."

Siobhan kept her eyes down, hoisting the bag onto her back. Andee said, "We know."

Siobhan lifted her shirt to examine her stomach, and saw that her skin was pink and inflamed. She must have been scratching in her sleep. They got Dina to stand and tied bags to her as well as themselves.

They reentered the woods. Nita, pulling up the rear again, held Dina's leash as the younger girl stumbled before her. Siobhan wore the compass around her neck, as Jan had, and pointed them due north.

. . .

THE GIRLS HAD LOST all interest in talking. Siobhan's lips were cracked and dry, and her mouth lacked the lubrication necessary for words.

Siobhan was having more trouble orienteering than she had the day before. "North" often pointed through closed thickets of bushes taller than the girls themselves. She followed thin breaks in the foliage, likely cut by animals, which began heading north before veering in all directions, and once, up a vertical, impassable cliffside. She followed a dry creek bed that gradually bent ninety degrees. She always tried to steer them north again, but she kept getting turned around. She worried she was leading the girls in circles. The trees seemed to repeat, a trunk split and seared by lightning reappearing again and again.

When she looked back to see if the others girls had noticed, if they were beginning to doubt her, she saw that they weren't paying attention. Their bodies walked mindlessly, blindly going through the alternating motions, one foot in front of the other. Their heads were down, chin bouncing on their chests, like a line of sleepwalkers.

Siobhan heard Nita make a small, surprised noise behind her. She turned and saw that Nita had slipped on a muddy patch, paused, and quickly righted herself. But Dina kept walking. She was yanked backward, her feet slipping out from under her with a yelp. The rope pulled out of Nita's grasp as Dina landed on her back in the mud, on top of her bound hands.

With an impassive expression, Andee said, "Let's take a break."

They found a relatively dry, mossy spot to sit. They drank the last of the creek water. It did nothing to slake Siobhan's thirst. It almost made it worse, like drinking sand.

Dina's back and hair were coated in clumpy smears of mud. "Can someone wipe the mud away from my eyes? Please?"

Nita obliged, cleaning Dina's face with her sleeve, tucking her filthy hair behind her ears. "You have to help me go to the bathroom," Dina added. "Or just fucking untie me." Her voice went high and unsteady on *fucking,* as though unaccustomed to its sound, the notes of its melody.

Siobhan had never felt so tired in her entire life.

Andee looked to Nita, who nodded. "Fine," she said. "We'll stand guard while you go. Siobhan, watch the food."

Andee picked the knots apart, and she and Nita helped Dina stand, still holding her elbows. Her wrists had swollen and were red and indented, like a roast that's been tied with butcher's twine. For no reason, a dumb sense of propriety, they guided her until she stood against a tree. They let go long enough for Dina to tug down her pants and underwear, pausing to shake the feeling back into her hands. Her feet were unsteady on the slick mud.

The other three turned away in different directions. Siobhan gazed purposefully into the distance. A pop of color caught her eye, pea-size orange berries that had also grown around the edges of Camp Forevermore. They'd been warned that the berries were poisonous, but they looked plump and alluring to her now.

In science class, Siobhan had been taught that people could go weeks without food. She counted in her head: it had been only something like sixteen hours since the bite of hot dog and sugary cocoa powder, and she was weak with hunger, reconsidering the pinched, sour-looking berries. Half of her mind had been on the trail mix all morning, going over each component one at a time: buttery cashews, clusters of honeyed granola, dense, sweet raisins. She'd patted the bag on her back, knowing it was in there. They would eat it soon. She lowered her eyes to the ground, where the girls had left boot prints in the squishy mud.

"Hurry up," Andee said.

"I'm trying," Dina said. "It's hard to go with all of you right here."

By Siobhan's feet, she noticed an imprint that looked different from the others. Like it had been left by someone who wasn't wearing shoes, all five bare toes pressed into the mud, wide in the pad and tapered at the heel. A large, stout man, she imagined, like a troll. "Hey," she said aloud, excited. She was about to point out the footprint to the other girls when she realized each toe well had another divot above it, a tiny hole. The point of a claw.

"What?" Nita said, her back still to the others.

"Uh." Siobhan hesitated. What good would it do to alarm them? She resolved to just head in the opposite direction from the way the tracks faced. "There're some berries over there. Maybe we can eat them."

Nita glanced behind her. "Those are poisonous. They tell you that the first day of camp."

"Oh, right. Of course." Siobhan swiped her boot through the mud, erasing the paw print.

THEY LEFT DINA untied as they continued on, Nita still following close behind her, and Andee showily between Dina and the pack on Siobhan's back. Siobhan's attempts at due north led them to where a long, deep ravine cut straight across their path. They turned and walked along the edge, looking for a place to cross, until they found a spot where it appeared relatively shallow and narrow, and they could see a small waterfall rolling down an embankment on the other side.

Nita approached the edge. "It's pretty sheer. It's not a long way to go down, but I don't know how we'd get back up again." She peered down. "Oh, there's a log down there. Maybe we can . . ." Nita suddenly staggered backward.

"What's wrong?" Siobhan asked.

Nita made a frantic shushing noise. She pointed into the

ravine. The girls gathered close to her, pushing through the saplings that blocked their view.

Two black bears were in the recessed ground below them, less than twenty feet away. "They're cubs," Dina whispered.

The two bears were on a log that had fallen into the ravine at an angle. They pawed at each other, knocking each other off the log, climbing back up again, in play. They were old enough that their fur had come in full and thick, while still a fraction of the size of a full-grown bear—about the same size as the girls themselves.

They were too small to have made the print that Siobhan saw. She felt the blood draining from her face, pooling in her feet, leaving her cold. She had led the girls here. "Their mother must be nearby," she said.

"We have to get out of here," Andee whispered.

"But which way do we go?" Nita whispered back. "We don't know where their mother is. We don't want to get stuck between her and them."

"Let's just get away," Andee said. Too loudly. The bear cubs looked up and stopped their game. One cub rose up on its back legs and peered at them. The other cub lumbered toward the girls on all fours. It reached the sharply slanted wall of the ravine and started to climb.

The girls scrambled away from the edge. Siobhan was closest to the cub, and as she tried to turn and flee, she felt something grab onto her, holding her in place. She screamed and flailed, trying to figure out what had happened, why she couldn't move. She finally realized that the strap of her bag had snagged on a branch. She struggled to untangle the strap from the tree, but couldn't turn far enough around. She tried to untie the bag from her body, her shaky fingers unable to penetrate the knot. She tried to wiggle her arms out of the straps that remained tied around her waist and hips.

The bear crested the ravine. It hoisted itself clumsily onto the edge where Siobhan was trapped. It looked different up close. Not cute. Almost lupine, its snout more pointed, its eyes small and mean, the kind of affectless curiosity Siobhan associated with teenage boys. She was still struggling, trying to free herself, her legs flopping, tossing her head wildly.

The bear toddled over to Siobhan. It went up on its hind legs and swayed unsteadily, before tipping forward onto its front paws again. It ran around her in a circle. It swatted lightly against her leg, testing her. Siobhan fought against the strap and felt her shoulder wrench out of place. She screamed again.

She thought she could see the girls' faces where they'd stopped a short distance away. They didn't look panicked, as she thought they would. They were staring straight at Siobhan. Dina was rubbing her wrists. She thought she heard Andee say, "The tent. The food." Their expressions were familiar; they were weighing a choice.

They were deciding whether to leave her here.

The cub paused in front of Siobhan. Something in the distance had caught its attention. Siobhan craned her neck to see over her own shoulder, to see what it was looking at.

On the far side of the ravine, at the top of the hill where water flowed down a carved, curving path, stood the shape Siobhan had seen from the beach — its majestic bulk and bristling fur, its thick haunches and forelegs, a demon queen in a glossy black coat, a shard of night invading the day.

The bear cub trotted just past Siobhan, back to the edge, to watch its mother's approach. Siobhan shut her eyes. She didn't want to see what happened next.

And then Nita was with her, Nita's hands were on her, unraveling the knots with practiced fingers, her face close enough that Siobhan could feel Nita's breath on her cheek, steady and sure. Not because of the mother bear, Siobhan knew, not because Siobhan was in even more danger, but because the cub had gotten out of the way.

When Siobhan could feel the last knot was almost loose, she braced her boot against the ground, wedging it beside a root to push herself forcefully free. The toe caught and she heard — felt — a loud crack in her ankle, a sound sent jolting through her body.

Still she ran. Pure adrenaline kept the bones of her leg in place. Nita was running alongside her. Andee and Dina fell in line. Siobhan knew without looking back what was behind her: the mother bear traversing the ravine, and the bag, with the tent and their last scrap of food, hanging forlornly in the tree.

THEY RAN and ran. The woods seemed to deepen and thicken around them, the canopy blotting out more and more of the sky. They weren't running the way they'd come, and the compass around Siobhan's neck spun as they took random turns, no longer trying to move systematically north, no longer following any plan at all. They ran even long after it seemed the bear hadn't followed.

This couldn't be the island they thought it was, Siobhan thought, the trees blurring past, her foot growing limp and stony, useless. The island with the town and the motel and the diner. They were in some boundless, uninhabited hell.

They came to a clearing, the reappearance of full daylight. A small, open field of grasses and wildflowers that was surrounded on every side by a wall of trees.

When they paused to take it in, Siobhan collapsed. She rolled back and forth on her spine, cradling her ankle in her hands and howling in pain. Her right shoulder blade burned, but that was nothing compared to the shattering, diamond-bright pain between her right shin and foot.

The girls knelt beside Siobhan. If only Siobhan's mother were here! She'd once had hair the color of Siobhan's, a wispy rose-gold that made the hair seem translucent, barely there, a trick of the light on their milky scalps. Siobhan had only ever seen it in pictures. Her mother had gone gray at a young age, and for all of Siobhan's life, she'd dyed her hair a deeper, more vibrant red, a purplish maroon that made her stand out in every room. Siobhan loved her mother's hair. She loved that she'd never seen anyone else with hair that color. She loved that she'd never lose her mother in a crowd. Her hair was a beacon, a lighthouse, forever guiding Siobhan home.

What she would give to see her mother walking out of the woods, into this clearing, her vivid hair flapping in the breeze like a flag of surrender. If her mother were here, Siobhan could finally give up. She could crawl into her mother's arms and cry, and her cry would signal that she was the center of the universe, her pain mattered more than anything else, and it was someone else's job to fix it, it was everyone else's job to fix it, she was too small and too helpless to do anything but cry.

But instead of her mother, Nita, Andee, and Dina hovered over her. The mean little faces that had almost — she was sure of it — left her strapped to the tree with the bears. "Can you walk?" Nita asked.

Siobhan swallowed hard. She pulled herself to a sitting position, and the pain in her ankle flared magnificently as it rolled a fraction of an inch. She shook her head.

Andee asked Nita, "What should we do?"

"I guess we're camping here tonight," Nita said.

"We don't have a tent," Dina said. "Or any food or water."

"I know that!" Nita snapped.

Siobhan closed her eyes, clenched her teeth. Her whole body shook and a tear traveled from the inner corner of her eye to the tip of her nose. She knew they were looking at her, but she couldn't help it.

"Hey, Siobhan," Andee said. Siobhan opened her eyes again, and Andee was waving a hand in front of Siobhan's face. "Does it hurt a lot? Like a lot, a lot?"

Siobhan nodded.

Andee reached in her pants pocket. She took out Jan's joint, still rolled in its Ziploc bag. Siobhan looked at her questioningly. "I grabbed it when we were packing up this morning," Andee said. "Good thing I did, huh? Or the bears would have it too."

Andee found the lighter in the remaining supply bag. "I've seen grown-ups do this a million times," she said. She tucked the joint between her lips, lit it, and then pressed it against Siobhan's mouth. Siobhan shook her head, drawing back. "It'll help with the pain."

Siobhan bit down harder on nothing. She was trembling violently, and the more she tried to tense and hold still, the more she shook. Her ankle hurt so much it almost wasn't pain anymore, and it wasn't really in her ankle anymore—it was a thrilling, murderous sensation that roamed from her foot to her knee to her brain.

"Will it really help?" she whispered.

"I don't know," Andee admitted. "Maybe. I think."

"God, it's scary seeing you like this," Nita said. "Please just try it."

Siobhan clamped her mouth around the paper. She immediately coughed so hard the lit joint fell into her lap. Andee caught it and held it pinched in her fingers. "Relax," she said. "Just take a deep breath in and hold it, okay?"

Siobhan took the joint into her hand this time, holding it the way Andee had, between her thumb and first two fingers. She inhaled. The smoke burned her lungs, like staying too long underwater, like she'd swallowed a lit match, but she held it in, as Andee had said. She counted to six before she couldn't stand it any longer. She exhaled. Smoke billowed from her mouth.

"There you go," Andee said. "Now do it again."

BASED ON TV PSAs and a rant by a gym teacher, Siobhan expected to hallucinate a melting, topsy-turvy world of kaleidoscopic color. As she waited for her flowerchild dream to kick in, she watched the other girls unroll the sleeping bags on the cold ground. The pain in Siobhan's ankle dulled slowly as she smoked the joint down to a nub, from feeling like it was on fire, like she would've gladly cut off her leg at the knee, to an ache that throbbed in time with the pulse in her ears. She could hear her heart beating, the blood sloshing around in her skull. She could smell herself, rank and earthy, crusted with sweat.

The four of them huddled together, two sleeping bags on the ground and two laid overtop their tangled bodies. She could smell all of them too, each bringing a different note to the stink. Together they smelled fungal, swampy, something that grows in the damp. Elbows and knees prodded Siobhan all over and jostled her ankle.

Siobhan turned her head. Daisies swayed nearby, the edges of the petals sharply in focus. Her vision had a new capacity for detail, a new acuity. A beetle crawled through the grass, and its iridescent back glittered, an alien green. She put her finger in the beetle's path and delighted in the tickle of its feet on her fingertip.

She fell asleep briefly but wholly, like she'd been drawn down into a pit of tar. When she woke, Andee and Dina were asleep beside her. Andee clutched Dina in her sleep. She murmured another girl's name into Dina's hair, a friend or a sister from Andee's other life.

Nita was sitting up, only her legs under the sleeping bag,

her upper body unprotected in the cool night air. The sky was still more indigo than the black of its darkest hours. Siobhan imagined she could see the stars reflected in Nita's eyes. She pushed herself up onto her good elbow. "Are you watching out for the bear?" Siobhan asked.

"No. Just thinking about stuff." Nita wasn't looking at Siobhan. "What do you think the girls did back at camp today?"

Siobhan didn't answer. She thought of her cabinmates, the heavy sleeper who had been in the bunk above hers. Already Siobhan couldn't remember what the girl looked like, exactly, or where she'd been from.

"I'm sorry I was a jerk to you before," Nita said. "At camp. You got on my nerves for no reason. Sometimes people just do." Nita ran her hand through the grass at the edge of the sleeping bags. "I'm glad you were with us. I wanted you to know that."

"It's okay," Siobhan said. She could hardly feel her ankle and shoulder at all anymore. She knew she had been angry before, but she couldn't remember why. She felt peaceful. Everything was okay. Nita had come to her rescue in the end. Sleep was near at hand, irresistible, the sucking pull of the tar, her injuries and a new queasiness in her gut drowned in the viscous black. "I knew about the bear."

"What was that?"

"I saw it last night, while we were eating dinner. And I saw its tracks today. I knew there was a bear somewhere."

"Why didn't you tell us?"

"I didn't want to freak you guys out. Dina was so scared of cougars and bears already. I thought she'd just lose it. I tried to steer us away from where the tracks led, but I guess I messed up. I'm sorry."

By the time Nita answered, Siobhan was half asleep, lucid but crowded by dreams and phantasms. "Don't be. I understand," Nita said.

"You do?"

"Yeah. You were trying to protect us. I get it." It seemed to Siobhan that Nita was whispering right into Siobhan's ear, her voice close and warm and syrupy. "That's what a leader does."

SIOBHAN WOKE AGAIN for only a moment, surfacing through the thick darkness. She perceived motion, voices. She remembered smoking the joint. Her mom would find out, she thought, and she'd be in trouble. Then she was submerged again, lost in that inky, consuming place. She felt something soft wrapping and compressing her; the mother bear was embracing her, pressing Siobhan between her paws and her fur-covered belly.

She woke for the third time choking on a scream. The pain in her ankle had returned in full force, pain both marrow-deep and crackling on the surface of her skin and every millimeter in between, like she was being eaten from within and without. Hurt, nothing but hurt, galaxies of hurt.

She spent a long time just trying to breathe, in and out, in and out, trying to regain control of her body and her senses. Other information filtered in. She was tucked into her sleeping bag, which had been zipped snugly around her. The sun was on her face.

She looked around as best she could without moving her lower body, trying to hold her bad leg perfectly still. The pain in her shoulder reasserted itself as she stretched her neck. *Hello,* it said. *I'm here too.* The girls had already packed up the other sleeping bags. She couldn't see where they'd put them. She couldn't see the girls.

She sat upright in shock, wincing and crying out again. "Nita?" she called.

All around her, only grass, weeds, flowers, the bordering trees. Their muted, sludgy colors, their speechlessness. "Andee? Dina? Where are you?"

She knew right away what had happened, but she couldn't stop herself. She surveyed the same scene, the empty land, over and over. "Hello? Guys? Are you still here?"

She shouted in all directions, into the woods, at the sky. "Nita! Andee! Dina! Anybody? Anybody!"

She remembered Nita asking her if she could walk. She remembered Nita kneeling behind Isabel, hands on her shoulders, promising Isabel that they'd be back soon, they'd get Jan to a hospital and she'd be okay. She knew what Nita had said to Andee and Dina in the night, as Siobhan lay in her drugged sleep. They could make it to town only by leaving Siobhan behind. They'd send help for her and Isabel. No one was ever going to find them in a clearing in this unknown heart of the forest. And what was the point of asking Siobhan, of telling Siobhan, and causing a scene? Causing her distress, making them all cry and fight and doubt themselves. Better to let her sleep. Maybe help would even arrive before she woke up. Better to leave right away, the sooner to get her that help, to help them all.

It made sense. It made perfect sense. It was the only way.

"Come back!" The trees hid no faces. Siobhan was more frightened by their abandonment than she had been by Jan's unhinged jaw and unblinking eyes. "Come back! Please don't leave me here!"

SIOBHAN'S VOICE GAVE OUT. Her throat felt raspy, her lungs singed. She hadn't needed to go to the bathroom since the day before. She remembered another fact from the same science lesson: people could only go a couple of days without water. She realized that her textbook and her teacher had likely been talking about adults, not children.

The grass still glistened with dew. Instinctively, her shoulder and ankle pulsing, she dragged herself backward using her hands, so her head and shoulders were on the ground instead of the sleeping bag. She licked beads of moisture off the blades of grass, took grass into her mouth and sucked on it. Her tongue and the roof of her mouth still felt like leather, dried out and impenetrable.

Clouds bounded across the sky in a strong wind, blocking and unblocking the sun. The same wind rustled through the trees, and the branches and leaves whistled like a human voice. She burrowed back down into her sleeping bag, a neatly wrapped snack for the bear.

She was hungrier and thirstier than she'd previously known was possible, but her terror was stronger. She knew she should stay put, where the girls knew she was, where they'd send help, but she just couldn't. She wanted above all else not to be alone.

She thought about a boy at her school who'd broken his leg skateboarding. He'd been back at school within a few days, where he'd let his friends try out his crutches during recess. Everyone else had watched as they went swinging and leaping across the blacktop.

She looked around for something she could use. A walking stick. She spotted a few fallen branches near the western edge of the clearing, jutting out from the woods, impossibly far away.

Siobhan carefully, agonizingly, rolled onto her stomach, her hands out in front. She took a few more breaths in this new position, straining to hold her bad ankle aloft, before she began dragging herself slowly across the hard, wet earth.

Weeds and wild grass tickled her face. Her clothes grew damp, smeared with even more dirt, the blood of insects crushed and scraped by her forearms and knees. Every few feet she stopped to rest and suck on more grass.

She didn't know how long it took her to crawl across the clearing. By the time she got there, she'd almost forgotten why she was doing it—she'd been focused on each determined instant, stilling her ankle and shoulder while the rest of her body fought forward and gradually wore itself out. She reached the branches and lay facedown on the ground, panting.

Eventually, she lifted her head. How was she supposed to stand up? She crawled farther, to a nearby pine tree. She pushed off her hands to sitting. She braced against the trunk, and with a single, heroic leap onto her good leg, she was standing on one foot.

Sweat coursed down the sides of her face. As Siobhan caught her breath, she looked down at the fallen branches. Only one looked like it could be used as a walking stick, with relatively few arms off a thick central column, probably the right height and thickness, and sturdy enough to hold her, yet not so heavy that she couldn't lift it. But now how was she supposed to pick it up off the ground?

Her back pressed against the tree, she slowly bent her leg. She lost her balance and caught herself on the foot of her broken ankle for an excruciating moment, before tilting her weight back into her one-legged squat.

Her fingers could just touch the stick she wanted. She clawed it closer to her and managed to grasp one end. She wedged the other end against the ground, and used the stick and the tree for leverage to straighten her leg once more.

She clutched tightly on to her new walking stick as she leaned her head back against the tree to rest. She was utterly exhausted. She couldn't face the endless, bewildering forest again, another hobbling march to nowhere. Not yet. Her sleeping bag, surrounded by the shining, open faces of buttercups, dandelions, and thumb-size daisies, looked like the last chunk of civilization on earth.

She used the stick to hop back to where she'd left her sleeping bag in the center of the clearing, pleased that her plan had worked and the walking stick functioned so well. She dropped the stick beside the sleeping bag. Her good leg, now completely spent, wobbled as she tried to ease herself back down. She fell hard onto her tailbone.

The clouds were thickening and turning a pale gray. She wanted to sleep, every cell in her body begged to rest. She was so, so tired. She escaped, however briefly, from this reality.

The sky had darkened when Siobhan woke from her fitful nap, but the clouds remained unbroken, the sun lowered and dilute. She thought she should retreat into the woods, dragging her sleeping bag and her stick, before the rain began. At least she'd have water to drink when it did.

She saw at once her mistake. In the middle of the flat clearing, there was nothing she could use to stand up. She held the stick with both hands and shoved it hard into the dirt, trying to pull herself up, rocking back and forth on her unbroken foot and her butt to build up momentum, but it was no use. She would have to crawl to the trees all over again.

She didn't have the energy. She didn't have the will. She lay back down. She covered her face with her hands so she couldn't see. Her body wracked with dry sobs. She cried for her mother, her father, God, every authority in the universe. Nobody was coming for her, and she couldn't save herself.

THE WIND DRONED through the branches and smelled like rain, but the sky remained sealed and taut. The heavy air taunted her. Her skin felt damp and a wet chill penetrated her clothes, but there was nothing to quench her thirst.

Siobhan slid deeper into her sleeping bag, pulling it over her head. In the darkness, listening to herself breathe, her teeth chattering and her whole body quaking, she thought again about the girls back at Camp Forevermore. Archery, bird-watching, swimming, inner tubes, hiking, arts and crafts, friends and sisters for life. And then they would go home. They'd go home, and they'd get to grow up, and she wouldn't.

Siobhan had always thought she was mature for her age, that she understood more than adults gave her credit for, but she saw herself differently now. She saw herself as grown-ups must have: new to the world, larval, her final self unrecognizable in this form. She thought about Isabel, Dina, Andee, and Nita, cursed them and longed for them. She knew somehow that they'd be okay, even Isabel. They'd survive and go on. Who would they become? What would they get to do and see? Who would they love?

Wind battered the cave-world of her sleeping bag. Siobhan thought about a field trip her fourth grade class had taken to the local natural history museum. There had been an exhibit about early humans. The guide told them that even the most ancient societies, before recorded history, had honored their dead. One of her classmates had shot his hand up and asked, "But how can you know that, if they didn't write anything down?"

Human skeletons have been found intentionally grouped and arranged, the guide explained, with the remains of flowers and other decorative items. The guide pointed to an unremarkable black-and-white photo of an archaeological dig, and beside it, an artist's rendering of what the grave would have looked like.

The drawing had been done in a broad, cartoonish style, with unfinished outlines and only pale touches of color, probably to appear less disturbing to children. Vague human shapes laid in a naturally occurring crevice, covered in flowered stalks and wreaths.

Siobhan remembered all the Forevermore girls lounging around the dock, the beach, and the nearby grass during the swim tests. Many had tied daisies together into bracelets and necklaces. Dina had been covered in ones gifted to her. Some girls had plaited the white flowers into each other's hair.

Siobhan poked her head out of the sleeping bag. The sky

had cleared, the air washed clean, having unleashed its rain elsewhere. She felt dizzy and off-kilter, the pain in her ankle changing again, tightening like a fist. She touched her face. Her cheeks were so hot they seemed to scorch her fingertips.

She lay on her belly and ripped out all the wildflowers and blades of grass that were within reach. She knotted the ends together into long chains and loops, hanging them from her wrists and neck. The flowers had barely any fragrance. They were only faintly sweet, even with dozens of them laid against her throat and chest. She pictured an archaeologist sweeping the dusty earth from her bones, someday far in the future, a small girl skeleton that never had the chance to grow.

SIOBHAN HEARD THE REST later, saw the footage: Nita, leading Andee and Dina, eventually stumbled upon a set of man-made steps, part of a hiking trail. The girls ran screaming and hollering all the way to the trailhead parking lot. No one was around, but two cars were parked in one corner, cars with the promise of people. Cars people would return to. They sat in the gravel beside the wheels to wait.

The three of them were on the local news that night. Wrapped in blankets from the big island's volunteer fire department. Small and incoherent, filthy, hair matted and snarled, stained knees, lisping and stuttering as they struggled with the reporter's questions. The reporter kneeled, her stick-and-ball microphone almost touching Nita's lips. They were told that Isabel had been rescued and Jan's body recovered. They were told that the search party had been looking in the wrong area, not expecting that the girls would have walked so far in the time they'd been missing, on so little food, on such little legs and lungs, and in the wrong direction — they'd been weaving first west- and then northward through the nature preserve and parkland, almost to the northernmost tip of the island, while the town hugged the southern coast. They looked up with the empty eyes of baby rabbits. They sounded stupid. They looked pathetic, utterly vulnerable. Condemned by secretive, dying Jan and criminally neglectful Forevermore, saved by pure chance. Anyone watching would think: Those poor girls! Thank goodness they were found.

WHEN THE FLASHLIGHTS CAME, the beams swinging back and forth and flickering behind the trees, an echoing chorus of voices calling Siobhan's name, she was so certain they were angels that she didn't bother to respond. Even when the town doctor opened up the island's only clinic in the middle of the night, examined Siobhan, and pronounced her fine — her ankle was broken in two places, she'd torn a muscle in her upper back, she was dehydrated, she had abrasions all over, she was in shock, but she was fundamentally okay, she'd be all right — she still didn't believe him. She'd known, as an unfamiliar adult form had reached down and plucked her from the grass, still wrapped in her sleeping bag and draped in flowers, that she'd been brought back from the dead.

SIOBHAN LIVED a quiet life, a typical life, of minor disappointments and ordinary loneliness. She became a researcher in child psychology. She spent her entire career in academia and avoided clinical work wherever possible. In the lab, she sent in her research assistants and collaborators while she observed from behind a two-way mirror. She offered to take on more than her share of the paperwork and computer analysis, so long as her co-researchers were the ones to actually talk to subjects, do the site visits, sit with the kids in their controlled rooms. More than once, a colleague or supervisor commented that, given her specialty, Siobhan should work on how awkward and stilted she was with children, especially one-on-one.

She preferred teaching college students. Looking out into a lecture hall of young adults, their laptop-lit faces recently arrived on the far shore of puberty, she felt relieved for them.

When Siobhan traveled for conferences, she sometimes woke in the middle of the night, and the unfamiliar hotel bed and outlines in the dark convinced her that she was still lying in that island clearing, still in her preadolescent body, a corpse wreathed in flowers. She had never left, and everything that had happened since was a dream, a girl's fantasy of adulthood, a film reel in the afterlife.

Every now and then, she would linger at the bar of the hotel hosting the conference, or attend one of the evening parties where name tags adhered to their chests or swinging from lanyards advertised their academic titles and affiliations, the possibilities for career advancement and conflicts of interest they were accumulating drink by drink. She would guide a warm body up to her room as insurance against the nightmares.

On one such night, she ran into her former graduate supervisor. He hit on her the way he had when she was his student, and she was considering it, even though he remained thirty years her senior, and the gap at thirty-three and sixty-three seemed, oddly, wider than it had at twenty-five and fifty-five.

Over watery rye-and-Cokes, she confessed that she often felt like what they were doing as researchers was confirming what they already knew. He lectured her angrily: That's the opposite of what we do! A scientist doesn't chase preexisting biases and folk knowledge, a scientist follows the data wherever it leads, a scientist learns new things about the universe and mankind!

She agreed in the abstract, but went back to her room alone.

Siobhan spent her days behind the two-way glass in her laboratory, watching kids interact with their parents, with her co-workers, with one another, with the traps and miniature worlds she built for them. Her theses and designs shifted over the years, but she could never prove what she wanted to. What she knew they were truly capable of. She stared into their eyes from where they couldn't look back at her.

ACKNOWLEDGMENTS

Many thanks are due to my stupendous agent, Jackie Kaiser, and the whole team at Westwood Creative Artists; my editors Jennifer Lambert and Lauren Wein, for their deft touch and understanding, as well as to their colleagues at HarperCollins Canada and Houghton Mifflin Harcourt, particularly Pilar Garcia-Brown, Lisa Glover, and Amy Edelman; the Writers' Trust of Canada, the Berton House, the Canada Council for the Arts, and the kind, generous people of Dawson City, Yukon; the Ucross Foundation; the Wallace Stegner House and the Eastend Arts Council; my brilliant, wonderful, supportive friends, writers and non-writers, too numerous to list here (but I hope you know who you are); my family, particularly my parents and sisters, who will always be my role models for how to live; and andrea bennett, my first, best, and dearest reader, my collaborator and companion through a creative life. Finally, thanks to JP Lobos, my great love: you made them all possible, but especially this one.